MISSING GIRL AT FROZEN FALLS

BOOKS BY LESLIE WOLFE

DETECTIVE KAY SHARP SERIES

The Girl From Silent Lake

Beneath Blackwater River

The Angel Creek Girls

The Girl on Wildfire Ridge

TESS WINNETT SERIES

Dawn Girl

The Watson Girl

Glimpse of Death

Taker of Lives

Not Really Dead

Girl With A Rose

Mile High Death

The Girl They Took

BAXTER & HOLT SERIES

Las Vegas Girl

Casino Girl

Las Vegas Crime

STANDALONE TITLES

The Girl You Killed

Stories Untold

Love, Lies and Murder

ALEX HOFFMANN SERIES

Executive

Devil's Move

The Backup Asset

The Ghost Pattern

Operation Sunset

MISSING GIRL AT FROZEN FALLS

LESLIE WOLFE

bookouture

Published by Bookouture in 2022

An imprint of Storyfire Ltd.
Carmelite House
50 Victoria Embankment
London EC4Y 0DZ

www.bookouture.com

ISBN: 978-1-80314-970-7
eBook ISBN: 978-1-80314-969-1

A special thank you to my New York City legal eagle and friend, Mark Freyberg, who expertly guided me through the intricacies of the judicial system.

ONE
SILENCE

There wasn't an ounce of deference in her daughter's blue eyes.

Lit up with defiance fueled by the fire that burned vividly inside her heart and gave its color to her long, tousled hair, Holly's eyes darted from her mother's face to the kitchen window. Outside, dusk hues were fading into darkness, inviting heavy shadows to the corners of the yard and seeding worry into Rachel's heart.

"Ten more minutes, Mommy, please," she insisted, fidgeting on the chair she'd taken with visible reluctance. "It's not night yet." Her fingers found the edge of the place mat and started tugging at a loose thread coming out of the seam. It would soon fall apart, like everything else that was in her way. "Please?"

Rachel bit her lip to contain a tense smile. "Dinner's ready, sweetie." After placing white, square plates on the table with quick, expert gestures, Rachel turned her back for a moment, long enough to retrieve the casserole from the stove and set it on the grate. When she looked up, content to see the roast had made it to the table without any spills or stains, Holly's chair was empty.

Testing the limits of her patience, her daughter hung by the back door knob. Her hands were squeezing the knob while slowly twisting it, her back almost touching the floor, her auburn curls sweeping the tiles. She stared at her mother with a wide, audacious grin on her freckled face as if to see if she could get away with turning the knob just one more bit until it gave under pressure, allowing the door to swing open.

Rachel's heart skipped a beat. That knob was loose, barely holding on even without an eight-year-old dangling from it with a vengeance. In Holly's mind, that rattling piece of hardware must've been the symbol of what held her captive in her mother's kitchen and deserved to be torn to bits. Even if that meant the little monkey could land hard on the floor while doing it, banging her head against the side of the cabinet. Or, more likely, she was just not thinking about any of that, in typical eight-year-old fashion.

Dropping the oven mitt on the table, she rushed over to the door and scooped Holly in her arms, using the opportunity to hold Holly tight for a brief moment before the child started squirming to get free.

Crouching, Rachel let her land safely on the ground while her eyes darted for a moment to the stove's clock. It was getting late.

With every passing minute, fear crept inside her like fog rolling in from the sea, swallowing everything in its path. She should've never said a word. She should've run, pretended like she was never there, and maybe they would've been safe. Holly would've been safe now.

Reluctantly, she opened her arms, breathing away the threat of tears. Without hesitation, Holly sprinted away from her, circling the table and filling the silence with laughter.

"Wash your hands before you sit down, young lady." The girl pouted, but Rachel didn't budge, pointing her finger at the sink. "Now." Then Rachel took her seat at the table with a long sigh, knife and fork in hand, ready to carve a couple of slices from the mouthwatering roast. The smell of buttery mashed potatoes and thyme-encrusted veal filled her nostrils, reminding her she hadn't eaten anything since morning.

Keeping her eyes on Holly's half-hearted effort to wash her hands while she typed a text message on her phone, Rachel almost missed the sound of a car pulling into the driveway. Yet the familiar noise sent icicles through her blood. In quick tiptoe, she went to the living room and looked outside through the sheers without turning on the lights.

"Oh, no," she whispered to herself. "Oh, please, no."

Rushing back into the kitchen, she grabbed Holly's jacket from the coat rack by the door, then stopped by Holly's side. "Remember what we talked about?" she asked her daughter in a low, intense whisper. She nodded, her eyes wide, her smile gone. "It's time. Here, put this on and go outside. Go hide in the toolshed, behind the tractor, like we discussed."

Holly's head bobbed again. She stood, hesitant, her earlier eagerness to go outside now vanished.

"Go." Rachel opened the back door quickly, and Holly slipped through. A gust of wintry wind blew inside with the scent of fallen leaves and the threat of November rain. "Stay there until I come to get you, all right?" Then she put her finger on her lips, pleading with her daughter to stay silent. "Breathe like I showed you, nice and slow, okay? Don't be afraid," she murmured, wiping a tear from her daughter's eye. "My brave little girl."

Holly whimpered and took a step back, sending her curls up in whirls as she turned to run barefoot on the frozen ground. Out of time for better options, Rachel took off her shoes and threw them over to Holly, then watched her stop just long enough to pick them up and slip them on before continuing to the shed. The sneakers were too large for her, but she bravely dragged her feet into the shed, pulling the door closed behind her with a rusty creak.

A sob climbed inside Rachel's chest, but she willed it gone as she closed the door and dealt away with Holly's plate, silverware, and place mat, shoving them quickly into the dishwasher.

What was she still doing there? It made no sense, but she didn't know where else to go. She'd wanted one more dinner for Holly and herself, one more day of normality before her entire life would be upended, maybe for good. But now she regretted it bitterly, only the latest in a slew of bad decisions she'd made.

She'd thought there was still time.

She'd been wrong.

The doorbell rang twice, seeming much louder than usual, sending ripples of fear through her veins. She slammed the dishwasher door shut and shouted, "Just a minute." Throwing the kitchen one last look, she braced herself and walked over to the front door.

For a moment, she considered not opening the door, blocking it with the back of a chair stuck under the handle as she'd seen in the movies. But she knew that would make no difference. It was better to try to talk her way out of it. Her only chance.

She opened the door and froze, suddenly at a loss for words, her throat constricted and dry.

The man stared at Rachel before coming in as if to gauge her intentions, as if expecting something more than the awkward smile she'd pasted on her trembling lips. He kept his hands inside the deep pockets of his trench coat, his shoulders broad, his expression stern, determined. The long flaps of his coat fluttered in the brisk wind like a captive bird trying desperately to flee.

"I—I know why you're here..." she said weakly. "But there's no need." The man continued to stare, his gaze cold, unyielding. "I decided it's better to let it all go and just disappear. I'll take Holly, and we'll just leave."

She looked at him briefly, then away. Her head hung low,

her eyes shielded by wavy strands of silky red hair. His face seemed carved in stone, immobile, indifferent. It was the indifference that scared her the most.

"Is that so?" he asked. His voice resounded strangely in the quiet room. "You just decided to drop everything and run away? And I'm supposed to believe that?" His laughter reverberated in the deathly silence like shards of glass.

She nodded frantically, feeling her heart thumping hastily in her chest. "I don't remember much anyway. I—I was wrong. I thought I'd remember, but..." Tears welled in her eyes. He reached out and touched her face. Jolting under his touch, she willed herself still. "I promise you I won't say a word."

A crooked smile tugged at his lips. "Cross your heart and hope to die?" he asked, crushing a tear under his thumb.

His question brought vivid images to her mind. A black SUV driving by on the street where she was parked. That vehicle slowing as it almost reached the corner. The window moving down in the light rain. A flicker of light and the sound of a gun going off. Twice. The hand that held the gun and the way it jolted upward from the recoil. The thump of a body falling onto the rain-soaked sidewalk, a young man, maybe twenty years old, perhaps younger. Blood mixing with rain and slowly flowing to the gutter. The black SUV accelerating, turning the corner, disappearing. Her breath, caught in her chest, searing and agonizing.

She shook her head. "Not a word, I swear. I'm just shook up, that's all." She pulled away slowly, knowing she was lying so badly her eight-year-old would've done a much better job. "I've embarrassed myself with those people... in the heat of the moment, I guess. I've never witnessed a murder before." She choked on the word, and her voice broke. "I thought I could remember the tag, but all I can remember was a black car. Or maybe blue. There are millions of them out there. I didn't see anything, really. I swear I didn't. Please, let me go."

"I'm not buying it." His voice was level, matter-of-fact.

She shrugged and shook her head again, lowering her gaze to the floor. "I already called them; I told them I can't remember anything." Lifting her eyes and meeting his for a brief moment, she added in a low, strangled whisper, "But *they* might think differently. I—we—are in danger if they think I've seen something. You know, the, um, killer. I wish I could tell them I didn't see anything. I'm no danger to anyone." Wringing her hands together, she took another small step backward. "I was too far. It was dark, raining. How could I have seen anything, right?" She tried to fake a chuckle, but it came out guttural, choked, grotesque.

A stifled sob escaped her lips. Her knees were feeling weak and shaky, and she let herself slide into a chair near the door, then buried her face in her hands. Her shoulders heaved as she sobbed, fear and desperation spreading throughout her body relentlessly.

He drew closer and touched Rachel's shoulder in a gesture that made her jump out of her skin. Gasping, she looked at him through a blur of tears. When their eyes met, she shuddered. His decision was made, and nothing she could say or do could change what was about to happen.

Still, she bolted from her chair and fled into the kitchen, flailing desperately, feeling the table surface for the long carving knife she remembered she'd set out earlier.

The man walked toward the kitchen table slowly, unfazed, determined. "Where's the kid?"

"She's not here," she stuttered. "I left her with my mom."

"Uh-huh," he replied coldly, taking out a gun fitted with a small silencer and aiming it at her chest.

Grabbing the knife with trembling fingers, she pounced, raising her hand in the air and leaping across the floor to reach him.

The gun went off twice, in rapid, silenced sequence, ripping through her flesh and setting off flashes of lightning inside her brain. Her body fell to the ground as the world around her turned dark. The knife clattered against the tiles and slid under the stove.

The man stared at her body for a few moments, then circled around the table and fired another shot into Rachel's head. The shock jarred her upper body for a split second, then nothing.

Just silence.

The man slid the gun inside his pocket and grabbed a dish cloth from the oven door handle. Whistling a familiar tune, he wiped any surface he might've touched since his arrival. The back of the kitchen chair across from where the woman had fallen. The front door handles. The kitchen doorframe. And, just for good measure, sections of the counter and the table.

Before leaving, he stared at the woman's beautiful face, serene in death, at peace. "What a waste," he muttered. He turned toward the table and peeled off a bit of roast crust, then ate it hungrily, licking his fingers. "And she could cook too."

He was almost at the door when he heard some noises outside, in the backyard. A crack, a thump, a stifled whimper.

"Damn it to bloody hell," he muttered and stormed through the back door, not bothering to care about the fingerprints he left on the rattling knob.

There would be time to clean those off later.

TWO
MISSED CALL

Kay stared at the suspect through the glass, bracing herself for when she'd have to go inside. Her fingers wrapped tightly around a tall, paper coffee cup to borrow warmth from its contents, she crinkled her nose and chuckled, looking at Elliot.

"This has to be a first," she said. "And he stinks like you wouldn't believe."

Her partner grinned and nodded once, a barely noticeable movement of the brim of his cowboy hat. "Want me to take him to processing?"

She gave the suspect one more look. He seemed awake now, not like earlier that day, when two deputies had to carry him from the cruiser, fast asleep. Disheveled brown hair that hadn't seen a comb in months and an equally unkempt beard covered most of the suspect's face. A dirty, gray T-shirt bore stains of a brownish substance that Kay didn't dare venture a guess about. His pants were worn out, stretched and slimy; the man must've been homeless for a while.

The smell of stale cigar smoke preceded Sheriff Logan's entrance in the small observation room by a mere split second. He'd grown heavier, Kay noticed, his abdomen pushing against the taut fabric of his shirt, threatening the integrity of several buttons. The circles under his eyes had deepened; probably, he was building up quite the sleep deficit, and the winter season was just starting. As always, winter brought snow, and with it hordes of tourists, either skiers or people who just loved being on the slopes and peaks of Mount Chester, once the first coat of white dropped from the sky.

And with them came a sheriff's office load of endless overtime. Petty thefts, bar brawls, drunk and disorderlies, break-ins, DUIs, the occasional rape, and sometimes murder. Dozens of car crashes, from fender benders to multiple car pileups to vehicular homicides, all because Californians couldn't drive on ice, and that was a proven fact.

"I thought he'd be locked up by now," Sheriff Logan said, stopping in the doorframe and giving the perp a quick look filled with unfiltered contempt.

"I wanted him fully awake for questioning," Kay replied. "I don't want some smart attorney to have the charges dropped because he was impaired at the time of the interview."

"What's there to question?" Logan grinned and scratched his buzz-cut, graying temple. "It's a first for me," he added, his grin widening to reveal tobacco-stained teeth. "To fall asleep at the crime scene."

Kay tilted her head just a little. "I like him for the Gravatt and Langton break-ins too. There are commonalities with those cases. Same time of day. Same point of ingress. Same MO."

"Fingerprints?" The sheriff's grin waned.

"Still waiting on those, but I thought I'd just ask him."

A quiet chuckle left Elliot's lips. He kept quiet, as always, but she could see his wheels were turning.

"He didn't quite fall asleep," Elliot finally said. "He was drugged. By Mrs. Donaghy. She somehow got him to drink coffee with her, and she spiked it with her own sleeping pills. That woman could charge hell with a bucket of ice water."

"Yeah... like three times the dose she gave him," Logan laughed. "I heard. Good for her. How did he get here?"

"The Donaghys tied him up with extension cords and called us," Elliot added. "Can you imagine Mr. Donaghy, at seventy-three, with his potbelly and bad arthritis, hauling this piece of scum tied up like a smoked ham to the front porch, 'cause 'he couldn't take the sight nor the stench of him'? His words, not mine," he added, his hands stubbornly stuck in his jeans pockets instead of making the usual air quotes.

Logan sucked in his abdomen, probably feeling a bit self-conscious on hearing Elliot's description of Mr. Donaghy's build. Kay turned away to hide a tiny smile.

"All right, I'm going in," she announced, leaving her coffee cup behind on a small side table and straightening her black turtleneck. She peeled her sleeves up to her elbows, then fished a scrunchie out of her pocket and tied her blonde hair in a pony-tail. Picking up a file folder with a few blank sheets of paper inside, a prop she sometimes used, she stopped in front of the door. "I'd say, ten, fifteen minutes," she added, looking briefly at Elliot. The brim of his hat moved ever so slightly. She didn't want Logan to know she and Elliot were going out for dinner later.

Although the entire town of Mount Chester knew. Especially the other cops.

The suspect barely flinched when she came in. Her breath caught in her chest; it was ripe in there. She walked straight outside to the thermostat, lowered it by ten degrees, and switched it to air conditioning. Then she came back in and sat across the table from the suspect.

"Mr. John Homer Boydston." She paused for effect. "How's your day going?" she asked, opening the file folder and shifting through the sheets of paper.

"Huh?" the man replied, staring at her with half-closed, bloodshot eyes. "How d'ya *think* it's going? I've been busted."

"Yeah, I heard." She closed the file and placed it neatly in front of her, then steepled her hands on top of it. "Why did you break into the Donaghy residence?"

He looked away from her toward the window, now a black square of glass with steel bars crisscrossed in front of it. It was dark outside, the days shorter and colder with the threat of more snow in the evening air. "I guess there's no point sayin' it wasn't me, huh?"

She feigned regret. "No, I'm afraid it would be useless. Let me remind you what happened." She waited until he made eye contact. "This morning at about ten, you broke into a house and started roughing up the two senior citizens who live there, demanding they give you money. You went through their drawers, Mrs. Donaghy's purse, and took everything you were able to find. Cash, jewelry, their car keys. At which point, Mrs. Donaghy offered you a cup of coffee, and you drank it. Then you fell asleep on their couch."

A flicker of understanding lit his bleary eyes for a moment. "She poisoned me!" he shouted, trying to stand. The chain running through his cuffs and locked onto the stainless-steel table rattled, holding him in place. Defeated, he let himself drop back on his chair, its legs screeching when dragged against the stained concrete floor. "She drugged me. I swear she did. I want to press charges."

"Mr. Boydston, you broke into their residence. They had the legal right to kill you in self-defense. They didn't. If anything, you should be grateful."

His mouth rounded in a silent O.

"Have you been read your rights?"

"Y—yeah, I know my rights. I've done time before."

"For what?"

He scoffed as if to doubt her ignorance. "Breaking and entering."

"All right, so you've done this before." She smiled politely as if to convey she understood him. "I'm going to guess that you broke into the Donaghy residence because you desperately needed money. Because you were starving."

He nodded enthusiastically, sending fresh waves of body odor her way. "That's—exactly, that's why. You got it."

"I've read in your file that you were fired from your last job for, what was it, stealing?"

He frowned, a feeble attempt as if his thick eyebrows were too weak to be summoned to ruffle.

"All right, so before we book you formally, let me tell you where we are. We have two other B and Es we're working on, the Gravatt and the Langton cases."

"Who?"

He probably didn't even know their names. Why would he bother? As far as she could tell, his MO was to drink himself unconscious or get high or both, then stalk an elderly couple and break into their home. He'd been shown leniency twice by the courts, but he'd repaid it by putting more people in the hospital.

"I have an issue here, Mr. Boydston." She leaned forward just a little to give her words more weight. Her gesture piqued his half-numb curiosity. "In both these break-ins, the elderly couples were severely injured, so the charges would be much higher. You see, my partner is from Texas. He's a hardened lawman who'd like nothing better than to hang the man who hurt those people, you understand?"

His face turned ashen and his lips quivered. "Hang?" He cleared his throat. "What do you mean, hang?"

"Oh, it's a figure of speech. We don't hang criminals in California. We execute them. Nice and neat, not like in old-time Texas."

He licked his lips nervously. "I didn't kill anyone."

"Well, that's the issue I'm having, Mr. Boydston. My partner believes the perpetrator who broke into the Gravatt home intended to kill the two people who lived there and made a mistake. Smashed their heads against the wall, but didn't use enough force to kill both of them."

The pallor deepened on Boydston's face. He swallowed hard. "Both?"

She ignored his question. "While I believe it was an accident, when you break into people's homes, they get scared. They run around like crazy, they trip over stuff. I think they fell and hit their heads." She paused, looking straight into the man's dilated pupils. "Only someone dumb as a post would kill someone for a hundred bucks, right? 'Cause that's all that was taken from the Gravatts, you see."

She paused for another moment, leaning back into her chair. "That's the issue I'm having. Was it premeditated murder, badly executed by someone stupid? Or just an accident during the perpetration of a minor felony?"

"It was an accident," he blurted, "I swear it was. I just wanted to hold him back, so I could go through the drawers, but he kept coming at me with that bat. I just only pushed him, n—not hard," he stammered. The chain rattled again when he clasped his hands together in an imploring gesture. "They weren't supposed to get hurt. I'm not stupid, you know."

"All right," Kay said, standing and grabbing the folder from the scratched table. "I'll let my partner know."

He lowered his face to the table until his chained hands could run through his messy hair. "Th—thank you, Detective."

She closed the door behind her and breathed deeply, then stepped into the observation room, just in time to see money changing hands.

"A bet?" she challenged the two, who looked sheepishly guilty as charged. "On what? This confession was way too easy."

Elliot shifted his weight from one foot to the other, lowering the brim of his hat enough to hide his blue irises. "On time. On how long it would take you—"

"Yeah, I get it." She pressed her lips together to hide a smile. That was her family, right there. Elliot, Sheriff Logan, the deputies. Her brother Jacob. "Who said what?"

A moment of silence, then Logan said, "I lost a tenner. I said you'd break him in twenty minutes. He said five. He came closer. You had him fessing up in six minutes flat."

"Wow," she said quietly, secretly flattered.

"He can pay for dinner now," Logan said, leaving the room with a brisk step, responding to a beckon from the dispatcher.

"I'll lock him up," Elliot offered.

Kay stayed behind, retrieving the cup of coffee and taking a sip. She watched Elliot take the perp from interrogation to the back for processing. Boydston squirmed for a while, then stared at Elliot's hat, his saucer-size belt buckle with the lone star on it, and fell quiet like a mouse, his gaze terrified. He must've figured out Elliot was the big, bad Texas lawman itching for a hanging.

While waiting, Kay checked her messages, frowning when she discovered a missed call from a number she didn't immediately recognize. The call had come a couple of hours earlier, but she somehow hadn't heard it. She checked the phone and found the side button had been slid on silent, probably by accident.

Tapping through to voicemail, she played the message.

"Hi, it's Rachel," a hesitant woman's voice said. It sounded fraught with tears. "I've been meaning to call you... for years. But I really need to speak with you now. I... hope you'll forgive me for what I've done. For everything. I know I have no right, but I need you. Please call me back."

Kay stared at the number displayed on the screen, her index finger hovering above it as she was trying to decide what to do.

"Who was that?" Elliot asked. "You seem upset."

She breathed deeply, realizing she'd been holding air in her chest while she listened. The sense of gloom that had engulfed her dissipated at the sound of Elliot's voice.

"Ah, just a blast from the past. She and I went to college together. She used to be my best friend."

"Wanna call her back? I can wait," Elliot said, taking a step back as if to offer some privacy.

She gave the idea another thought but realized she wasn't ready for that conversation yet. "No... let's grab dinner. I'll call her later."

THREE
THE FALL

Holly rushed toward the shed, her feet hurting over the pebbles that lined the surface of the concrete pathway. Then her mother's shoes landed in the grass by her side with two thumps. She stopped and picked them up, the grass wet and cold under her feet. She slid them on. They were still warm from her mother's feet. When she got back inside later on, Mommy would shout at her for not having her socks on.

She hated socks.

Socks were ugly and smelly and mean.

They slipped down all the time and had to be pulled up. They hid in the farthest corners of the drawers, making it difficult for her to match two of the same kind. They made her trip and fall. And sometimes, they made her feet too warm.

But she missed socks right now, wished she had them with her, the two ugliest ones, knitted by Grandma in thick, coarse, gray wool.

Teeth clattering, she hid inside the cold, damp toolshed, holding on to the back of the lawn tractor with frozen hands. It was pitch black inside. Wind gusts rattled the corrugated vinyl walls, howling and hissing against the foliage of the red cedar.

Berries and tiny branches dropped at times, bouncing loudly against the roof of the shed.

Then something moved against her leg and she shrieked. A tiny shriek, ending swiftly with her own hand covering her mouth.

Something was in there with her. It could've been a spider. A big one. Heart thumping against her chest, she started feeling a bit lightheaded, seeing things that weren't there in the pitch blackness of the shed.

Then she remembered what Mommy had taught her.

Placing her hand on her chest, where the scar was, she breathed deeply, counting seconds with each breath. The pacemaker felt like a lump under her skin, a familiar staple that meant she could live a normal life. That's what Mommy said.

And that meant she could climb the red cedar in the back of the yard. She'd be better off up there. No one lived up that tree, except some squirrels and an old owl, and she didn't mind them. Spiders lived in the shed. Big ones. Wolf spiders, black widows too.

Slowly, holding her breath, she pushed open the shed door and snuck outside. Dragging her feet, she rushed to the old tree and climbed, first on a rock, then on the fence beams, then she reached the fork, about seven feet above the ground. Another couple of branches up, and she was completely engulfed in dense, rustling foliage, where no one could see her. Wind blew angrily, but she held tight, both her arms wrapped against a thick branch.

Then she looked toward the house.

The light was on in the kitchen, and she could see clearly inside: the table, the casserole, and the red bowl of mashed potatoes.

Heart racing in her chest, she saw Mommy rushing in, faltering, grabbing the steak knife from the table. A man appeared. Her mother lunged at him, but he was faster.

Two shots she barely heard.

She gasped, unaware of the tears falling down her cheeks.

Her mother's body falling to the ground, out of sight.

Another shot.

Her foot slipped out of the Converse and lost grip. The branch she was holding on to gave way, and she fell, foliage rustling. She cried when she hit the ground; the thick branch shielded her head from hitting the rock but dug deep into her side, tearing the down jacket and spreading tiny feathers into the wind.

Then she pressed her lips tightly together, careful not to make a sound, sobbing quietly. Mommy would be mad. She was supposed to wait in the tool shed.

After a while, when cold had already started nipping at her bare feet, she heard the door open. Heavy footfalls drew closer, but she didn't dare look. She held her breath, waiting to hear Mommy's voice calling her name.

When the man picked her up, she stopped sobbing, scared out of her mind. As he was carrying her away, past the house, she asked, "Where's Mommy?"

Only the howling wind answered.

FOUR
SURRENDER

The shooting range behind the Franklin County Sheriff's Office was deserted at that early hour. The range master was usually around after seven-thirty, but Kay didn't see him in his office or on the grounds. Maybe he was warming up somewhere.

The morning was cold and breezy; rolls of vapor unfurled with every breath. A trace of ground frost lined the trimmed grass with silver; soon there would be snow covering the fading green of the thick blades, just as it had already lined the higher elevations of Mount Chester. The sky was still blue, a perfectly crisp shade of California clear sky, making that upcoming snow a different day's problem.

"Ugh, it's got teeth." Elliot stomped his feet a few times to warm up. "It ain't hog-killing weather yet, but it's not too far either." He pulled his hands out of his denim jacket pockets, blew air on them, and then rubbed them together vigorously.

"That's nothing," Kay said calmly, setting down her coffee on a wooden bench. "By now, you must know it can drop to twenty degrees here. Sometimes even below that."

"Up there?" He pointed at the peaks of Mount Chester, almost entirely covered in snow.

"No, down here," she smiled. "I thought you'd been living here for the past... how many years?"

"About nine," he muttered, then blew more air into his hands, holding them cupped at his mouth. "But we repress traumatic memories, right?"

She laughed. "Exactly." She was impressed. "And you've only worked with a shrink for a partner for about two years."

"Two years, eleven months, seven days," he said, surprising her again. "And I thought you were a behavioral analyst, not just any shrink."

At a loss for words, she unzipped her leather jacket for long enough to take her weapon out of its holster, then quickly zipped it up all the way to her chin. She checked the magazine, racked the weapon, and took aim at a paper target barely hanging from a stand, twenty yards away.

Methodically, she fired all the rounds in slow cadence, making every shot count, as the range master used to say during her initial certification class. Surprisingly, her FBI weapons certification carried only limited weight in Franklin County. She had to get recertified when she'd moved back from San Francisco and joined the sheriff's office almost three years ago. Maintaining that certification required regular practice, signed off by the range master.

After she fired the last shot, she placed the weapon on the bench and trotted toward the paper target. It was wrinkled and stained by moisture but still showed clearly the holes she'd put in the center of the target. Several were off a little, up and slightly to the right, but all her shots had scored good points. Beaming with satisfaction, she tore the paper target from the stand and started folding it.

"Hope he'll sign off on this." She folded the paper until it could fit into her chest pocket.

Elliot took a few steps to the left, where a series of small steel plate targets hung from holders. He shot her a mischievous grin, stretched his neck left and right, then took aim. Whistling an upbeat tune Kay didn't recognize, he punctuated with quick shots fired into the steel targets. The bullets hitting them clanged loudly with various tonalities, somewhat matching the tune he was whistling. Without skipping a beat, when he emptied a mag, he dropped it and reloaded another. In less than a minute, he was done firing twenty-four rounds.

"That's gotta be a shooter from Texas," the range master exclaimed, appearing out of nowhere. He was a retired deputy, about seventy years old, who walked with a permanently bent back from a car pursuit gone bad. He'd ended up in a ravine after his cruiser had tumbled at least twice, and, to add insult to his injuries, the perp had managed to get away. "Perfect aim, Detective."

Kay shot him an inquisitive look. "How could you tell?"

"By the sounds he made. He played the first measures of 'The Yellow Rose of Texas.' You didn't recognize it?"

She shook her head, amazed. "The plates have different pitches?"

Elliot smiled and lowered his head, hiding his eyes under the brim of his hat just as his cheeks flushed a little.

"It's where a bullet hits the plate that gives the sound its pitch," the range master explained, tugging at a dark blue knitted hat to lower it over his ears. "The closer to the edge, the higher the pitch. The plates themselves are all the same."

"Oh, wow," she whispered. "I guess that beats my performance by a long shot," she added, handing the range master the paper target she'd put holes into earlier.

"This is good. It meets the proficiency requirements," the range master said, examining her work. "You shot a few too high. I'm willing to bet you shot these last when the recoil was getting the best of you. You're taking the finger off the trigger way too fast. That makes you jerk the gun." Then he looked at her encouragingly. "We all have our strengths and natural talents."

"Oh, well, then, if we're in a situation, I guess I'll let Elliot do the shooting, while I just talk the perps to death."

They burst into hearty laughter. The range master patted her on the shoulder. "You're not bad at all, Detective. You pass with flying colors. Actually," he gave the paper target another look, counting points in his mind while his lips moved soundlessly, "you scored one hundred and eight points out of one hundred and twenty possible. That's ninety percent proficiency. You're great."

"Yeah, but I'm not 'Yellow Rose of Texas' great, am I?" she said, chuckling. Elliot looked at her for a split second, a sparkle in his eyes as he smiled.

Her phone rang loudly. She took it out of her pocket quickly, recognizing the ring tone for the office dispatch.

"Good morning, Detective," Lizzie, the dispatcher, said. She was twenty-three or so, smart as a whip, and rumored to be the sheriff's niece. "Sheriff Logan wants you in the office, on the double."

"Copy that," Kay replied. "We're five minutes out." She ended the call and turned to Elliot. "Come on, partner, we have a case." She frowned for a moment, realizing the dispatcher had said nothing of the kind.

They found the sheriff in the observation room, staring through the two-way mirror at the back of a broad-shouldered man seated in the interviewer's chair. He wasn't cuffed. He wore a good quality charcoal suit, on the expensive side, with the collar of a white shirt showing, and black, shiny shoes that looked new.

The sheriff's arms were folded at his chest, and his expression was one of bewilderment. "He's surrendering," he said, without any other introduction, as soon as Kay and Elliot stepped in. "There's a warrant out for his arrest, issued in San Francisco County."

"What for?" Kay unzipped her jacket and took it off, abandoning it on an empty chair nearby. She approached the glass and looked at the man from behind. Something in his demeanor, in the shape of his haircut, seemed oddly familiar.

"Murder."

The word left a brief trail of silence in its wake.

"So, what's he doing here?" she asked, a feeling of doom descending into her heart. For a brief moment, she thought of the call from Rachel that she'd missed last Friday. After dinner, Kay had tried to call her but got voicemail.

The sheriff looked at Kay with a raised eyebrow and two deep tension lines flanking his mouth.

"He wants to surrender to you. He says he's your husband."

FIVE

REUNION

"Brian."

The muted whisper left Kay's pale lips without her noticing.

As if he'd heard her, the man turned around and looked straight at her through the two-way mirror. Then he stood and approached the glass, stopping inches away from it. Kay took an instinctive step back, although she knew he couldn't actually see her.

With the sight of his handsome face, memories came crashing back.

He hadn't changed much in the nine years since she'd met him. A touch of silver on his temples, but the rest of his hair had remained raven black, not giving an inch to a receding hairline. A hint of a smile fluttered on his lips as if he somehow knew she was there, watching him.

She'd fallen for Brian Thomas Hanlin nine years ago and almost instantly regretted it. They were not a good match. She loved his acute intellect, his innate curiosity, his sense of adventure, and the way his entire being seemed to vibrate in her presence, wanting her, loving her passionately, sweeping her off her feet with the tiniest kiss.

She'd thought he was the one. And, for a short while, she'd been deliriously happy.

What she'd loved the most about him turned out to be his biggest flaws. His innate curiosity went on to exploring other women whenever she wasn't looking. His sense of adventure drove him to try casual relationships without end. The fiery passion she relished was nothing but insatiable libido.

For as long as she could lie to herself, she didn't want to see it.

After a whirlwind romance and only a few months of dating, she'd said yes to him in her final year, just a few weeks before completing her master's degree in psychology. After graduation, she joined the FBI and started on an accelerated path to earn her PhD with the bureau's support. But before she could start working on her degree, only one month after they'd been married, she went to Quantico for twenty weeks of training at the FBI Academy.

While she was on the East Coast, he called every day and visited every other weekend. She thought he missed her.

She'd never been more wrong about anything in her entire life.

And with that realization came the pain. Suffocating, mind-numbing, soul-crushing pain.

One month after her return from Quantico, they were divorced.

She hadn't seen him since.

But even now, when she closed her eyes, she could recall the sight of him touching another woman's elbow at the Thanksgiving party, the way that woman leaned into him, the way he lowered his lips close to her ear and whispered something that had her swooning. It all came back, a memory so acutely painful she gasped.

He had some bloody nerve to show up on her doorstep like this.

Letting out a long, tense breath of air, she removed her weapon holster and put it in Elliot's hands. "Hold on to this for me, please."

"Kay—" he started, but she didn't let him finish.

"Let me deal with this," she said, unable to raise her eyes to meet his.

Anger trembled in every fiber of her being as she opened the door and entered the interview room. She hadn't thought of him in years, but it all came back, the hurt, the shame, the unbearable feeling of rejection that comes implicitly with being cheated on. She'd moved on; she thought she'd healed. She and Elliot were—

Damn.

"Brian," she said, the moment she entered the room. "I'd say this is a surprise, and not a pleasant one."

The air smelled of his favorite aftershave, an elegant, musky scent. Recognizing the scent she once used to love only fueled her anger. Her bedsheets used to smell of that. And of him.

He turned to face her and smiled widely, showing two rows of perfectly white teeth. He'd had some work done. He started over toward her with open arms, but she put her hand up in the air firmly, and he froze midstep.

"Stop right there." She pointed at the dented chair reserved for suspects. "This isn't some sort of reunion."

He sat without objecting, although he gave the chair a bit of a disgusted look. It was grimy. Maybe janitorial should've cleaned it more often. But she didn't care; she hadn't exactly invited him over.

Kay couldn't bring herself to sit just yet. Restless, she paced the room like a caged lioness, her face scrunched in searing anger and rekindled shame.

"You look good, Kay," he said. "Fresh mountain air agrees

with you. You haven't aged a day." His charm was just as effective as she remembered it to be, maybe a bit more polished even. But he was wasting it on her.

She dismissed his compliments with a hand gesture. "Ah, save it. What do you want, Brian?"

His megawatt smile vanished. "Oh, so you have to be like that?"

"What do you want?" She repeated the question slowly, but her voice was menacing.

"How's Jacob?" he asked, instead of doing what she'd asked him to do for bloody once.

Her hands propped up on her hips. "What the hell do you care? You never liked my brother."

"That's not true. Why do you say that?"

"Are you kidding me? You used to call him the hillbilly bear. Remember that?"

He smiled with a hint of embarrassment, lowering his gaze for a moment. "Yes, but with lots of love, Kay. You never heard me say a bad thing about him. Not ever."

She folded her arms at her chest, not convinced. "He's on vacation in Florida with his, um, family." There was no reason to tell him about Jacob's girlfriend and her adoptive daughters. She gritted her teeth, realizing he'd manipulated her into answering questions, into doing what he wanted. Again. "What do you want, Brian? Last time I'm asking. You have five seconds, then I'm walking away."

He lowered his gaze for a moment while tension built in his jaw. "There's a warrant out for my arrest."

She finally sat across from him, ending her restless pacing. "I heard."

A beat of tense silence. "I need your help," he blurted, his voice tinged with fear. "I didn't do it. And you're the only one I can trust."

"Are you serious right now?" she snapped, painfully aware

that perhaps Elliot and her boss were watching from the observation room. "How about my trust? Was I ever able to trust you?"

He didn't flinch. As always, it was as if her remarks couldn't touch him, sliding off him like raindrops on a window.

"Look, I know I've done you wrong, and I'm sorry—"

"Oh, now that you need me, you're sorry? How dare you?" Her voice climbed, her pitch grating, irritating to her own ears.

"I expected this... your anger." The charmer's smile returned for a split second. "And I will sit here and take all of it for as long as you want to dish it out because I know I deserve it and then some."

She stared at him in disbelief. The Brian she knew would've never not defended himself, would've never not attacked back, making her feel insecure and nothing short of a bitch. Was he for real?

"You're everything that stands between me and a life sentence, Kay. They're determined to lock me up and throw away the key. For something I didn't do."

She focused on her breathing for half a minute to soothe her frayed nerves. "I'm not an attorney, Brian. Maybe you can recall what I do for a living." She looked into the brown eyes that held her gaze calmly. They seemed so honest, so innocent. "You need a good lawyer. You must go through the process once the warrant has been issued. You know that just as well as I do."

He shook his head violently. "No. They'll kill me in there." He reached across the table and grabbed her hands. She pulled away as if his skin burned her, shooting him a warning glare. He backed away. "You're a cop and a damn good one. I've seen you work. You have a strong sense of right and wrong, of justice and fairness. I don't know anyone as honest and as brilliant as you."

He paused for a moment while Kay's thoughts raced from past to present, trying to decide what she could believe.

"Help me find the killer, Kay," he eventually whispered.

Suddenly, he seemed tired, defeated. "That's the only defense I need." He clasped his hands together tightly until his knuckles turned white. "Look, when I came here and surrendered, I put my life in your hands."

Silent, she looked at him for a while, weighing her options. She could just walk away. There was an active warrant out for his arrest, and that meant he wasn't going to leave; he'd be handed over to San Francisco Police Department for processing, and that would be it. She'd be well within her rights to do that; she didn't owe him anything.

But what if he was telling the truth? He must've known how badly she resented him for what he'd done, and yet he'd come to her for help.

"If you lie to me, Brian, I swear—"

"I won't," he said, looking straight into her eyes with candor. "This is different. I know I lied to you in the past, and you're right not to trust me worth a damn, but I promise you have nothing to worry about."

She couldn't believe herself. As if watching a train wreck in slow motion without being able to pull herself to safety, she heard herself say, "Tell me about this murder they're charging you with."

SIX
A COP

From the observation room, Elliot watched the loaded exchange, not realizing he'd clenched his fists. In minutes, Kay had transformed into someone he didn't recognize. In the tone of her voice, in the glistening anger sparking in her eyes, he could see she'd been deeply hurt by that man. He would've gladly gone in there and punched the daylights out of that slimy piece of scum.

Yet, he studied him with curiosity. He was someone Kay Sharp had said yes to. Where did that leave him? Two turns left past yonder, most likely. She'd never mentioned a husband, and she obviously still had strong feelings about the man, although not the kind he'd ever wish on himself.

And how stupid could that man be? To have someone amazing like Kay for a wife and screw it up so royally that she left and never looked back? She'd never mentioned him once, not even by accident. Not even after a couple of beers.

The man was annoyingly good-looking, well-dressed in a city slicker kind of way, and well-off by the looks of things. Kay didn't seem to care about those things; that much he knew. She appreciated honesty and kindness in people. Perhaps that's why

Mr. Slimeball was in her past and Elliot in her present. And future. Maybe.

Because she'd given in to his demands quite easily. He'd slathered more compliments on Kay than strawberry jam on a Sunday sandwich and had softened her up enough to make her willing to consider helping him. Elliot watched the scene helplessly, knowing he couldn't, under any circumstance, intervene.

Smooth son of a bitch.

"Did you know Kay was married?" Sheriff Logan asked. Like Elliot, he'd been standing there, watching, the expression of disbelief still etched on his features.

"Had no idea," Elliot replied.

Logan shook his head and sighed, the smell of stale cigar still strong on his breath. "I wouldn't want to lose her because of this." He gestured toward the glass with frustration.

Elliot's brow ruffled under the brim of his hat. "What do you mean?"

"Things could go many ways, and not all good. She could decide to return to San Francisco with him." Logan shot Elliot a quick glance. "She might not come back."

It seemed Logan wasn't all that clueless about where Elliot and Kay stood on a personal level.

It was tough to keep a relationship secret in a small place like Mount Chester. Even if that relationship was a little more than a work friendship, people were still talking about the two of them. They'd be seen having dinner at one of the three restaurants in town, hiking Wildfire Ridge, or having a picnic by Blackwater River Falls, and it was immediately on everyone's lips. Rumor mills worked real smoothly in small towns.

Everybody knew everybody, and everyone talked.

"Maybe you can do something about it," Logan continued. "Remind her why she stayed," he added, seeming a little uncomfortable asking.

Elliot nodded once, wondering if he had what it took to hold

Kay back. He'd better figure it out, faster than prairie fire. The thought of losing her was not something he was prepared to handle. "I'll do my best, boss."

Logan patted Elliot on the shoulder on his way out. "Keep your eyes peeled wide on this guy. He's a murder suspect and he's uncuffed. You never know."

Just then, Lizzie popped her head in the doorway. "Sheriff, I have someone here who wants to file a missing person report, a Mr. Lorentz. What do I tell him?"

"Tell him the detectives will be right there," Logan replied, then knocked on the two-way mirror twice, seeming almost relieved he had a reason to interrupt Kay's awkward reunion with her ex.

The scraping of metallic chair legs against the concrete floor preceded Kay's departure from the interview room. She closed the door behind her and joined them in the observation room.

Her eyes darted sideways, avoiding Elliot's. "What's going on?"

"We have a case," Elliot replied. "A missing—"

The sheriff cut him off. "What are you going to do?"

Kay seemed puzzled.

"About him." Logan gestured toward the window at Brian, who sat calmly in his chair, waiting.

Kay shrugged and lowered her eyes. "I honestly don't know yet. He needs to give me case details, and then we'll see."

"You know damn well you can't investigate a case in San Francisco, right?" Logan's voice was tense, fueled by a different kind of angst than Elliot's. "You don't have jurisdiction."

"Yes, I know that," she replied, closing her eyes for a moment. "I'm not going to investigate. I'll just look at the evidence and formulate some conclusions, see where that takes us."

"Who would those conclusions serve, Detective?" Logan

asked. "I'm sure the case investigator in San Fran doesn't want a biased opinion from the suspect's wife."

"Ex-wife, Sheriff." Her voice was ice-cold when she clarified her status.

"I'm willing to bet my next paycheck he doesn't want you anywhere near his evidence. Your involvement could blow up their case. Have it thrown out of court by any attorney worth their salt. They'll have your badge, and nothing I say or do would change that."

"Ah," Elliot whispered, but no one heard him. That was the fire ant crawling up on Logan's leg. Engulfed in his own anguish, Elliot hadn't thought of that scenario. They could lose Kay for more than one reason. And the smug, selfish bastard in that room wouldn't give a dead bullfrog's fart if his situation cost Kay her career.

"Who is he, anyway?" Elliot asked, looking at Kay. She kept looking away. There was already a chill in the air between them, and that man had been here less than an hour. What had started as a good day was turning into a disaster.

"Like I said, Elliot, he's my ex." She glanced at him so quickly before looking away he nearly missed it. But he caught enough to read the sadness she was trying to hide.

"No, I meant, other than that, why do you believe him when he says he didn't do it?"

A long, weary breath left Kay's chest before she replied.

"He's a San Francisco PD cop."

Fabulous, Elliot thought. *A cop.*

Charged with murder.

SEVEN
MISSING

Kay stood in the observation room doorway, wishing she'd wake up and realize it was a nightmare, the kind that happens years after a conflict, just a banal resonance of the subconscious mind to old, unresolved trauma. But no, it was real. Brian Hanlin was here, in flesh and bone, and she dreaded the moment she'd have to go back into that room.

"Let's take this at my desk," she offered, shooting the interview room a loaded glare and grabbing her jacket from the chair.

"I could handle it if you'd like," Elliot offered, his voice lacking conviction.

She touched his arm in passing, in silent gratitude. "Job comes first," she said, giving Logan a reassuring look. The sheriff walked away, his back a little hunched as if bent under the weight of his thoughts. On the way to his office, he stopped by a deputy's desk and instructed him to keep the witness in the interview room under close supervision.

Beckoning Lizzie to bring Mr. Lorentz over, Kay sat behind her desk and breathed. The familiar chair with her jacket hanging on its back, the scratched desktop littered with paperwork and small objects she used every day, the keyboard she instinctively drew closer as if getting ready to type, all those things were elements of her strength, foundational blocks of her existence. Memories of the good life she'd made for herself here, in her native Mount Chester, like the stapler she got as an anniversary gift from the sheriff. Promises of a happy tomorrow, like the bouquet of wildflowers Elliot had given her the day before, probably picked from the meadow behind his house.

Elliot leaned against the desk and crossed his legs at the ankle, studying her silently. He'd plunged his hands into his pockets and hadn't said much. She wanted to ask him what was wrong, but she knew already. Brian was what was wrong. And Brian wasn't a conversation she wanted to have with Elliot while waiting for a new case interview in a bullpen swarming with deputies.

Lizzie brought over a man with a despondent look on his face. Kay stood and invited him to take a seat by her desk. He was about fifty years old, dressed in a worn-out gray suit and a blue shirt, his navy-blue tie loosened, and his top button undone. His pale forehead was covered in beads of sweat, although it was cold outside, close to freezing. His pants and sleeves had grass blades and dirt stuck to them as if he'd been crawling on all fours through the woods, but he didn't seem to care. His hands were trembling, maybe from his emotional state or perhaps from physical exertion, because he was also panting heavily, out of breath, as if he'd run all the way to the precinct from who knows where.

Kay waited for him to take a seat. "Can I get you something, Mr.—"

"Lorentz. Gabriel Lorentz." He wiped his brow with the back of his hand in a quick gesture. "It's about my daughter, Taylor. She's missing."

"Since when?" Kay asked, the tip of her pen hovering above her notepad.

"Since six forty-seven this morning," the man replied after checking his phone.

"Mr. Lorentz, it's only been three-and-a-half hours—"

"You don't understand," he replied frantically, grabbing Kay's forearm in a pleading gesture. "Her watch messaged me that she'd fallen and wasn't responsive. I went there and looked everywhere, and she was gone."

Kay looked at Elliot briefly. "Let me see the message you received," she asked, then took the phone from the man's trembling hand. The message read, *The owner of this watch has taken a hard fall and is not responding to their watch. The estimated search radius is 125 feet.* Then the message continued with specific latitude and longitude coordinates.

She showed Elliot the phone screen. The information was compelling enough to elicit an immediate search. Several wearable devices were able to detect when the wearer took a hard fall. It seemed Taylor's had done its job.

"Doesn't this kind of message get sent after a nine-one-one call is made?" Elliot asked.

"Y—yes, maybe, I don't know," Mr. Lorentz stammered. "When I got there, I started looking, just like the thing said, a search radius of one hundred and twenty-five feet. I called her name, looked for footprints." His hand covered his mouth for a brief moment. "Even blood. There was nothing. She just vanished. But before that, the watch said she fell."

Kay put her hand on his arm reassuringly, then looked at Elliot. "We need to pull that nine-one-one call with dispatch report and find out what happened, if they sent anyone."

"You got it," Elliot replied, then disappeared.

"They didn't send anyone," Mr. Lorentz said. A sob choked him. "There wasn't anyone when I got there. I might've been a few minutes late. I was in the shower when the message came, and I didn't hear it right away."

"What time did you get there?"

"Seven twenty-five," he replied apologetically. "I should've had my phone with me in the shower. I knew she was out running, but I just—" His shoulder heaved under the weight of a shattered breath. "You never expect these things to happen to you. Never."

"Where is this spot, exactly?"

"By Frozen Falls, if you know it. The GPS put me about twenty yards from the Frozen Falls rock, two yards from the edge of the blacktop."

"That's low in the valley, right?" Kay asked, surprised the watch had had enough signal strength to send the message. The signal was weak there, on the stretch of highway north of Katse Coffee Shop. One bar, two at the most, and sometimes none. Maybe the watch had failed to call nine-one-one or had delayed the function until the signal was restored.

"Right," he nodded vigorously. "One mile north past Katse."

"Where do you live, Mr. Lorentz?"

"South of Katse, two-and-a-half miles, on the west side. We have a small farm."

"And Taylor? What time did she leave, and where was she going?"

"She went for a run at six-ten, maybe six-fifteen." He sprang to his feet as if getting ready to bolt. He seemed anxious, panicked almost, his patience for Kay's questions running thin. "She sometimes runs, okay? She likes to run around the hill in the morning, when the traffic isn't too bad. Let's go out there. Please. We need to find her."

"How old is your daughter?" Kay asked as gently as she could. They still had a few things to clarify before heading out there with a K-9 unit to try to find Taylor. Was there another unit investigating, after the nine-one-one call? Had they found something? Maybe she'd been found and taken to the Redding emergency room.

"She's nineteen, and she's a good kid. Not many kids these

days let their fathers know where they are, with these wearables and phones and all that. But she does. Always. Let's go, please. Help me find my little girl. She might be hurt out there, bleeding. There are bears in those woods... wolves too."

Elliot approached from dispatch with a heavy stomp in his step, the kind Kay had only seen when he was angry or upset.

"Excuse me, Mr. Lorentz," Kay said. "I'll be right back."

The man watched her leave with his jaw slacked in dismay. She met Elliot halfway across the bullpen by an empty desk.

"Turns out, the device made the nine-one-one call, and Redding dispatched it here. Deputy Leach took it. He went there at nine after seven, spent exactly four minutes looking around, and then disposed it as a crank call." Elliot briefed her in a low whisper. "I spoke with him just now, and I don't think he gave enough of a crap to look. He completely forgot about it."

Kay shook her head. At some point, someone had to do something about Leach. In his place, they could have a deputy who wanted to make a difference. Maybe Leach was good enough for speed traps and traffic, but for the rest of the job, he was a liability. One day, his laziness could cost someone their life. Perhaps it already had.

She took out her phone and typed a quick message to dispatch. Moments later, the phone chimed with the response.

"We have to search for the missing girl, Elliot, as soon as possible. I've already sent the request for a K-9 unit. They should be at the scene in about forty-five minutes. Let's hope it's not too late."

"And the guy in the interview room?" Logan asked, giving her a start. She hadn't noticed him approaching. At six-foot-four and 240 pounds, the sheriff could be unexpectedly light-footed. "What are you going to do about him?"

Brian. The returned bane of her existence, one wanted for murder no less.

For a moment or two, she'd forgotten all about him and the mess he was dragging her into.

"Let me finish with Mr. Lorentz. He's quite anxious for us to start searching for his daughter, and that's my first priority. Just a few more details; it won't take long. Then I'll need to ask you for a few days off."

The sheriff groaned and slapped the side of his thigh in frustration. "What do you want to do?"

"Brian needs to be taken to San Francisco anyway, in police custody, and I can do that. Make sure he gets a good lawyer, that sort of thing."

"Procedure calls for SFPD to get their butts over here for the transport," Logan pushed back, rubbing the ridges on his forehead with stubby, tobacco-stained fingers as if he wanted to smooth them out.

"If we bend the rules just a little, no one will complain, I promise you that."

"And you're comfortable hauling a family member in cuffs in the back of your vehicle?"

"Ex-family member," Kay clarified. "He's a cop, Sheriff. I really can't imagine he'd go around killing people. It's not who he is." She paused for a moment, looking at Logan intently. His demeanor, his entire body language, showed how much he resented what she was planning to do. "When I joined the FBI fresh out of college, he was already a sergeant with SFPD. He's got tenure, and he's a good cop. If he's being framed, I believe I can figure out—"

"Detective, you're putting your career at risk by asking as much as a single question from a witness," Logan said. "Don't do anything stupid that we'll both end up regretting."

She put her hand on her chest, refraining from giving Logan a hug. He meant well. "I promise." Letting a long breath of air escape her lungs, she looked at the worn-out carpeting for a brief moment before meeting Logan's direct and doubtful gaze.

"He was a philandering cheat as a husband, a liar, and a heart-breaker. But I can't think of a single lie he'd ever told except when covering up his many affairs. I believe he might be telling the truth this time."

He stared at her for a long moment, then nodded. "All right, you do what you got to do, Detective. I'll consider the trip to San Francisco on the books; after all, it's police business to turn over custody of a suspect. Just watch your back out there."

Kay breathed with ease, throwing the interview room a tense, worried glance. She'd decided to take Brian to San Francisco and she wasn't going to change her mind, but she was dreading it. All of it. His presence, in the same space with her, breathing the same air. His aftershave, leaving its musky trail in her Interceptor, invading her senses, stirring up memories of endless nights of passion and ardent kisses. All the things she'd wanted to say to him and never had, knowing how pointless it would've been, still weighed heavily, aching to be said.

Most exasperating of all, she didn't trust herself in his presence.

The entire thing couldn't be done fast enough. And, for some reason, she wanted to call Rachel again. Maybe she'd pick up this time.

But first, she wanted to ask Mr. Lorentz a few more questions. She rushed over to her desk. He was visibly relieved when she returned.

"Mr. Lorentz, we're organizing the search as we speak."

"Thank you," he whispered, his voice fraught with tears.

"You told me your daughter allowed you to know her location via her phone and watch, correct?"

"Yeah, there's an app, and I checked. See?" He held the screen in front of her. "It shows her last known location where the emergency coordinates were, but the phone and the watch are both off now. I've been checking every five minutes."

That could mean anything, including that she'd entered an area of spotty coverage. "And she has her phone with her?"

"Always. She loves listening to music while she runs. I told her it's dangerous, she won't hear cars coming, honking, but she wouldn't listen."

"How far does she usually run?"

"About five miles. She's in great shape and very ambitious. And she likes that stretch of highway because it goes down then up again. Nature's variable load workout, she calls it."

"All right, Mr. Lorentz. We're waiting for the K-9 unit to get here. My colleague, Detective Young, will be right back to take you to the search location."

"H—how about you?" he stammered, the look of despair on his face renewed.

"I'll be coordinating a few things from here and working with the technical team to try to locate the devices. Please give us a moment."

He tried to stand and leaned against the desk, seeming disoriented, turning even paler. More sweat broke out in tiny beads at the roots of his hair, on his forehead. Before Kay could catch him, he landed hard on the floor, seizing.

Kay knelt by his side and slid her folded jacket under his head. She loosened his tie and undid a couple of shirt buttons, then shouted, "Someone, get EMS in here!"

EIGHT
ROAD TRIP

EMS was getting ready to leave when Kay finally made it to the interview room. It was empty. She shot Deputy Hobbs a quick look. He was the one Logan had tasked earlier with keeping tabs on her ex.

Hobbs tried to keep a straight face. "If you're looking for your, um, suspect, he's loaded in your vehicle, Detective, all ready to go."

She thanked him with a nod. It would be a while before the rumor mill would come to a stop after Brian's unexpected jaunt through her life. Until then, everyone would smirk, whisper, and make all sorts of comments. Nothing she could do about that.

Circling by her desk to pick up her jacket, Kay frowned at the sight of the stained carpet where Mr. Lorentz had collapsed with a hypoglycemic seizure. She blamed herself for not catching the signs earlier. He'd been pale and sweaty despite the cold weather, anxious, restless, sometimes slurring his speech. All the symptoms had been there, and still, she'd missed it.

On a normal day, on a day without Brian Hanlin on her mind, she wouldn't have missed it. Any parent whose child had taken a hard fall then disappeared would've been anxious and trembling and panting, but not pale. Not sweating so much. The poor man must've exerted himself looking for his daughter until he nearly died.

She rushed outside, eager to get Brian out of her life again. The EMS bus was still there, Mr. Lorentz sitting on the rear bumper with an IV in his arm. He stood when she approached, seeming steady on his feet, his sweat gone, his color back to healthier hues.

"Detective?"

"Mr. Lorentz, my partner is right behind me. He'll meet the K-9 unit at the emergency coordinates provided by the device, over by Frozen Falls. Two other deputies are already on-site, grid-searching."

Mr. Lorentz pulled the needle out of his arm, waving off the EMT who was trying to stop him. "I'm good. Let me go." He rolled down his shirt sleeve and hung his jacket on his shoulders. A red dot stained his sleeve. "I'm not going to sit here anymore; we've wasted enough time. I'm coming with you."

Elliot heard the last phrase, coming out of the precinct with his car keys in hand. Kay searched his eyes, then turned to Mr. Lorentz. "All right, Mr. Lorentz, you'll ride with my partner."

She waited until Elliot reached them before turning to leave.

"Kay," Elliot said, then stopped as if unsure what else to say. She smiled weakly. "I'll be fine, Elliot. And I'll be back before you know it," she whispered. Looking into his eyes, she felt tempted to call SFPD and tell them to pick up their suspect, and the hell with Brian Hanlin. But what if later she heard he was convicted and sentenced to life in prison over a crime he didn't commit? How would she be able to live with herself?

Her ex ruined everything he touched; that was for certain. Just by showing up.

"Finally," Brian said as soon as she climbed behind the wheel. He was slouched in the back seat, in the middle, leaning sideways. "Your chubby colleague didn't bother to tell me why I'm cuffed here like a perp."

Starting the engine, she peeled off, heading for the highway. "Typical procedure for murder suspects in custody, if you recall."

He scoffed and grinned, probably uncertain what would work best on her, sarcasm or charm. He settled for the latter. "But is this really necessary, Kay? Having me chained like a drug-dealing thug?"

It probably wasn't. Dreading the argument that would not end until he was uncuffed, she reached into her pocket and fished out the cuff key, then handed it over. "Don't make me regret this, or I'll have you chained with barbed wire."

The handcuffs clicked and rattled when he dropped them onto the floor. Brian sighed, relieved. "That's much better, thanks. Now, aren't you hungry?"

It was as if they were married all over again. "Damn it, Brian, this isn't a social call. I'm turning you over to San Francisco Police Department, not taking you out on a picnic."

He leaned forward, resting his forearm on the back of her seat. She could feel his breath touching her hair. "San Fran is two hours out, and they're not exactly waiting for me with a meal and a cup of coffee, right? I've been locked up since seven-thirty this morning, and no one bothered to ask." He paused for a moment, probably noticing her eye roll in the rearview mirror. "Last I heard, people were fainting and seizing in your custody from low blood sugar."

He wasn't going to stop. She could've duct-taped his mouth, but he had a point. She'd skipped breakfast that morning, running late for her shooting range practice with Elliot, and had settled for the coffee he'd brought.

Still, she was caving to Brian's whim, and that infuriated her to no end.

Groaning, she speed-dialed Katse Coffee Shop on her media screen. Tommy MacPherson, the owner, picked up after the first ring.

"Hey, Tommy, it's Kay Sharp."

"Good morning, Detective," he replied, raising his voice a little to cover the chatter in the background and the whistling of a nearby cappuccino maker. "What can I do for you?"

"I need two large croissants and two cups of coffee to go."

"Two croissants for me, please," Brian intervened. "And have them warmed up."

Kay clenched her jaw for a brief moment. "Okay, three croissants. But make one of the coffees a really watered-down decaf, please, Tommy. Some people don't need stimulation. And can you bring them outside to my car? I'm hauling a suspect." She pulled into Katse's parking lot as she spoke.

"Sure. A minute or two, Detective."

"That's mean," Brian said the moment she ended the call. "You didn't use to be like that. You were sweet and gentle, wanting to make people smile."

"Well, you changed all that, Brian. I met you, and five seconds later, I found out some people were scum."

Tommy knocked against her window, startling her. She lowered the window and took the bag of croissants from him, then one cup of coffee. Courteous as usual but probably eager to sneak a peek at her passenger, Tommy reached inside to hand the second cup of coffee to Brian.

"Here you go, Mr. Sharp, your decaf."

Brian started laughing. "Thank you."

Kay fumed. "His name isn't Sharp," she clarified, her eyes cold as ice staring Tommy into backing off, apologizing.

"I'm so sorry, Detective. Everyone's saying, um, never mind. I made a mistake." He held his head down and his hands raised as if Kay was going to shoot him. It wasn't his fault people talked.

"It's okay, Tommy. Please charge this to my card."

"Sure thing." He took another step back. "What's going on down there?" He pointed down the road toward the valley. "Heard someone was missing?"

"Taylor Lorentz, if you know her. She disappeared early this morning when she was jogging. Know anything about that?"

"Yeah, no, I mean, I knew her, just in passing, 'cause she runs by here quite often. But I didn't know she was missing."

"Well, call me if you hear anything."

"Will do. And sorry about the..." He gestured toward the vehicle with an embarrassed look on his face. "The whole name thing."

Her appetite had vanished; she drove off toward the highway, flooring it. In the rearview mirror, the distant red and blue lights of several vehicles flashed where the search for Taylor Lorentz had begun.

A loud slurp disrupted her thoughts.

"Ugh, this coffee is seriously lame," Brian complained. "You're vengeful, aren't you? Still bitter, maybe? Just a little?"

"You seem awfully relaxed, Brian, for someone who's about to go to jail. What the hell is in that brain of yours? Do you realize how serious your situation is?" Lowering the window a couple of inches, she forced a cold, soothing breath of air into her lungs. She rested her eyes for a split moment on the contour of the rocky mountain peaks against the azure sky, borrowing from the mountain's serenity. Brian had always been a little irresponsible.

"I have you on my side," he replied, his voice somber. "I know you won't leave me."

"You don't know that, Brian. I came this close to calling SFPD and washing my hands of you." She held her hand in the air, her thumb about an eighth of an inch away from her index. "That could still happen."

A few moments of sullen silence told Kay she'd hit the spot.

"Who's the victim?"

He didn't reply right away. Checking the mirror, she noticed his head hung low.

"My fiancée," he eventually said. "We were to be married in December. She wanted a Christmas wedding, everything white, everything perfect." His voice broke a little. "Maybe you don't want to hear this, Kay, but I loved her. I really did."

She let the loaded remark go. As far as she was concerned, he could love anyone and get married to anyone. She'd stopped caring a long time ago. Yet the tiniest shard of jealousy pricked her heart, making her wonder if he'd cheated on his new fiancée too. If he'd loved her more than he did Kay. If this dead girl had been the one for him.

She chased the unwanted thoughts away. It was better to just stick to the case.

"Why are you suspected of killing her? What do they have on you?"

"I doubt they have anything—"

"Are you still a cop, Brian? Were you ever? A judge must sign that warrant based on evidence and witness statements. It doesn't get issued just like that, because someone wants it."

It felt just like when they were married, and she'd tried to get a straight answer out of him when she'd asked him where he'd been.

"I made detective second grade two years ago, after several undercover stints. So, yeah, I'm a detective, just like you. A suspended one with a murder warrant out on his name, but a detective nonetheless," he said, a touch of pride in his voice but also frustration and bitterness and fear. "I meant to say they have my fingerprints at the scene, but she was my fiancée, so they would've been there, right? And I had no alibi for the time of her death. I don't think they have anything else; there's nothing else they *could* have."

He hadn't touched his croissants. He held the bag in his hand still, the paper rustling every now and then, the aroma of warm, buttery pastry filling Kay's nostrils.

"When was she killed?"

"Last Friday, around six in the evening," he replied, the sadness in his voice returning. "Maybe I've made some enemies in the SFPD. I rose through the ranks, and I put some really bad people away, some of them connected. Organized crime, drug networks, a couple of dirty cops." The paper bag rustled, then he took a bite from a croissant and chewed it. "This is good," he mumbled, his mouth still full.

"Do you think you're being framed? Or they just pinned it on you because 'it's always the spouse'? The lazy cop's quick collar?"

He took another bite. "I don't know. Might be."

"You must have some idea who killed your fiancée," she said, honking furiously at a Dodge Ram driver who wasn't paying attention. She'd been driving behind him for a minute with flashers on. Startled, the driver veered out of the way so abruptly he almost hit the guardrail.

Brian cleared his throat the way he always used to do after eating, then took a swig of coffee.

"She was supposed to enter WITSEC the night she was killed. A US Marshal was going to pick her up at seven."

"Okay, run that by me again," Kay said. There were several unusual things about his story. "From the top."

"She'd witnessed a crime, an apparently random street shooting the day before, and had already spoken to the ADA about it."

"Why did they believe her life was in danger?"

A beat. "Not sure. I wasn't there for the entire conversation. The details she gave must've been pointing them at some suspect on some active case, I guess. They didn't want to share any of that with me. That ADA, he's an asshole, a big one, power tripping like none other."

"If they deemed her to be in danger, why did she go home? She was killed at home, wasn't she? You said your prints were there."

"Yeah, she was killed at home."

"Hers? Or yours?" She'd nearly said ours.

"Hers." He bit his lip for a moment, seemingly thinking about what to say. "I don't know why they let her go. I didn't realize how serious it was because they didn't tell me what they suspected. She wanted one more day to put things in order before going into WITSEC. One more day of normality, she'd called it. I don't believe she'd realized how serious her situation was."

"What did she tell you?"

"She hated the idea of going into WITSEC, even for a short period of time. She'd seen a shooting, then did what she thought was the right thing to do without asking me first. I would've told her to just walk away. Screw the justice system when it comes to our families, right? Witnesses put themselves in immense danger. I would've told her what testifying really meant, and she'd still be alive now."

They drove in silence for a while. Kay wondered why the SFPD had been so quick to issue a warrant for Brian's arrest when this was clearly a case of witness tampering.

"Then why you, Brian? Why name you as prime suspect? Doesn't the ADA put two and two together?"

"It's not the same ADA. A different one is on my case, an ambitious, politically motivated little bitch."

"Who investigated your fiancée's murder?"

"An old-timer, a detective from our precinct with a hard-on

for me, apparently. I can't be sure he's not on the take. I don't trust the guy." He crushed the empty paper bag and abandoned it in the cup holder on the center console, next to Kay's untouched croissant. "I think I'm being set up, Kay. If you can't figure out who did it, I'm finished. I will die in prison."

NINE
HER NAME

Kay waited by the SUV while fuel flowed into the tank, whirring at a brisk pace and filling the area with a faint whiff of gasoline vapor. They were almost at the Golden Gate Bridge, not more than twenty minutes away from Brian's precinct, and she'd thought it best to stop. Once they headed into the city, there would be no stopping until they reached their destination.

Against her better judgment, she'd allowed Brian to enter the gas station unescorted to use the facilities. Almost ten minutes had passed, and she was getting worried. Had he bailed on her? Had he suddenly decided he didn't want to go to jail and hitched a ride out of Marin County going wherever?

The pump handle clanked and stopped. She put it back on the pump and grabbed the receipt. When she looked up from her wallet, Brian was there with a smug smile and a tall, iced cappuccino topped with a swirl of whipped cream covered in chocolate syrup and caramel.

Two thousand calories in a plastic cup. Just what she needed.

Unfortunately, he was about finished downing a stiff black

coffee, and that meant he'd soon be argumentative, hostile, and even more impulsive than his normal self.

"Thanks," she said, pushing away the hand bearing the peace offering.

"I insist. If you're not going to drink it, I'll have to sacrifice myself."

All he needed was a sugar rush. With a frustrated groan, she took the cup from his hand, more to keep it away from him than anything else. Although the caramel-covered whipped cream dunked in coffee was mouthwatering.

She sat behind the wheel while he climbed reluctantly into the back seat after her angry gesture deflated his initiative to ride in the front seat.

"Do you have a lawyer?" Giving in to temptation, she tasted the coffee. It was delicious, by any standards, even if it was gas-station brewed.

"There's someone I could call, yes. I can't afford much of a lawyer, but I guess I can call in a favor or two."

She turned toward the highway ramp. Traffic was picking up, turning dense. "Have them meet us at the precinct. Say, thirty minutes?"

He didn't say anything. After a while, Kay looked in the rearview mirror and saw he was texting on his phone. He probably had someone already lined up; he must've figured out he needed an attorney by now. A few moments later, a chime interrupted Kay's thoughts.

"She says she'll be there, although she might be a little late." He sounded relieved.

"She?" Kay couldn't help a chuckle. "Of course."

"Oh, come on," Brian pushed back loudly, slamming his hand against the back seat. "Now I can't have a professional relationship with a woman because that means I'm screwing her?"

Kay muttered an oath. Why was it he brought out the worst

in her? She still resented him, still hated him for what he'd done to her, for how insignificant and powerless he'd made her feel. Sometimes, she wished she could duct-tape him to a chair to yell at until she was out of breath and finally done cleansing the stain of Brian Hanlin off her soul. "You can have whatever relationships you want with whomever you want. It was wrong of me to make that comment."

For a while, the wheels whooshing on asphalt and thumping rhythmically was the only sound she heard.

"It's okay," he said after a while, sounding glum. "Like I said earlier, I'll take whatever you want to dish out."

She didn't reply, still lost in thought. What was she going to do after she delivered him to the San Francisco Police Department? Where would she go? Who would she talk to? Sheriff Logan was right. She couldn't barge in and take over an investigation. She didn't have the right to request access to the crime scene, speak to the victim's family, examine evidence, any of that. There was no plan.

She headed toward the precinct. They were only a few minutes out, but the traffic was heavy. Soon, he'd be taken away for processing, and probably the next day, he'd have his arraignment and post bail. Between today and tomorrow, she'd have time to think about what to do, how to get to the bottom of it. A nice long stroll by the ocean to clear her head of the madness he dispersed, and she'd come up with something.

He deserved to burn in hell, not rot in jail for a murder he didn't commit.

"One thing to another," he said, the somber accents in his voice still heavy. "I guess I should tell you her name."

She looked straight at him through the rearview mirror, a sense of doom descending in the pit of her stomach on realizing he'd somehow managed to not bring up his fiancée's name until then. How did he pull that kind of crap off?

"It's better to hear it from me, here, than during arraignment. You'll be there tomorrow, right? For the arraignment?"

"Who was she, Brian?" she asked coldly, feeling her throat dry, constricted.

He paused for a moment. Kay held her breath.

"It was Rachel," he whispered. "I know what you'll say—"

"You miserable sack of lying shit!" she shouted, slamming both her fists against the steering wheel. "She was my best friend! And you didn't think of mentioning this until now?" She stopped for a moment, panting, stammering, more words wanting to be spoken than she could speak. "Y—you lied to me eight years ago when I asked if you'd been sleeping with her. I know what I saw at that party, but you swore to me—" She choked on her anger, feeling the threatening burn of tears in her eyes. She wasn't going to cry... not there, not with him watching.

"It wasn't like that—"

"Shut up," she said. "This morning at the precinct, and on the road here, when we talked about the case, what were you thinking, withholding her name? That I wouldn't find out? That you'd somehow get away with it?" She breathed deeply, willing herself calm, but she wasn't succeeding. "You've always been a coward, Brian. A coward and a liar and a cheat. And I don't know what the hell I'm doing here."

She brought the SUV to an abrupt stop in the SFPD precinct parking lot and cut off the engine.

"Kay, please—"

"Don't you dare," she said, turning toward the back seat and drilling into him with her glare. "Don't say my name or move an inch until I get back. Don't say a single damn word or I'm out of here, and if they fry you, so be it. I don't care anymore."

She stared at him until he lowered his eyes and clasped his hands together, apparently subdued. Then she climbed out of the vehicle, in a daze, not sure what she wanted to do. All she knew was she had to get away from him as quickly as possible.

"Wait, where are you going?"

"To grieve the loss of my best friend," Kay replied coldly, then slammed the car door as hard as she could.

TEN

BLOOD

Elliot pulled over by the side of the road, behind Deputy Novack's vehicle. Two other marked cruisers were there, and another blocked northbound traffic access. Half a mile north, a fourth cruiser blocked southbound traffic, holding back several vehicles that were probably headed into Redding. They weren't going to get there any time soon.

He got out of the SUV and shivered, then zipped his denim jacket all the way up.

It was cold as a mother-in-law's heart.

The wind was howling at the bottom of the valley, rolling down from the versants of Mount Chester with icy gusts. Tall firs bent at the tips, their branches shaking off needles and cones, littering the road. A few miles east, the rocky peaks were covered in fresh snow, glinting in the sun. If it weren't for the perfect blue sky, Elliot would've thought a snowstorm was coming.

He'd taken Mr. Lorentz to his home first to pick up a clothing item of his daughter's for the sniffing dog, and also get everything he needed to keep his blood sugar under control. Lorentz had grabbed a couple of protein bars and his insulin kit, then burst into tears while he watched Elliot seal Taylor's pajama top into a plastic evidence bag.

"We'll do everything we can, Mr. Lorentz," Elliot had encouraged him, helping him to the car. "It's very soon, and we have the best K-9 unit coming in to help." He started the engine and asked, "Is there a Mrs. Lorentz we could call?"

"My wife passed on last year. Cancer. She fought it bravely, hung on for as long as she could," Mr. Lorentz said weakly, his voice breaking off at times. "Taylor is all I have left in this world, Detective. I can't bear the thought of losing her."

The drive from the Lorentz farm to the emergency coordinates took less than two minutes. Elliot drove past Katse doing seventy miles per hour.

As soon as he pulled over, Elliot turned to his passenger and said, "Please stay here, Mr. Lorentz. It's warm in the car, and we need you to be safe while we do our work."

"But I can't sit here and do nothing—"

"Please, Mr. Lorentz, trust me. It's better this way. If we have questions, we know where to find you. As soon as we find anything, I'll be here to let you know." He looked into the man's tear-filled eyes, trying to instill some hope into his weary soul.

"Okay, I'll stay here."

Elliot thanked him and rushed over to Deputy Novack. He was a good cop, thorough and resourceful, next in line to make detective if he wanted it. Tall and fit with a bony frame lined with lean muscle, he never took off his Ray-Bans, even when it rained. Elliot suspected it was because he looked very much like Stephen Dorff playing Sheriff Bill Hollister in a popular TV show, and Novack was milking the look for all it had, five-day stubble and all. That didn't make Novack a bad cop, though. Not a vain person, he was probably just as much entertained by the resemblance as his colleagues were.

"Tell me what you have," Elliot said. He stomped in place vigorously. His Texas birthright included hating cold weather and not tolerating it too well. His feet had gone a little numb, and he'd only been there a few minutes.

"We started gridding here, by the road, and going inland in twenty-foot-wide swatches, north and south, but it's just the four of us. We didn't get far and didn't find anything yet."

The grasses were tall and thick by the side of the road. Several red fuchsia flowers still stood tall, sprinkled alongside the road. A few nights of ground frost had started to wither the grass, turning it into red-spotted yellowish humps of mangled blades and withering wildflowers. Several footsteps were still visible, probably Lorentz's or the deputies. If this was a crime scene, it was trampled and compromised already. He couldn't blame a desperate parent for trying to find his daughter; he would've done the same thing.

Pulling out his phone, he checked his location GPS coordinates. They were a little off from what the emergency message had indicated. "Do you have the exact location pinned?"

"Yeah, it's over there," Novack pointed down the road a few yards.

They'd marked the spot with a small, red flag on a wire. Elliot walked over there while Novack resumed searching the woods by the highway. The device had warned about a 125 feet radius, but Elliot decided to trust the technology.

At some point in the recent past, when they were working on a different case, Kay had explained how GPS works and that it needs a direct line of sight with three positioning satellites for accuracy. Devices between tall buildings or near a mountain could have the results skewed. Or something like that... He didn't speak tech the way his partner did.

Squinting at the clear blue sky as if to see how many satellites were up there, he took his hat off and studied the scenery. Tall firs lined both sides of the highway. Mount Chester rose toward the east, its versants close enough to take a good chunk of that direct line of sight off the table. Things weren't looking good for accurate positioning.

But devices are consistent, not moody and finicky like people can be.

He checked the phone's GPS readings for his location and had the coordinates shown on a map with terrain this time. The device, using the same geolocation system that Taylor's device—and all others—had used, showed his location with stunning accuracy. Less than ten feet from where he really was, judging by the distance to the Frozen Falls rock and on which lane of the road his blue dot was showing.

That was precise enough. There must've been swarms of geolocating satellites right above their heads, doing their jobs.

If Taylor had been running, heading north, because she had only recently left the house and she usually ran five miles, she would've been on the east side of the road. Elliot walked over to the edge of the blacktop and started looking carefully, examining every blade of grass, every inch of asphalt, and moving in an opening spiral from those precise coordinates.

About six feet north, on the very edge of the road where the asphalt had crumbled, he found a drop of blood. Kneeling to get closer, he examined the drop for directional clues. Several tiny other droplets surrounded it, barely visible to the naked eye. A slight tail was formed, its direction pointing in the direction Taylor was going.

East.

Into the woods.

She'd taken a hard fall, got hurt, and walked into the woods. But why? It made no sense. If she'd been hurt falling and she was bleeding, she would've stayed on the side of the road to flag down a car and get help. She would've called home. She wouldn't have gone into the woods to hide.

Maybe her fall wasn't a fall after all.

He raised his arm in the air and whistled loud enough to

make all his horses come home. "Over here," he shouted when he saw Novack was looking his way.

A yellow evidence marker bearing the number "1" was placed by the blood droplet, and Deputy Farrell started taking photos. Novack and two other deputies combed the tall, bent grasses, careful not to miss any shred of evidence.

"I found something," Novack called. He stood on the edge of the road a few feet south of the blood drop. Elliot rushed over there and saw what Novack was showing him. Two barely visible trails, running parallel and closely together, disturbed the grasses starting from the asphalt and disappeared into the woods. As if her body had been dragged away from the road.

"Oh, crap," Elliot muttered, staring at the drag marks. He didn't want to let that first blood drop discourage him, but the evidence looked grim.

He followed the drag marks until they vanished, the grass scarce where the shade of the tall trees kept the sunlight from reaching the ground. A thick layer of fir needles took its place, but the drag marks weren't visible anymore. From that point, there was no way to determine where to look, but they had a starting point.

He was about to leave when something caught his attention. On the reddish-brown cover of dry fir needles, was a light brown scrunchie made of velour-like fabric. Several strands of hair still clung to it. Picking it up carefully with a gloved hand, he placed it inside an evidence pouch, zipped it, and placed it inside his pocket.

The sound of arguing voices caught his attention. He looked up and saw Mr. Lorentz fighting Deputy Farrell to break loose from her grip.

"I know you found something," he shouted. "What did you find?"

"Mr. Lorentz, please, let us work," Farrell pleaded, holding him back by both his arms.

Elliot signaled her to let the man go. He'd been through more than his share of hell that morning. The detective returned to the road and instructed Novack to comb through the area.

Almost running, Mr. Lorentz closed the distance between them breathlessly, a look of paralyzing fear on his face.

"Tell me, what did you find?" he asked as soon as he reached Elliot.

"Nothing to worry about for now, sir. Just a blood drop that could be older or could belong to someone else. Nothing definitive yet." Experience had shown him that honesty worked best in cases like that. "Now, please, wait in the car."

The man shook his head violently. "No. Please, I'll wait here, won't make a sound, but please, don't send me back."

Elliot groaned. Procedures were clear; the man had no business being in the middle of an active investigation. He'd already bent the rules to breaking point just by having him in his car, farther up the road. "I'm sorry, we simply can't. I hope you understand. Every moment we spend arguing with you, we don't spend looking for Taylor."

That statement had the effect of an ice bucket poured over the man's head. Instantly subdued, he whispered in a trembling voice, "I understand, Detective. I'll go back to the car and wait."

"Just a second," Elliot said, extracting the evidence pouch from his pocket. "Is this something Taylor would've worn?"

A sob choked Mr. Lorentz. He quickly covered his mouth with his hand as if to try to keep it bottled inside. "Y—yes, she has a set of three. Her mother gave those to her. She was wearing that one when she left. Where did you find it?"

"Please, Mr. Lorentz, let us work. I'll come to find you the moment I know anything." He patted the man on his shoulder, squeezing it a little for encouragement. Dragging his feet and keeping his head hung low, Mr. Lorentz started walking uphill toward Elliot's car.

He didn't get too far before a cruiser bearing the K-9 insignia pulled in. When he saw the police dog jump out of the cruiser, Mr. Lorentz froze in place, his hand on his chest, his mouth ajar, staring.

Elliot pretended not to notice him.

Soon they'd both learn what had happened to Taylor Lorentz.

ELEVEN
MEMORIES

Without looking back, Kay walked away from her Interceptor with a brisk step, wishing as much distance between her and Brian as possible. Once she reached the parking lot entrance, she looked left, then right, trying to figure out where to go.

A few yards outside the parking lot, she found a sidewalk partly obscured by two parked vehicles. She sat on the curb and hugged her knees, wishing she could curl up in a ball and lie down somewhere dark and quiet.

With the memory of Rachel, tears came rushing to her eyes, and a sob swelled her chest. Burying her face in the crook of her arm, she cried until she couldn't breathe anymore. One by one, forgotten memories flooded her mind, each more painful than all the rest.

Rachel had called last week and left her a message. Kay hadn't called her back right away, not until later that night. Her calls had gone straight to voicemail; the same had happened the following morning.

And now she was gone.

Still crying, she found Rachel's message on her phone and

looked at the date and time. Last Friday, at 4:42 p.m. If she'd returned her call right then, Rachel might still be alive.

Her finger hovered above the play button for a moment, then tapped. Her voice came to life.

"Hi, it's Rachel. I've been meaning to call you... for years. But I really need to speak with you now. I... hope you'll forgive me for what I've done. For everything. I know I have no right, but I need you. Please call me back."

The same voice had said the very same, "Hi, it's Rachel," the day they first met. Kay was starting her sophomore year at UC Berkeley and had been assigned a new dorm room after summer break. She'd climbed two flights of stairs to find the room empty. Within minutes, she'd got herself minimally settled and changed clothes; her shift was starting at her new job. Four days a week plus weekends, she was going to wait on tables at a busy, posh pizza place a mile down the road.

She was about to leave when the door swung open, and a spirited girl with fiery curls and freckles on her nose stormed inside, holding her hand out in a wide-grinned greeting.

"Hi, it's Rachel," she'd said. "Your new roommate."

Her smile was infectious, her laughter irresistible. Her effect on heartbroken Kay, who still carried the weight of her childhood memories like balls on a chain she couldn't break free of, was immediate. Although she'd always thought it would be impossible for her, Kay started to heal.

They'd become inseparable, Rachel and her. On weekdays when the school load was light, and she didn't work, she was guest of honor at the Epling family home. Rachel's father had passed, only her mother remained, and Rachel made sure she'd visited every week. Her dedication to her mother made Kay feel guilty for not doing the same; her situation was different. She couldn't bear to visit the home where so much suffering had been endured at the hands of her father. Soon enough, Rachel had stopped asking Kay about her family.

They shared the same major, psychology, and attended the same classes. They helped each other study and tackle the challenging load of balancing classes and working to support themselves through school. On weekends, after the pizza place closed and Kay was free, they'd go dancing or attend parties with other students, nothing too crazy, just enough to feel young and free like one is supposed to feel in college.

Years flew by quickly. Rachel had a bad relationship in her junior year, and Kay had held her in her arms while she sobbed after her boyfriend had vanished with her dismal savings and a pearl necklace she got from her mother the day she turned eighteen. She furiously refused to press charges; Kay suspected Rachel secretly hoped he'd come back to her, and she'd forgive him, and they'd live happily ever after. A little more mature than her friend, Kay had tried to tell her life didn't work that way. Heartbroken and disillusioned, Rachel sobbed her way through the junior year exams.

Then senior year started. Summer had been good, and they managed to sneak in a couple of weeks of actual vacation between extra shifts at the pizza place and taking early classes. Kay had her mind set on joining the FBI after graduation because she'd witnessed the bold rescue of a hostage group during a bank robbery from the café across the street. She was vying to be inside, to do something that mattered to people's lives. She couldn't graduate fast enough.

The money was in counseling the executives of Silicon Valley, but she wanted her work to have more meaning than that. Rachel was going to counsel the overworked, rich, and powerful, as she liked to quip, then she'd grab Kay and see the world together on her big, fat dime.

In her final semester, fate decided to put Brian Hanlin in Kay's path. A nine-one-one call was made by the faculty after finding an office had been broken into overnight.

He turned heads wherever he went, and he knew it.

Dressed in uniform and with a hint of a smile in his eyes, he'd taken his time at the scene, taking statements, names, and phone numbers. Almost all the female students smiled and batted their eyelashes when he spoke with them. Some of the men too.

When Kay's turn came to be interviewed, she was tired after a long day. All she wanted was a long shower and a book to read in bed. With her, Brian's charm didn't work that well.

Then Sergeant Brian Hanlin was gone, leaving the entire dorm with dreamy eyes for at least a few minutes after his cruiser departed.

He never called any of them with follow-up questions.

Except for Kay.

The follow-up question was about how Kay liked her coffee.

And so, the cool-headed senior was swept off her feet by the exuberant, charming, and absolutely irresistible Brian Hanlin.

Her relationship with Brian evolved like a brush fire, all-consuming and intense, leaving nothing in its wake. Rachel had fallen in second place, but she understood or claimed she did. She'd been quite honest when she'd confessed that she envied Kay for her relationship with Brian. In retrospect, knowing what Kay knew now, Rachel had been a little too interested in her boyfriend than Kay would've liked.

But they stayed friends, besties, and when Kay had said yes to Brian Hanlin in front of a very small audience, Rachel had been her maid of honor, blushing and tearing up when it was her friend's time to kiss the groom.

From the dorm room, Kay had moved into Brian's house, a three-bedroom, detached house with a small backyard he'd inherited from his parents. Soon after their honeymoon ended, Kay was able to graduate early, while Rachel still had to go the entire semester with the rest of their class.

They had returned from Las Vegas, where they had a hotel suite for a week, and Kay was deliriously happy. She liked everything about her new husband, except, perhaps, the attention he always got from women, young and old. Back then, she thought none of it was his fault; he was a charismatic individual, handsome, intelligent, and well-built, who knew how to carry himself and how to strike a conversation.

In hindsight, Kay blamed herself for not noticing Brian had been almost as interested in other women as they had been interested in him. He'd probably been walking by her side, Kay's hand in his, and had smiled at other women, had made eye contact with them in the fascinating, lascivious way he lit a fire in Kay's blood whenever their eyes met. The evidence must've been there... but Kay was blind to it, refusing to see anything that wasn't about her perfect new life with her perfect new husband.

After graduating, despite it being earlier than the rest of her class, Kay wanted to celebrate with Brian and Rachel. She'd made reservations at a fancy steakhouse, Espetus, in San Francisco and was excited to be with the two people she loved the most.

Yet the much-anticipated dinner was clouded by Rachel's distance. She seemed cold, reserved, not her usual self. Her eyes veered away every time Kay looked at her, staring toward the floor as if guilty or ashamed.

The signs had been there... but Kay, absorbed by her happiness, had not yet paid heed to them.

Somewhere in-between cuts of mouthwatering meats, seeing how happy Brian was for her graduation, she decided to break the news of her other major achievement. Rachel knew she'd always wanted to join the FBI, but she'd never told Brian. They'd talked about it in principle, and he'd wished her good luck in her endeavors, but she'd saved the news of her acceptance as a precious gift for him, something to make him proud of her.

While the waiter was uncorking a bottle of champagne, he'd

asked, "What are your plans, sweetie? Corporate human resources? The pay is good. Plenty of big names here to choose from."

Smiling widely, she reached out and grabbed both their hands. Brian's, with her left, and Rachel's cold, almost inert one, with her right. "I have more exciting news for you. I've been accepted by the FBI. I'm leaving for Quantico in a couple of weeks."

Brian's hand withdrew with a jolt. "Oh, so now you're gonna be a fed, huh?" He'd gulped down the champagne without raising the glass. "Where does that leave me, then? Just a cop, a measly sergeant, doing his beat. And when us cops are too stupid to solve a case, no worries, captain can call in the feds."

Rachel's frozen fingers snuck out of her grip. Her best friend's gaze was lowered, and her cheeks had caught fire. Probably with embarrassment, on her behalf, Kay had thought back then. Now she knew better.

That night Brian had yelled at her the entire drive home for not saying anything about her intentions, for keeping secrets. She'd apologized and cried her first tears since she'd met him. She had truly believed she was to blame. Now she wondered how she'd graduated from a four-year psychology program totally unable to spot a narcissist.

Her blissful happiness was a thing of the past. She and Brian made up shortly after her botched celebration. He apologized, she apologized, they made passionate love, and then he invited her for a redo of the Espetus dinner, Rachel included. Kay passed. A few days later, she was leaving for Quantico, tearful at the airport terminal yet relieved to be breaking off from the tension between them.

On the flight to the East Coast, she cried again, face leaning against the plane window, turned away from the elderly woman who snored in the middle seat. Since the FBI announcement,

Brian had started coming home late every day, refusing to answer her questions, snapping at her if she insisted. At times, his clothes smelled of the faintest trace of perfume, various brands. He always maintained his innocence and had sworn he wasn't cheating on her. And she believed him.

Suffering through the most lucid moment since she'd met Brian, Kay realized she didn't know whom she'd married.

Quantico engulfed her in a flurry of classes, tests, physical training, and graduate courses she continued to take toward her PhD in psychology. Brian called her every night and visited once every other weekend or so, convincing her he missed her dearly. The twenty weeks of the FBI Academy couldn't be over soon enough.

She missed him too, so much it scared her.

Classes ended the week before Thanksgiving, and Kay was thrilled to be back home for the holidays. Brian picked her up from the airport with a dozen red, fragrant roses and wrapped her in an embrace she didn't want to end.

At home, a Thanksgiving invitation from Mrs. Epling, Rachel's mother, was waiting on the dining room table.

"Wanna go?" Brian had asked casually.

"Absolutely," she replied cheerfully, then kissed his lips. Thanksgiving at Rachel's mom's had become a tradition over the past three years.

"Okay. We'll figure out what to get her. Probably a pie and a bottle of wine would be fine."

A few days later, they arrived at the Epling residence. Through the living room window, she could see a few people drinking, laughing, and mingling near the festive set table. Rachel wore a backless black dress and heels and was chatting with a young man Kay didn't recognize. When Brian rang the bell, she turned and walked over to the door, and Kay could see her silhouette better.

Rachel was pregnant.

Visibly so... at least seven months.

And she'd never said a word to Kay, although they'd spoken on the phone while she was gone.

Kay congratulated her and gave her a big hug, deciding not to ruin her mood by questioning her about the pregnancy and the secrecy surrounding it. Rachel thanked her with a muted voice.

Cherishing being among friends, Kay enjoyed the evening and drank a couple of glasses of wine, chatting lively with former peers. She'd missed the official graduation party; she was at Quantico when it took place. They had a great time, although she'd been missed. Some circled around her with all sorts of questions about being a fed. Was it as cool as in the movies? Not really, she'd explained. These days, it was mostly data and video surveillance analysis and all sorts of science and technology. No *Silence of the Lambs* in her career, she didn't think. But she still loved it, looked forward to the excitement of making a difference.

Kay remembered that particular moment as if it were yesterday. In the foreground, she was answering questions about her exciting new career. In the background, Brian was speaking with Rachel, standing awfully close to her. His hand left his side and raised to touch her face, to remove a strand of red hair and tuck it behind her ear with a tender, familiar gesture. She smiled and lowered her eyelids, leaning ever so slightly into his hand. He then brought his lips closer to her ear and whispered something. They both smiled, sharing a quick, heated glance before Brian walked away.

Kay watched speechlessly. Breath caught in her chest while pain tore at her heart with sharp, merciless claws. She left there that night keen on getting the truth out of Brian for once. Silent for the drive home, the moment they reached the house, she asked, "Are you sleeping with her, Brian?"

He feigned ignorance like the pro cheater that he was.

"With whom?" His demeanor showed no fear of being caught, just frustration, irritation with her question. It wasn't the first time she'd asked. It wasn't the first time he'd lied, either.

"With Rachel," she replied calmly, giving him, for the hundredth time, the benefit of the doubt. "Is that baby yours?" The words hurt her chest as she spoke them. It couldn't be true.

"No, sweetie," he said, dropping his tie on a chair and rushing to give her a reassuring hug. "I swear, I'm not."

That night, she didn't sleep a wink, remembering all the details she hadn't paid attention to when she should have. The heated glances Brian exchanged with women all the time. The women's reactions, even if he'd sworn to her repeatedly, he wasn't cheating on her. Rachel's aloofness, her distance, and the fact that she hadn't called Kay once the entire time she was at Quantico; only Kay had called Rachel. With a bit of effort and browsing her phone's call history, she could easily map Rachel's relationship with Brian by the timeline of her guilt.

And it had been going on for a while, even before Quantico.

Heartbroken and unwilling to live a lie, Kay filed for divorce the next day.

She never saw Rachel again, never heard from her, until her voicemail a few days ago.

Still, she deeply regretted not calling her back sooner.

Maybe she'd still be alive.

TWELVE
CAPTIVE

"Where are you, Mommy?"

She barely dared to raise her voice above a broken, tear-choked whisper. She listened for a while and didn't hear a sound. She'd woken up from a nightmare, shivering, her face stained with dry tears.

The bed was narrow and hard, covered with a scratchy blanket. It smelled of something funny, like clothes forgotten too long in the closet or the old tent they used for camping trips. It had the same color as the old tent, a dark shade of olive green like the soldiers wore in movies.

The pillow was lumpy and smelled of bleach. It didn't have a pillowcase; it was bare, the canvas in narrow gray and blue stripes, crooked here and there where it was worn out and stained with tears.

It wasn't like Mommy would've made it.

Mommy made sure the sheets were fresh and smelled good, that Mickey and Minnie were on her pillowcases, and the blanket was soft. She was there when Holly woke up, every time.

Where was she?

Trembling, she sat on the side of the bed and reached down with her toes until she touched the cold, concrete floor. Holding on to the lumpy mattress, she slid down. Her mother's shoes were gone; she looked everywhere for them, even under the bed where a few dust bunnies lived.

The room was almost dark; the only light came from a small window close to the ceiling, crossed with bars thicker than her finger. She could see a patch of blue through that window and a few blades of grass, as if the earth touched the sky in those few inches of space.

She was in a basement. The window, too small to fit through and too high for her to reach, must've been close to the ground, so close that grass touched it. A small snail dragged its home across the surface, leaving a slimy trail behind.

Disgusted to see the snail's underside, Holly looked away.

A large fireplace took up the best part of the opposite wall. It was darkened by smoke and soot, the hearth barren, discolored where intense heat had touched the concrete. Someone had done quick work of sweeping it clean, leaving ash and cinders behind in the hearth.

In the corner, a door allowed a sliver of yellowish light to come in through a crack. Holly grabbed the handle with both hands and tried to open it. But it remained closed, not even rattling or moving under her weight. Finding more courage, she banged her fists against the door and called out.

"Mommy? Where are you?"

She stopped and listened. Only silence filled the darkening room. The patch of blue in the window was fading into evening hues. She banged some more, hoping her mother would hear her. Hoping she'd come to get her like she'd promised.

But this wasn't the tool shed, and she wasn't hiding behind the lawn tractor like she'd been told.

After a while, resigned and tired, she climbed onto the bed and curled on her side, her hands between her knees, shivering.

Tears fell on the pillow, staining it anew. Her heart thumped against her chest faster and faster as she remembered what she'd seen from the red cedar in the backyard.

Her mother, shouting, running through the kitchen. A flash of light, a loud bang, then another. Her mother falling to the ground.

Then she slipped and fell from the tree and didn't remember anything after that.

Did Mommy get up from the kitchen floor? Who scooped her up after the fall?

A shaky whimper came off her lips. Shivering, she closed her eyes and cried until she fell asleep, easy prey for nightmares to haunt.

THIRTEEN
ATTORNEY

Still sniffling, Kay walked to the SUV and opened the back door. There was no point in delaying what needed to be done. Now that she'd decided to help Brian defend his innocence in Rachel's murder, she needed to get it done so she could move on with her life. Dredging up ancient history served no one.

"Get out," she said, looking elsewhere, not at Brian. In the rush of things, her sunglasses were left on her desk at the precinct.

"You've been crying," Brian said. He reached as if to touch her face with a caress, but she shook her head, closing her eyes. Crushed between eyelashes, tears rolled down her cheeks.

He withdrew. "I'm so sorry, Kay," he whispered. "I never got to tell you, but I really am. I broke your heart."

She wished he would stop talking but, at the same time, took his words in as a wounded warrior would take morphine, thirstily absorbing every word, desperate for the soothing they brought.

"Hearts like yours should never be broken," he continued, slowly drawing closer. Kay refused to open her eyes but felt his breath on her face, the smell of him intoxicating, dangerous, and deadly. "My sweet, sweet Kay. I never stopped thinking of you. All these years—"

It took all her willpower to step back and remind herself where she was and why. She looked at him coldly. "Where's your lawyer, Brian? It's getting late."

He held her gaze for a loaded moment, his eyes intense, burning, yearning. Behind him, the SFPD precinct and its exterior finish in marine shades of blue, gray, and aqua ceramic tiles reminded her of an oversize public restroom turned inside out, lending the situation a touch of sobering ridicule.

She looked away, hiding her efforts to control the urge to run her fingers through his hair, to draw him close. Taking in a breath of chilly, salty air, she leveled her head. Maybe that's why it tore her apart when she'd left him. She'd been addicted to him, to his heady touch, and somewhere underneath all that anger and pain, she craved another fix.

"Not on my life," she muttered, feeling ashamed of herself and her momentary lapse of judgment. What was it about this man that made women lose their minds?

"Sorry," he said, "I didn't catch that."

Good. "Call your lawyer, Brian. Tell her we're waiting."

She studied him while he made the call. He was attractive, even more than she remembered, because men age differently than women, some adding sophistication and charisma with their laugh lines. He was a chronic philanderer who thrived on his conquests and lived for the hunt, but also someone she'd fallen in love with. Had it only been physical? What did she see in him back then?

She remembered still. They used to have such a good time together, laughing, exploring, talking till dawn. He made her happy, and she was easily addicted, vulnerable after the life she'd lived with her abusive father, yearning to be loved. Life with Brian had helped her heal and understand that the abuse she had endured at the hand of her parent was not her fault. Of course, on a rational level, she'd always known that, but with Brian, she'd felt it.

Until it all went away because Brian's love was nothing but a lie.

She'd left him, but she'd felt rejected, unworthy, expendable. Perhaps the memory of that agony drove her to keep Elliot at a safe distance. She probably wouldn't survive another heartbreak like that.

"She's five minutes out," Brian said, ending the call with his attorney. "Kay, I wanted to—"

She put her hand in the air, and he stopped talking. She just didn't want to hear it anymore. His words were comforting, but that was the intrinsic danger of letting him talk. Just how much she needed to hear those words.

Instead, she looked at him squarely and said, "If you ever lie to me again, by omission or in any other form, I'll be gone so fast I'll leave you twirling in my wake." She paused for a moment, then asked, "Is that clear, Brian?"

"Crystal." He plunged his hands into his pockets. "I swear I'll be truthful, one hundred percent."

She drew closer until she could see his pupils dilate slightly with her approach. "Did you kill her, Brian?" He didn't flinch; only his jaw slacked. "Did you kill Rachel?"

The tiniest reaction in his pupils, a slight dilation, could've been a normal surprise response. "I swear I didn't," he replied, his pitch low, somber. "I already told you that." He sighed and pressed his lips together for a moment. "I can't say I blame you if you don't believe me. I'm just grateful you're here."

A blue BMW 7 Series drove into the parking lot and stopped, parallel with Kay's Ford.

"There she is," Brian said, "my attorney, Carly Hosking."

Finally.

The tall blonde was someone Kay recognized, mostly from her FBI days, testifying for the prosecution on various organized crime cases. She was a hot commodity, rumored to charge north of a thousand dollars per hour. Dressed in a black Chanel suit with white trim and stiletto pumps, she took her time collecting her things from the trunk of her car while wrapping up a phone call.

"Hosking is your attorney?" Kay asked in disbelief.

Brian nodded.

"How come you can afford her from a cop's salary?"

He chuckled bitterly. "I don't. Cops charged with murder aren't good cases to take these days, but she's doing it pro bono," he whispered quickly as Hosking was approaching. "I gave her a shit ton of business over the years. I collared a lot of connected scum."

Carly Hosking stopped in front of them with a polite nod and a professional smile. Her hazel eyes stayed cold, focused.

"Doctor Kay Sharp, my ex-wife and former FBI Special Agent, meet Carly Hosking, my attorney," Brian introduced them. Kay shook a hand with long fingers, one adorned with a sizable diamond ring, at least two carats, mounted in white gold. She had a strong, ambitious grip Kay liked.

"You should wait outside for now," Hosking said, checking the time. "It's almost six; I won't be able to get an arraignment on schedule for today. Let me see what I can do."

Brian turned a shade of sickly pale. The thought of spending the night in prison, awaiting arraignment, had probably hit home.

"She can hold her own in court," Kay said, watching Hosking as she clicked her heels and swayed her hips on the way to the precinct entrance. "She's one of the best. You're lucky to have her on your side, Brian. You're getting a million-dollar defense."

Seemingly nervous, he licked his lips and swallowed. "No, I'm not. She only agreed to represent me with the surrender and arraignment. After that, I'm on my own. I'm broke, and I'm screwed."

FOURTEEN
SEARCH

"I'm not buying she fell and crawled into the woods," Elliot muttered. "It's dumber than a barrel of dirt, and she knew better. She grew up in these parts."

"But you're thinking foul play?" Novack asked, pushing his Ray-Bans up with the tip of his finger. "Not runaway?"

Elliot gestured toward the blood drop. "She would've turned off her devices to get herself a head start. Nope, something happened with this girl. Hope she's still alive."

"What do you think it was?" Deputy Novack asked, studying the bloodstain up close. He was chewing gum slowly, methodically, as if it carried some meaning or helped him think.

Elliot watched Deputy Deramus attach the long lead to Spartan's collar. The dog whimpered quietly and sat, his bushy tail sweeping the asphalt in wide, enthusiastic movements.

"Vehicular, if I had to guess," Elliot replied, glaring at the asphalt unstained by any skid marks. "Otherwise, we're shit out of luck."

"What do you mean, Detective?"

"Taylor Lorentz decided to run today on a whim; there was

no pattern to her behavior. No one knew about it. That means, if it wasn't vehicular, it was completely random."

"And we're never going to catch the bastard," Novack growled under his breath. "No skid marks? Can that happen in a hit-and-run?"

"That's what I'm looking at." Elliot took off his hat for a brief moment, enough to scratch the roots of his hair, then put it back on. Crouching by the bloodstain, he showed Novack the directionality of the drop. "I don't see any evidence of a crash. Say the driver was on his phone or something, didn't see her, the road is narrow, the light was low. I can believe all that. But when the vehicle hits something, the reflex of any driver is to hit the brakes hard. This one didn't."

"There are no shards or breakage either," Novack added.

"This is Leach's favorite speed trap place; everyone's flooring it downhill. That car would've been doing seventy, and there would've been evidence of a crash and long trails of burned rubber from the brakes."

Novack looked at the bloodstain, then at the edge of the woods. His wheels were turning in the right direction.

Elliot stood and stomped his feet several times to get his pantlegs to come down off the calf of his boots. Moving helped keep the chill at bay. "On top of that, there's not enough blood for a hit-and-run at that speed."

"Unless the hit threw her on the side of the road, where there's grass to break her landing," Novack ventured. "Then the driver stopped and dragged her into the woods."

"Yeah. Not buying it. He would've braked hard. But let's find her first. Then we'll see what's what." Elliot threw the K-9 handler another look to see why it was taking so long. The deputy was on the phone.

Everyone and their mother were on the damned phone these days. Working with them was like herding cats to do a sled dog's job. Wasting time was a thorn in his side, knowing that girl was out there.

With a determined spring in his step, Elliot closed the distance to Deramus, who ended the call when he saw him approach.

"Good morning, Detective." John Deramus greeted Elliot with a hand extended right above the dog's head. Elliot shook it warily, but Spartan had no objection. "Do you have the scent item?"

Elliot pulled the Ziploc bag with Taylor's pajama top and handed it over to the deputy. "There's a bloodstain by that marker, but let's start here. Let's see where Spartan leads us."

Deramus pulled the pajama top from the bag and held it under the dog's nose. "Sniff it, yes, good boy," he said in a low, muted tone of voice. The Malinois inhaled the scent with snorts and impatient whimpers, then started tugging at the lead.

Elliot followed Deramus and Spartan straight to the blood-stain, where the dog stopped and whimpered for a moment, snorting a couple of times, then headed into the woods. The Malinois was quick, holding his nose several inches above the ground and the lead line taut. Deramus ran behind him, his duty belt rattling and bouncing with every step. The deputy was in good physical shape, probably the result of working with a police K-9. Elliot, already panting after a few minutes, envied the apparent ease with which the deputy and his dog kept up the rhythm of the search. Behind Elliot, Novack and two other deputies were falling behind at different rates.

The dog stopped and sniffed the Frozen Falls rock forma-tion. It was tall, standing about thirty or forty feet above ground, emerging from the side of the hill like a cascade turned to stone by a witch's spell. Made up of dark granite with embedded crys-tals of black nephrite jade that sparkled like ink when the rays of the sun fell on the crystals at the right angle, Frozen Falls was a little-known tourist attraction. Most tourists gathered on the mountain or at the ski resort; few ventured so far off the beaten trail of seasonal attractions to discover Frozen Falls.

Some did. Among them, few had tried to extricate black jade crystals from the rock, going at it with tire irons and hammers and who knows what else, but the granite was enduring and rarely released the crystals in the hands of the pilfering tourists. A layer of grayish green serpentine rock a couple of feet overhead had been targeted the most, its shiny surface chipped here and there.

But Frozen Falls wasn't just an oversize and eye-catching boulder; water sprang from the side of the hill, washing the rock formation with clear water. When it rained, the falls covered the rock formation completely. Over the dry months of summer, the spring dried out completely, leaving the rock barren, a dark gray with horizontal serpentine inserts and jade crystals. For a couple of months every winter, the spring froze, lining the rock with a stretch of white ice with bluish hues, running the length of the rock and ending in a small puddle at the base.

"Got something," Deramus announced, pointing with his finger at a bungled white wire that clung to a small bush. "Spartan flagged it."

Elliot slid on a glove and crouched by the bush. It was a pair of earbuds, the type many still used even if wireless versions had been available for years. He opened an evidence pouch and let the earbuds fall in, then inserted the remaining wire until he reached the end. The wire didn't end with the usual plug; it had been severed. Elliot sensed a faint smell of burned plastic. Holding the wire end under his nostrils, then feeling the rough, hardened edges with the tip of his gloved finger, he confirmed the wire had been severed by something hot.

Rushing to catch up with Deramus and his dog, he put the evidence pouch into his pocket. Spartan was leading them around Frozen Falls, heading into the ravine that opened up behind the rock formation at the foot of the hill.

Elliot was still a few yards behind when Spartan barked twice and sat, signaling he'd found something.

FIFTEEN
BACK

The truth was, Brian was scared.

Kay could see it on his face, now that the mask had dropped a little since Hosking had mentioned spending the night in jail.

He stood, leaning against the grille of Kay's Ford, his back hunched, his hands plunged inside his jacket pockets. He stared at the cracked pavement, jaw clenched and knotted, saying nothing, just waiting, a picture of despondence and anguish. Kay had few words of encouragement for him; she didn't want to commit to anything she didn't know she could deliver. But she was going to try. Whatever he'd done wrong to her, however agonizing, wasn't worth his life. If he was being set up, she'd do her best to get to the bottom of it.

If only he'd stop being an irritating, arrogant, and selfish son of a bitch, and level with her for once.

With a muted groan, Kay realized she was being childish, expecting him to suddenly transform into a mature, responsible, and honest adult. It wasn't in his genes. Short of a DNA transplant, it wasn't going to happen.

"I never would've dreamed," he muttered with a bitter chuckle, "that you'd hold my life in your hands one day."

"I don't, Brian, stop sensationalizing everything. You and I both believe in the justice system because it works. Trust that it will work in your case."

"How about the many innocents spending their lives in jail?" He turned to face her, his features scrunched in fear and angst. "How did the mighty American justice system work for them, huh?"

Kay refused to argue with him. She checked the time on her phone. Hosking had been inside the precinct for almost an hour.

And there weren't any messages from Elliot either. She would've expected some news in the Taylor Lorentz case by now.

She started typing a text message to her partner.

"Got some more important business you need to attend to?" Brian asked, his voice dipped in narcissistic outrage. For a moment, she'd dared put herself first.

Shaking her head, she let the phone drop into her pocket and looked him in the eye. "I have a ton of more important business, Brian, but I chose to help you. That doesn't mean you own me."

He stepped back. "I'm sorry. I'm just..."

"I get it. It's not easy. Just endure through it, and we'll sort this out."

A click-clack of stilettos on pavement got her attention. Hosking was coming back.

"I negotiated the surrender of my client for tomorrow morning at nine," she said loudly, still closing the distance to them. "He doesn't have to spend the night in jail."

Kay's jaw clenched. What was she supposed to do with him until tomorrow?

A long breath left Brian's chest noisily. "Whew. You're amazing, Carly. You're the best."

She touched his forearm. "I'm not done yet." He fell silent, his smile waning fast. "The arraignment is also tomorrow, at noon. Expect to post bail. I believe I can get you released, but for murder cases, the bail is rarely under half a million dollars."

Brian scoffed. "How the hell—?"

"You'll figure something out," Hosking replied with the certainty and serenity about financial matters that only rich people have. "I'm not the least bit concerned."

"But I don't—"

She patted his forearm in a repeat of the earlier calming gesture. "You'll find someone to lend you the money. Something to sell. But first, let's find out how much you need, and that will be tomorrow." With a professional smile that didn't touch her eyes, she turned to Kay. "Will he be staying with you tonight? Or will you let him go?"

Kay pressed her lips together for a moment. "Technically, he's a prisoner I'm transporting."

"I've arranged his surrender," Hosking replied, playing with the BMW key fob she'd fished from her black Gucci purse. "Legally, you're off the hook."

"I don't believe so," Kay replied. "If he decides to run between today and tomorrow, I'm sure my boss won't be too thrilled I let a wanted suspect flee."

Hosking shot the blue sedan a yearning look. "Well, this could be debated until we're both old and gray, but suit yourself. It makes no difference to me what you do with him as long as he's here tomorrow morning, nine sharp." Her smile widened. "No pun intended."

She turned and left without allowing either of them to say anything. Within seconds, the blue Beemer exited the parking lot, turning left on Turk Street.

"I promise I won't run," Brian said. She gave him a long stare.

He could've been truthful, but Brian's mind worked in ways she'd rarely found logical. Maybe he was truthful now and had every intention to be there as agreed, but later tonight or tomorrow morning, things could change. He could decide to make a run for Mexico. He could blow his brains out, desperate and alone and intoxicated.

She wasn't going to take any chances.

"Get in," she said, climbing behind the wheel of her Interceptor.

Hesitating, he opened his mouth to protest, but she glared at him. "Get in, Brian. Don't make me regret this."

He climbed into the back seat and fastened his seatbelt. "Where are you taking me?"

"Home."

He breathed with relief.

"My home, not yours. We're going back to Mount Chester."

"Thank you," he whispered, reaching and squeezing her shoulder. She stiffened under his touch but didn't pull away.

"Nothing to thank me for, Brian. You'll be spending the night in lockup, but at least you'll be safe."

"What?" He popped his head between the seats, too close to her face for comfort.

She wished her SUV was equipped with a wire mesh partition between the front and back seats, the way deputy cruisers were. That thing would've come in handy. It was a long drive home.

"You're being ridiculous, Kay. I'm not going to run and just throw my life away, become a fugitive for the rest of my days. You know damn well there's no statute of limitations for murder. I have every interest to clear my name."

She slammed on the brakes, stopping at a red light. "You're a murder suspect with an open arrest warrant. I'm a cop. I'm not letting you go, Brian. End of story." The light turned green, and she peeled off. Running into traffic on the road to the highway, she lost her patience and turned on the red and blue flashers.

"It's my way or the highway straight to hell for you in this one. No other option."

"Fine. Whatever."

In the rearview mirror, she could see Brian pouting, sullen and grim, leaning back against the seat with his arms crossed at his chest.

"Well, then, now that we've settled this, I have more questions for you."

"I'm sure you do," he mumbled, seemingly struggling to keep his resentment contained.

She paused for a moment, focusing on the heavy afternoon traffic, which her red and blue lights could barely shift. The question she was about to ask was a difficult one; it tore her up inside. The answer would put a timeline to his cheating, one more accurate than the timeline of Rachel's guilt.

They had crossed the Golden Gate Bridge heading north in complete silence, both lost in their thoughts. Once the traffic cleared somewhat, she turned off the flashers and filled her lungs with air, steeling herself.

"At that party, Rachel was pregnant. Did she have her baby?"

"What?" he mumbled as if awakened from deep sleep. "Yes, she did. A little girl named Holly." He ran his hands over his face and rubbed his eyes.

"Where is she now?" Kay asked. Fear unfurled in her gut. No one had mentioned a child. And by no one, she meant Brian, the man who invented lying by omission. She hadn't spoken with anyone else about the case.

"She's with Rachel's mother, in Union City, across the bay. She's safe."

Kay breathed. "Is she yours?"

Silence, punctuated by tires whooshing against the pavement, thumping at times. Infuriating silence.

"It's a simple question, Brian."

"Yes, she's mine," he replied, his voice barely above a whisper.

"Argh, damn you to bloody hell," she muttered, her memories still fresh and painful.

She'd just returned from Quantico the week before Thanksgiving, and she'd been gone for five months. Had she not completed the twenty weeks of training as an FBI agent, she might've missed the subtle clues in their body language, in their facial expressions that night, and he would've continued to play both fields unbothered. "When's her birthday?"

He didn't reply, just lowered his head, resting his forehead in his hands. The humble, shame-filled posture aggravated Kay, who knew it was yet another way in which he lied to her.

"It's your kid, Brian. You must know her birthday." Sarcasm colored her voice, doing little to hide the inflections of pain. After all those years, even though she thought she was safe, he could still hurt her.

"December thirtieth," he blurted, almost shouting. "And no, she wasn't a preemie, all right? What else do you want to know? I cheated on you, and you already know that. What's the point in digging up all this crap? I thought you were here to help me, not kick me when I'm down for your own morbid curiosity."

She barely heard any of that. She'd stopped paying attention after he'd mentioned Holly's birthday.

It meant he'd been sleeping with Rachel for at least two months *before* they got married.

All this time, she'd held on to the memory of her wedding day, thinking it must've been the only day she could be sure he'd been truthful to her. She'd been wrong.

The vows he'd taken had been lies from the start. And by her side, during the ceremony, she'd had his mistress as a maid of honor.

Against all odds, he'd managed to hurt her again.

SIXTEEN
CRIME SCENE

She lay in the grass, her eyes wide open, staring at the clear sky as if she could still see the azure. Her face, beautiful and serene even in death, was pale as if the bitter cold descending from the mountain had drained the color from her cheeks. Her lips, slightly open as if to whisper a last goodbye, carried the pink blush hues of her lip gloss, untouched by the elements, still pristine. Wind gusts blew her hair at times, shielding her eyes with silk-like, ash-blonde locks for a moment, then letting them reflect the azure once more. A couple of fir needles had entangled in her hair. A few more had landed on her alabaster skin, a sign that the elements had begun their irreversible conquest. Several drops of blood stained her face. Her chest was soaked where the bullets had ripped through flesh, delivering an instant demise.

Elliot froze in place, several feet away from Deramus and his dog Spartan, studying the area carefully, hoping to find a usable footprint. A thick layer of dry fir needles lined the ravine, doing nothing to preserve a print. Strong wind gusts toyed with the needles incessantly, lifting them up a few inches in the air, swirling them, then letting them drop back on the ground, while new ones shed by the tall firs came down in bursts.

He checked his phone after a chime drew his attention. Dr. Whitmore was a few minutes away. He couldn't touch the body until then, couldn't check to see if the shots had been through and through, but he crouched by her side, nevertheless.

It was Taylor Lorentz.

Just as her father had described, she'd worn a gray sweatshirt over a red sports bra. The watch that had sent the alert was a barely visible bulge under her sleeve. A bullet had crashed into the iPhone she'd carried in her breast pocket, doing its best to try to save her life. It had stopped that one bullet, but there had been two more. A short piece of white wire hung from the phone, where the bullet had cut through the earbuds lead, severing it and melting the plastic edges of the insulation.

"We'll canvas the area, look for the murder weapon," Novack said. "There's snow in the forecast for later."

Elliot stared at the blue sky in disbelief, but the chill in the air and the smell of frost agreed with the deputy. "Maybe." He stood, brushing the fir needles off his pants where his knees had touched the ground.

"I guess that's it for us, then," Deputy Deramus said, extending his hand. Elliot shook it.

"Yeah, thanks."

Deramus left with Spartan, quickly disappearing into the woods toward the road. A few moments later, the silhouette of the coroner's van became visible between the tree trunks, faint glimpses of it.

"You're still thinking random?" Novack asked, looking at the girl's bloodied chest.

Elliot pushed his hat down on his head, making sure the wind didn't blow it away. "Got nothing else to think. If you can figure out why someone would shoot this girl while she was out running at six in the morning, go right ahead."

"Yeah. It's not a crash either. You were right—no brakes."

"I saw this type of thing in my last year in Austin," Elliot said, rubbing his hands together to warm them up. It was taking Doc Whitmore a while to get there from the van. He wondered why.

"What, random, side-of-the-road shootings?"

"Gang initiations, that's what they were, back in Austin." He picked a green fir needle off a branch and chewed on it. It smelled of Christmas and the eastern hemlock tea he'd had a cup of when he'd visited Kay's Pomo Indian friends. It made everything better.

"Shooting people to prove their worth?"

"Something like that, yeah. The victims were random as far as we could tell, and in most cases, we never caught the shooters." He looked around, studying the terrain some more. "No gangs here, in Mount Chester. We're too far for anyone to drive up from the Tenderloin and shoot this girl as an initiation rite. It would be worthless, laughed at."

Novack scratched his forehead. "Why?"

Rustling of leaves and stepped-on twigs announced the arrival of the county medical examiner.

"Because, my young friend, gang initiations are supposed to show audacity and grit in the proselyte," Dr. Whitmore replied, approaching Taylor's body. "Potential for a bold and lucrative life of crime. There's no daring to shoot someone in the middle of nowhere. There's no risk... hence there's no glory." He set his bag on the ground and pulled open the zipper. "What have we here?"

As if he'd been given a cue, Novack vanished, joining the other deputies on the evidence grid search.

"Taylor Lorentz, nineteen years old," Elliot briefed him. "Her watch reported a hard fall this morning, at six forty-seven."

"Oh," Dr. Whitmore said. A whisp of sadness touched his

eyes. He crouched by her side and gently removed a strand of hair that had blown over her face. "I knew her." He looked at Elliot over his shoulder. "Her mother passed last year, you know. She was a close friend of my wife's. I met this poor young thing at the funeral. It was a cold day, just like this one, no snow yet, but close. Shelley had hoped Taylor would stay in touch and allow us to help her with life, with her father. He's gravely ill."

Elliot plunged his frozen hands into his pockets. "I'm sorry, Doc. Please give Mrs. Whitmore my sympathies."

He shook his head and gritted his teeth. "I understood this kind of thing in San Francisco with all the drugs and the gangs and the guns. I can't count how many victims of such senseless crimes landed on my table during my tenure there. But here?" He extracted the liver temp probe but hesitated before proceeding, his hand hovering over the girl's abdomen. "We chose to retire here to never see this again." Ending his tirade with a bitter scoff, he abandoned the liver probe for a moment and examined the wound.

"The shots were grouped tightly," Elliot said. "Close range?"

The medical examiner studied the wound closely, exposing some skin. "There's no stippling, so I'd say over two feet away." With a gloved hand, he extracted the phone from the pocket carefully, then flipped it over. The tip of the bullet had penetrated the phone casing completely but had stopped short of piercing her skin. "This is a nine mil. At under five feet, it usually goes through several phones before it stops." He bit his lip and frowned. "I'd have to run some tests in my lab, but I'd say these shots were fired from ten to twenty yards away."

Elliot whistled in appreciation. "Some grouping from twenty yards out, Doc. You don't see that very often."

"Yep, you don't," he muttered, sealing the phone and its bullet into an evidence pouch. "I'm willing to bet the deputies won't find the murder weapon lying about in some shrub." He picked up the liver probe again and exposed the skin of her abdomen. "Corneal clouding has begun to set in," he said, checking the time on his wristwatch. "The liver temperature confirms the time of death somewhere between seven and eight this morning. What time did her watch send the alert?"

"Six forty-seven," Elliot replied.

"Well, she died at that precise moment or shortly thereafter." He cleaned the liver probe and packed it inside his kit. Then he knelt by the girl's head and beckoned Elliot. "Here, help me flip her over."

Once her back was exposed, Doc Whitmore checked the discoloration of the skin where her body had rested on the ground. "She'd been dragged; there's some abrasion. The bullets are still inside the body." He stood with a groan. "Let's load her up. Can you spare a deputy? My assistant had a dental appointment."

Elliot looked around to locate someone to help the aging coroner. Doc Whitmore was pushing seventy. His hair had turned completely white, his neatly trimmed beard also, but he was still coming in to assist whenever the county had a murder or a suspicious death to investigate.

He thought of asking Novack to help, but he wasn't anywhere to be seen. Instead, he saw Farrell a few yards away and Hobbs another few yards east of her.

"Denise," he called out to Deputy Farrell, "ask Hobbs to help the ME with the body, okay?"

"You got it."

"If you're here, who's watching Mr. Lorentz?"

Slack-jawed, Denise Farrell looked at Elliot and shrugged. "He seemed okay. I thought you needed us all here, looking for the vic."

"Oh, for crying out loud," Elliot said, rushing toward the highway. "You had one job to do," he continued to stew, although Deputy Farrell was out of earshot. It wasn't like her to abandon a task, so he put a lid on it.

When he reached the road, he found Mr. Lorentz sitting on the asphalt, leaning into one hand as if he was just trying to get up. Grabbing his phone and speed-dialing dispatch, Elliot rushed to his side. "Lizzie, get me EMS at the scene, fast as lightning."

Mr. Lorentz had his mouth open and panted, guttural sounds coming out at times. He'd been sobbing so hard he'd run out of breath. His hand pointed shakily at the markings on the coroner's van.

"My baby... she's gone," he wailed. Tears streaked down his face, blotching his deathly pale skin.

"I'm really sorry for your loss," Elliot whispered. He tried to help him get on his feet but then gave up and sat on the asphalt by his side. It was better than having him collapse and injure himself. "Help is on the way, Mr. Lorentz."

"No," he said. "I'll stay with my little girl."

"You shouldn't see her being loaded into the coroner's van; I promise you." Shifting slightly, Elliot put his own body between Lorentz's and the van, obscuring the view. "You should remember the good times, the laughter, and the sunshine. Not... this."

The man's quivering hand found the strength to grab Elliot's jacket lapel, scrunching the thick fabric between bony, arthritic fingers. "Tell me... how did she..." His voice trailed off as his breath shattered under the weight of a new sob.

"She was shot," Elliot replied as gently as he could, wishing Kay was there. She'd know how to make his pain more bearable. "She died instantly."

"Why?" he asked, his voice a fraught whisper. "She wasn't supposed to run today. No one knew where she was but me." Holding on to Elliot for support, he turned and looked straight at him. "Promise me..."

"I promise," Elliot said, not needing to hear more. "I won't rest until I find who did this and make them pay."

Moments later, he watched the EMS crew load Gabriel Lorentz into the ambulance. He held the man's hand with both of his while they took his blood pressure.

"He's diabetic," Elliot said to the EMT who was checking his vitals. "He already had a seizure today. Glad you made it in time."

The man shot him a quick, intense glance from underneath a furrowed brow.

"Not a moment too soon."

SEVENTEEN
WITNESS

Kay breathed hastily, lowering the window a few inches for some fresh, frigid air to help her fight the tears that threatened to overwhelm her. Anger consumed her insides, swelling her chest, strangling her with a chokehold she couldn't shake.

"Why, Brian?" she asked, flooring the gas pedal. "Why did you marry me in the first place?"

He slapped his hands against his thighs in consternation. "Jeez, Kay, what do you want me to say, huh?"

"The damn truth for a change. It's not gonna kill you."

He paused, lowering his forehead into his hands again, probably thinking about what to say, how not to damage her commitment to helping him clear his name.

"You were special," he whispered. "You're probably not going to believe me when I say this, but you still are special to me. And I care about you deeply."

She scoffed loudly and ran a burst of siren to get a slow-moving truck out of her way, wishing it were louder. "Yeah, right. And that's why, because I was too special for you to bear, you sought comfort in Rachel's arms."

"No, it's not like that," he pleaded, putting his head forward again and looking at her directly, not through the rearview mirror. "Look at you now, dropping everything and helping me, your cheating ex, clear up my name. Only someone truly special would do that."

Or someone incredibly gullible, Kay thought, *a complete idiot.*

"But I wasn't special enough for you to stay true to me, was I?" Her voice sounded more bitter than she would've wanted. She didn't understand her bitterness; until that morning, she hadn't thought of Brian in years, with the exception of a brief moment after receiving Rachel's voicemail last Friday. But the wound of his betrayal was there, still bleeding, raw, painful as if it were just yesterday.

"What can I say? I'm a dog." He chuckled quietly. "I've always had this in my blood. I can't stop." He reached out and touched her arm. "But you—"

She jolted and pulled away as much as she could without letting go of the steering wheel. "Don't touch me."

He withdrew instantly. "I'm sorry."

For a few miles, they drove in silence. Kay focused on pushing the old memories away, sealing them inside a lockbox in her mind, ordering them to never emerge again. One still tugged at her heart, refusing to give up. How could she have been so wrong about Rachel? She'd seemed an honest, light-hearted person, a true friend. How could she have said yes to being her maid of honor while she was screwing Brian?

Her eyes checked the rearview mirror and landed on Brian's face. He'd closed his eyes and relaxed his features; he could've been asleep.

The expert manipulator had achieved his goal and could relax. He'd talked Kay off the ledge, had told her what she needed to hear so she wouldn't dump him in the first precinct along the way and be gone, never looking back.

Because Brian Hanlin always got what he wanted.

Maybe it was time to test his commitment to being truthful.

"Why did Rachel go through with it?"

His eyes opened wide. "With what?"

"With the wedding. With being my maid of honor, doing all that girly stuff, pretending she was happy for me while she was sleeping with you. I can't understand why."

He shifted in his seat, visibly uncomfortable with the question. "Well, if you must know—and I really don't know why you're not letting this go already—I talked her into it."

"What? Why?"

"Really, you have to ask?" He muttered an oath. "So you wouldn't figure out we were having an affair. If she'd stopped talking to you, if she'd said no to being your maid of honor, you would've not found peace until you uncovered the truth. You were an excellent cop, Kay, even before becoming one."

Kay swallowed hard. "Was she pregnant then? At the wedding?"

"I guess she was... about two months into it. For what it's worth, I didn't know. She told me the day we came back from our honeymoon." He chewed on the tip of his finger for a brief moment, a gesture he'd copied from Kay. "She was devastated, cried her eyes out when I insisted she show up for the wedding acting perfectly normal. She *begged* me not to make her do it."

"Okay," Kay sighed, "poor little Rachel. Forgive me that my heart isn't breaking for her right now."

But it *was* breaking, Kay realized, blinking back tears. Brian had been a heartless asshole with both of them, not just Kay. Forcing Rachel to sit through her lover's wedding and play a role in it. It must've been hell. How she wished her friend had had the courage to tell her what was going on.

"She called me," Kay announced calmly, passing by a sign putting Mount Chester sixty-four miles away.

Brian jolted. "When?" He was invading her bubble again, leaning into the space between the front seats.

"Last week, on Friday. She caught me during a suspect questioning, and I couldn't take the call, but she left me a voicemail. By the time I called her back, she was gone."

"I had no idea. Had she ever called you before? Since... then?"

"No, never." Kay passed a tractor trailer filled to the brim with ripe tomatoes. "How come her kid is with Mrs. Epling?"

Brian leaned back against the seat and breathed. "Didn't I tell you Rachel witnessed a shooting? She wanted to testify. I wasn't with her when it happened; I was still working. By the time I got there, she'd already spoken to the cops and told them what she'd seen. They made her promise she'd come in the next day to make a formal statement."

"You still didn't tell me how her daughter ended up with her grandmother. Walk me through what happened with this crime she witnessed and her subsequent testimony."

He groaned. "It's beginning to blur up in my mind. I haven't had much sleep lately." He ran both his hands through his hair, one after the other. "Thursday evening, she was parked on the side of the road, waiting. Then—"

"For what?"

A beat. "For me. We were going to meet for dinner, but I couldn't get away from work on time. Some collar took too damn long to book."

"What did she see, again?"

"A drive-by shooting, gang-related. Some street corner drug pusher got popped. To make it worse, Holly was with her."

"Okay, then what happened?"

"The cops came. By that time, she should've been long gone, but she stayed. She knew better than to get involved in gang-related crime as a witness, but—"

"Where was this? What street corner?"

"On Haight Street." He cleared his voice. "And Gough."

A pang of painful memory caught her breath. "That's where we used to—"

"Yeah, the Brazilian steakhouse you and I used to visit. She liked that place too. It's good."

"Okay, never mind," she said, wishing she really didn't mind. "So, the cops came, then what happened?"

"Our precinct took the call. She recognized one of the cops, a friend of mine, got out of the car, and started running her big mouth. 'Officer, officer, I saw it all.'" He covered his mouth with his hand and stifled a sob. His mockery was nothing but a mask for his pain. "By the time I arrived, they'd taken her statement, arranged a meeting with the ADA the next morning, the whole shebang. It was too late to make her backtrack at that point. But I didn't give up."

A convoy of trucks bearing the Walmart logo zoomed by heading south toward the city, noisy and fast, lifting dust whirls in the air. Kay rolled up the window. "What did you do?"

"I insisted she recant the next morning. I begged her to tell the ADA she didn't remember much. I managed to scare her just enough to have her drive across the bay that evening to her mother's, to leave Holly with her while I went back to the precinct to find out more about the shooting." He paused for a moment, staring away from her, seemingly collecting his thoughts. "You know, who they suspected, how big of a risk was that testimony to her."

"You didn't have dinner?"

"By the time the whole circus was done, the place had closed for the night. But we didn't feel like eating anymore. She took Holly to Mrs. Epling's. I went back to the station." Another sob shuddered his breath. "Oh, God..."

"Then what happened?" she asked gently.

"We were supposed to meet in the DA's office the next morning. She got there early and didn't wait for me. Silly little goose... In the ten minutes until I got there, they had talked her into testifying and entering WITSEC with Holly. Moments after I arrived, they introduced her to the US Marshal who was going to take her."

"What triggered them into offering WITSEC? It's not that common to be offered to someone who just sees a random shooting on a San Francisco street."

What Kay meant was it rarely ever happened. With limited resources for the Witness Security Program, district attorneys usually had to go to bat for witnesses to enroll them in the program. Or detectives, knowing that otherwise the witness would not testify, and their perp would walk. But it seemed that Rachel had not shied away from giving a statement.

"I don't know," Brian eventually answered. His voice was fraught with sorrow. He'd kept everything bottled in until then, but reliving the events seemed to have pushed him further than he could handle. "The moment I showed up, they clammed up and said they would take her into protective custody immediately. That's when she flipped and begged them for a few hours, one more day of normality, to set her life in order before having to disappear." He shook his head in disbelief, eyes lowered, lips pressed tightly together. "They arranged to pick her up at seven."

"Then what happened?"

"She went to her house to get ready, and I went back to the precinct to..." he cleared his voice again, "well, to spy on the progress with the shooting case. I wanted to understand what she'd seen, whom she'd seen, that her life would be in so much danger. Yes, whenever you open your big mouth and testify about a murder, any murder, you put your life on the line. But something felt weird about the entire situation."

Something did feel weird; Kay had to agree. They'd offered WITSEC too quickly. They'd refused to discuss matters with Brian present, although he was a cop and, technically, almost a family member of the witness.

"Then what happened?" she asked, although Brian looked like he needed a break.

In the rearview mirror, she could see his head hung low. When he spoke, she could barely hear him. "I found her when I got there, at about six."

"Oh, my goodness, Brian, I didn't know you were the one who found her. I'm so sorry. That must've been terrible." A tear rolled from the corner of her eye. A philanderer or not, Brian had been in a relationship with Rachel all those years; it must've been devastating.

"I found her on the kitchen floor in a pool of blood. The table was set, food untouched. She'd made us a roast. You see, I wasn't going with her into the program. We were saying goodbye for a while." He sniffled and breathed deeply, steadying himself. "She was shot execution-style from close proximity."

"In the back of her head?" Kay asked, pushing away from her mind the image of Rachel lying on the kitchen floor, dead.

"No... Why?"

"Because that's what cops usually call execution-style. One round to the back of the head."

He frowned, then ran his hand over his face. Kay threw glances in the mirror any chance she had, studying his body language. "You're right. No... she took one in the forehead and two in the chest. They were thorough."

"What did you do next?" Kay kept her voice subdued, resisting the urge to squeeze his hand and offer some comfort.

"I called nine-one-one. They got there in just a few minutes."

Kay squeezed the steering wheel as tight as she could, focusing. She needed access to evidence, crime scene, and witness testimonies. That wasn't going to happen. The investigation seemed to have been wrapped in a hurry by someone who didn't care who they were charging, as long as they could move on to some other case.

"Have they released the crime scene yet?"

"I don't know," he replied morosely. "I've been busy running from my coworkers and staying out of jail."

"Were you interviewed? Formally?"

"Yes, that first night, when I found her. Last Friday."

"Did you have an attorney present?"

He rubbed his forehead nervously. "No... They're the people I work with. I thought I could trust them. I was a fool. Motherfuckers," he muttered, his bitter voice trailing. "They set me up. Yesterday, a friend of mine from the force gave me a heads-up about the warrant. I ran... then I came to you."

She mulled things over silently for a while. It seemed they had rushed through the investigation, in a hurry to lock Brian up. The autopsy report would usually take more than the five days that had passed since last Friday. In San Francisco, the coroner had bodies lined up, sometimes waiting for weeks before getting looked at. Brian had found her body, had a legitimate reason to visit her home, and leave fingerprints all over... What was this about?

"Did they find the murder weapon?"

"Not that I know of."

She couldn't bring herself to ask if he had all his weapons accounted for. He was smart enough to figure that out by himself. "I need to see that crime scene. Who's the detective on the case?"

"A bitter old coot, Detective Brockett. He's hard-core, a brute, and quite narrow-minded. He served in the Marines for twenty years. He's been suspected of ties to the local mafia, but there was never any evidence. Just whispers, coincidences, that sort of thing."

Fabulous. The old coot would kick her right off the premises the moment she dared ask for permission to visit the crime scene. If he was dirty, as Brian hinted, she had to be careful not to make things worse. For both of them.

"There's something else," Brian said, only moments after they'd passed the Mount Chester city limit sign. "How will the killer know that Rachel never got to tell me what she saw that night?"

Silence dropped heavy between them.

"They *don't* know," he added in a resigned voice. "I could be their next target."

EIGHTEEN
SOUP

The sound of silverware clattering against porcelain woke Holly from a deep slumber. Eyelids still clinging shut, she imagined Mommy fixing something good to eat in the kitchen. Her stomach churned and growled, reminding her she was hungry.

She smiled before opening her eyes, and called, "Mommy," then stretched and waited, with her eyes shut, for the kiss on the forehead to come.

No one answered. No one touched her skin with tender fingers and soft lips that smelled like strawberries.

The memory of where she'd fallen asleep invaded her mind, brutally awakening her senses. Her smile vanished as she sat abruptly, eyes open wide, staring at the woman seated by the bed.

She was chubby and breathed funny through her mouth as if she'd had to climb stairs or chase the bus. Dressed all in black, she wore a short-sleeved top and a frumpy, wrinkled skirt that hung on her as if too large for her size. A tiny cross on a silver chain escaped from underneath the top, hanging on her big chest. Her face was round and sweaty, her jowls hanging a little on the sides like a bulldog's. Her black eyes were staring at Holly impatiently.

Instinctively, the little girl wriggled away from her until she reached the edge of the bed.

The woman had pulled a chair to sit by the side of the bed. A tray with a bowl of red-colored soup that smelled like stew was on the bed by her side. She'd been stirring the soup with a spoon, with short, impatient movements that had thrown several droplets on the tray, a few more on the blanket. By the bowl, a couple of slices of brown bread looked stale and smelled of acrid grain.

"Don't be difficult," the woman said. "I know you must be hungry. It's been a while since you ate, hasn't it?" Her raspy voice reminded Holly of Cruella de Vil. She probably smoked just like Cruella too. Holly could smell it on her breath.

Holly's stomach agreed, prodding her with a pang of pain. It didn't smell as good as the soup Mommy made, but she decided to try, just a little. Legs folded underneath her, she drew close to the tray and picked up the spoon.

It was thick and smelled of chicken and tomatoes and bell peppers. After a second spoon, Holly had to admit it wasn't too bad. She slurped it quickly, but then she stopped. Mommy had said never eat anything from the hand of a stranger. It wasn't the first time she'd disobeyed, but it was better to stop before it was too late. She'd be mad.

"Have some bread," the woman said. "It will fill you up."

She took a tiny bite out of a slice and found it tasted as bad as it smelled. Afraid of the woman, she didn't spit it out; she swallowed it with a spoonful of soup, then pulled away a little, regretfully abandoning the spoon in the bowl.

"Where's Mommy?"

The woman sighed and rolled her eyes but then smiled encouragingly. "I was hoping you would tell me."

"She's not here?" Holly burst into tears. "She's not coming to get me?"

"What did you see?" she asked, leaning closer to Holly's face and reaching out to tuck her auburn hair behind her ear.

Holly pulled away, sobbing, hugging her knees and hiding her face.

"When you last saw your mother, what did you see, sweetie?" The woman's voice was warmer, more understanding. "Come on, your soup is getting cold."

"I was in the kitchen, and Mommy was making dinner," Holly whispered in a crying voice. She shot the woman a fearful glance. "I didn't see anything else."

"But you weren't in the kitchen when they found you, *boba*."

Fear spread through Holly's blood like ice water. The woman must've been there, seeing her leave the tool shed, where her mother had told her to hide. Seeing her disobey her mother, climbing up that tree. Heart thumping in her chest, she put her hand over it, like Mommy had taught her, to soothe it down.

She couldn't tell the woman what she'd seen.

The woman stood from the chair with an angry groan and then sat on the bed, closer to her. The tray tilted, almost spilling the soup left in the bowl. "*Dime*, where did you see *tu puta madre* last?"

Holly started sobbing hard. "I don't understand."

The woman brought her face inches away from Holly's, holding her chin with fingers thick like sausages and just as greasy. "Okay, I'll spell it out for you. Where were you when your mother was killed?"

Stunned, Holly fell silent. Mommy couldn't be dead. She'd just fallen on the kitchen floor. She'd get up soon and come get her. She had to believe it. Mommy said believing makes things happen.

She had to believe it.

She'd stop crying because Mommy was just fine, and she was coming. There was nothing to cry about. She had to believe.

After a while and several other words Holly didn't understand, the woman left with a stomp in her every step, taking the tray with her. She slammed the door behind her and bolted it shut from the outside.

Scared out of her mind, Holly held her breath, listening hard as her heavy footfalls faded away. Then she heard her say a few words to someone, a man who talked back too quickly and quietly for her to catch what he said.

Most of what the woman said she couldn't make out, but then she must've spoken louder because a few words came across clearly.

"The little bitch won't say a word. I could bet a pretty penny *la chica* saw something, but she's too scared to tell me. After all this time, she still doesn't trust me, *estúpida*."

Terrified, Holly leaned against the wall, her hand pressed tightly on her chest to soothe the desperate beats of her heart. Panic overwhelmed her when she realized she'd seen the woman before. Eaten that soup before. Heard the terrible lie that her mother was dead.

Forcing herself to breathe slowly, just like Mommy had taught her, she kept her hand pressed on the small lump on her chest and whispered her commitments. No eating food from strangers. Don't say a word. Breathe slowly.

If I believe Mommy will come, she will.

NINETEEN

HOME

"You'll be safe here," Kay said, pulling in front of the Franklin County Sheriff's Office.

After Brian's comment about the potential danger to his life, she'd been checking the rearview mirror obsessively to see if anyone was following them. No one was. A few miles later, she breathed with ease, just as they were passing by a new La Quinta Inn & Suites hotel built last year.

"We could stay here," Brian had said, his voice tentative, unconvinced, probably aware his request would immediately be turned down.

"No, we couldn't," Kay replied. "You're an arrestee in police custody. You don't get to spend the night in a hotel. You spend it in lockup. You know the rules, what the hell." She was getting tired of his incessant bickering, his insistences, his refusal to accept his new reality.

She was getting tired of *him*.

"To tell you the truth, I was hoping I'd lay low here, in no man's land, while you figure out who killed Rachel." He leaned forward, sticking his head between the front seats again. She caught his grin in the corner of her eye, the smell of Altoids on his breath. "I'm more than ready to skip the entire surrender and arraignment business we have on the docket for tomorrow."

She'd sped on, eager to drive the remaining few miles and be done for the day.

"I won't harbor a fugitive, not even by as little as stashing you in county lockup," she groaned and rolled her eyes. "And this no man's land you're talking about is my home."

As soon as she cut the engine, she got out of the warm SUV into the evening chill, the cold wind sending shivers down her spine. She opened the back door and extracted him, then took him inside the precinct.

The place was almost deserted. Lit dimly by the hallway lights and a desk lamp in the dispatcher's cubicle, it was eerily silent. It smelled of stale popcorn and yesterday's coffee. A hint of bleach came from the restrooms, which was Brian's first destination. She waited outside until he was done, then escorted him to one of the two cells and showed him inside.

Rubbing his eyes, Deputy Hobbs faltered over, coming from the back. By the deep wrinkles stamped on his sweaty face, he'd fallen asleep somewhere, probably in the supply room, on one of the cots.

"Hello, Detective," he said, sleep slowing his words a little. "I thought I heard something."

"Brought you a customer," she said, feeling tired and achy all of a sudden.

Hobbs frowned in the dim light. "Isn't he—"

She chuckled bitterly. "Yeah. It's him." The bane of her existence. She locked the cell and gave Hobbs the key. "Keep an eye on him. He could be in danger. He's been involved in a gang shooting. Of sorts," she added, feeling the need to further clarify but lacking the energy to do it. "And if he says I said it's okay to let him out to do anything, it's not true. He's to stay locked up at all times until tomorrow morning at six, when I'll pick him up and take him to San Francisco." She sighed, dreading another long drive with Brian in the back. "Again."

"Copy that, Detective," Hobbs said cheerfully. "Should I concern myself with some food for him?" His eyes glinted a little when he asked. He was probably looking for a reason to order pizza on the sheriff's dime.

She held back a smile. "I'd say, yes. Order something."

Brian held on to the bars, watching the exchange closely, his eyes rounded in disbelief.

"Can't believe you locked me up like I'm a perp, for fuck's sake," he muttered. "I'm a cop, and you know me. We could've stayed in that damn hotel, taken a shower, felt like human beings for one more night before they lock me up tomorrow. I might never get out of there, Kay. They might shiv me in there before I learn where the pissers are. You know damn well what happens to cops in prison."

Usually preoccupied with appearances, it wasn't like him to use bad language, not unless he was pressing on a suspect. He was probably tired, visibly scared, perhaps at the end of his wits.

"You'll be safe in there," Kay said, taking a few steps away from the cell. "Deputy Hobbs will take good care of you."

He slammed his hand against the bars as hard as he could. They rattled a little. "Come on, don't leave me here! It's not like we haven't slept together before. I'll take the floor."

Loud cackling erupted from the next cell. A dirty face with bloodshot eyes, almost entirely covered in locks of sweaty, grimy hair, emerged from under the blanket. "Trouble in paradise?" he asked, slurring his speech something fierce. His words filled the air with the smell of stale booze and vomit.

"Who's this?" Kay asked.

"A drunk and disorderly, Novack's collar. We let him sleep it off till morning."

"Fabulous," Brian snapped. "He stinks of piss, Kay."

The drunk went over to the side of his cell and extended his hand between bars, almost touching Brian's shoulder. "I've never been locked up with a pig before. Welcome to the joint. D'you got balls for life on the inside?" He reached as far as his arm would go but couldn't touch Brian. He'd pulled away, cursing under his breath. "It ain't so bad, you know. Three hots and a cot, even for losers like you." Then he cackled again, clapping his hands in excitement. "Sure, you might have to suck some cock on occasions, but hey—"

"Shut the hell up." Brian glared at him and withdrew to the far end of his cell, his fists clenched at his chest as if ready to pounce. "Kay, please—"

"Have a good night, Brian. I'd suggest you get some rest. It's a long day tomorrow and not an easy one."

She patted Hobbs's shoulder on the way out, eager to get out of there, to be rid of Brian, all the memories, and the unnerving scent of his bloody aftershave.

Stepping outside, she stopped at the top of the stairs and breathed in the cold air, clearing her lungs and her mind. She gazed at the stars for a while, wondering how they sparkled more vividly that night, probably because of the cold air. She'd seen them like that hiking on the peaks of Mount Chester. They were beautiful, distant beacons of light that warmed her soul.

When she lowered her eyes from the sky, Elliot was there, leaning against the side of her Interceptor and staring at her with a hint of a smile on his lips. Her heart swelled. It took every bit of willpower she had not to rush into his arms and bury her face in his chest.

"I was getting worried about you," she said, unable to stop smiling. "It's not like you to not respond to a message."

Frowning, he looked at his phone. "I don't have a message from you. I was about to call you when I saw you'd returned and I thought I'd wait." Kay thought he blushed a little, but the light coming from the single parking lot lamppost was dim and yellowish. "Just to make sure you're okay."

She checked her phone and found the message she'd typed unfinished and unsent. Brian had interrupted her, and she'd somehow forgotten all about that. Raising her eyes from the screen to look at Elliot, she smiled apologetically. "My bad. I didn't hit send."

He drew a bit closer. "Did you have time to eat?" He checked the time on his phone. "I bet Hilltop would still make us some burgers."

Her smile widened. "You're on, partner."

TWENTY

DINNER

The smell of fresh fries was wasted on him, ditto for the mouthwatering cheeseburger set on a large white plate on the table in front of him. Elliot's gaze was focused on Kay's pale face, her haunted eyes, the dark circles under them that weren't there in the morning at the shooting range. Only fourteen hours ago, his partner was laughing and joking and passing her weapons proficiency in the early sunshine, not a care in the world.

He could teach that piece of shit who had stumbled back into her life a valuable lesson, Texas-style.

Kay's fingers were wrapped around the hot cup of tea she'd requested instead of her usual beer. Like him, she was ignoring her food, seemingly lost in her thoughts, breathing in the steam bearing the scent of fresh chamomile.

One damn day, that's all it had taken that smug son of a bitch to wipe the smile off her face.

She raised her eyes and, for a moment, looked straight into his. He could get lost in those eyes; they did things to him he couldn't explain. With a hesitant smile, she said, "I'm really hungry, you know." A light chuckle. "I'm hiding it well, but I am." She threw the untouched plate a look. "This looks great."

Elliot ran his fingers through his hair, wondering why she hadn't once mentioned an ex-husband. He'd asked himself that a thousand times already, but no answer ever came. Just suppositions, theories, and a sprinkle of wishful thinking.

But if he learned the son of a bitch was a wife-beater, he'd be dead meat waiting to be salted dry before the end of the day.

"Do you believe his story?" he asked, keeping his voice from reflecting his thoughts.

Kay glanced at him. "Who, Brian?"

He nodded and shrugged. *Who else?*

She bit her lip for a moment, probably thinking what to say, although she must've thought about it already. Since the ex had shown up on their doorstep at the precinct, she'd been withdrawn, quiet, secretive. As if embarrassed of something, deeply ashamed. There was a tension between them that didn't use to exist, replacing their unspoken chemistry, obliterating it almost without a trace.

"That's one hell of a question," she eventually said, stabbing a fry with her fork but stopping short of putting it into her mouth. "He's a cop, a decent one. He's mostly worked organized crime, drug rings, smuggling, that sort of thing. In San Francisco, where the stakes are high." She looked down for a moment, her entire face shrouded in sadness. "The woman whose murder he's charged with was my best friend. Well, former best friend." Her cheeks caught fire. "His fiancée," she added, visibly uncomfortable, shifting in her seat and abandoning the fork with the stabbed fry on the side of her plate. "And former mistress, back when we used to be married." A pained sigh ended her statement. When she looked at him again, her eyes were tearing up.

Aw, hell. Yeah, the son of a bitch deserved a good pounding, no doubt about it. Maybe jail was just what the doctor ordered for the cheating sleazebag.

"I'm so sorry, Kay," he said, reaching for her hand. He squeezed her frozen fingers, and she welcomed his touch for a long moment. Then she pulled away slowly.

"It's okay," she replied after a while. "Ancient history." Taking a sip of tea, she gave the fork a quick look but didn't touch it. "Not a whole lot of reasons to believe him or help him, as you can see. But he's not a killer. Anyway, the case points in a different direction altogether. So, there's that."

His brow furrowed a little. Had she been investigating the case? "What do you know so far?"

"Rachel, that's the girl's name," she clarified with a glance, "had witnessed the shooting of a drug dealer the night before she was killed. She gave a statement to the cops, met with the ADA, and was supposed to enter WITSEC that night." She shook her head. "I honestly can't think of a single reason why they'd arrest my ex for it. They're setting him up." The stabbed fry found its way to her mouth, finally. She chewed it slowly at first, then enthusiastically. "This is good," she mumbled as if she'd never had fries at the Hilltop Pub before. "Tell me about Taylor Lorentz," she asked, stabbing a few more fries with a determined jab. "Did you find her?"

A long moment of silence took over. Elliot pushed aside his plate.

"That bad, huh?" Kay asked gently. As always, she could read his mind like an open book.

"She was shot in the chest and dragged into the ravine behind Frozen Falls." He ran his hands through his hair again, realizing his gesture was a tell that Kay could read but still doing it. "There's no apparent motive and nothing to point at anything other than a random shooting on the side of the road. We found blood where it happened."

She looked at him intently with a slight frown, chewing.

"You're saying someone drove by and just shot her for—for what? For fun? For the heck of it?"

"Seems that way, yeah." He took a swig of beer, the cool liquid quenching his thirst and soothing his angst a little. "No one knew she was out running that day; it was a spur-of-the-moment decision. Six in the morning, not a whole lot of traffic then."

"Poor Mr. Lorentz," Kay whispered. "How's he taking it?"

"As expected. He's in the hospital; he had a complete breakdown when we found her body."

"Wow. What are you planning to do?"

He looked at her for a while, taking advantage of her averted gaze to study her weary face again, her hunched shoulders, the paleness of her skin. If there was ever a time his partner had needed his help, that was it.

"I'm actually going to call the boss in the morning and ask for a couple of days off. Then I'm coming to San Francisco with you."

Visibly surprised, she looked straight at him. "What? Elliot, no. There's no need for that. Plus, Logan will blow a gasket. He can't have both his detectives off with an active murder case on the table. But thank you so very much."

"The case you're describing, the mess your ex is in, sounds like a dangerous affair to me. You need someone to watch your back. You know you can trust me," he added, wondering why he'd said that the moment the words came out. Her trust in him had never been the issue.

"With my life," she replied with a warm smile, touching his hand briefly. "I'm not going to get in any trouble—"

"Famous last words."

She laughed. "No, I mean it. I can't investigate this anyway. All I'm planning to do is speak with the ADA and draw his attention to the other case, the shooting Rachel witnessed." She must've seen the confusion on Elliot's face because she continued, "It's different ADAs. They don't seem to talk much with each other. It's San Francisco; what can I say? Things get lost in the shuffle. I've seen worse." She shrugged and collected the last of her fries with her fingers. "That's all I can really do. But you're needed here. Taylor Lorentz deserves your full attention now, when the case is fresh. The first forty-eight hours, remember?"

Stubborn and independent and feisty and fearless. The woman drove him insane.

A smile tugged at the corners of his mouth as he realized the qualities he was grumbling about in his mind were the same ones that made Kay so damn attractive.

"All right," he said, knowing any insistence would be instantly dismissed. "But call me the moment you need me. If your hairs start standing on end for no reason, just call."

"You got it," she replied, taking a reasonably large bite out of her cheeseburger and chewing it with her eyes half-closed. A few moments later, she asked, "Okay, Taylor Lorentz. What are you going to do? Any leads yet?"

He took another swig of beer, eyeing his untouched plate. Hunger was starting to gnaw at his stomach. "I'm visiting Doc Whitmore tomorrow to see what he's got so far. Maybe we'll get lucky. There was a bullet that got lodged in her phone, might be some usable prints on that. Then, you know, the usual. Find out about her life, who would've had any reason to want her dead. Maybe someone was stalking her and took the opportunity to shoot her when she left the house so early in the morning, by herself, and chose to run through a deserted stretch of woods." He bit about a quarter of the mouthwatering, cheese-covered hamburger and chewed it quickly, then washed it down with another swig of beer. "If there are no fingerprints or DNA, and there's no real connection with the vic, we're shit out of luck. If it was random... we might never find who did it."

The random scenario scared the wits out of him. He'd

worked a random shooting case in Austin he couldn't close. He was still haunted by the memory of the young boy's mother, who blamed him for her son's killer walking free. That open case file had stayed on his desk for years. For the little boy who'd been shot from a passing car, there was no justice still.

Kay shook her head and held her hand up in the air. "Random today isn't what random used to be, especially here, in our neck of the woods. Far less traffic than a big city. Fewer cars that drive by, even if there are fewer cameras." Wiping her fingers on a paper napkin, she finished her meal, pushing aside a perfectly empty plate. "We'll catch him, partner, don't worry. If it was random, the unsub drove there. He didn't walk. And driving leaves trails we can follow."

He finished his burger quickly and his beer right after that. "Why don't you come by tomorrow morning for a horseback ride? I hear it's going to be beautiful. Clear skies, a bit chilly though, but no snow yet."

A wave of sadness washed over her face. "I can't, Elliot. Not tomorrow. Rain check? I have to take Brian to San Francisco at six in the morning."

"He's back here?" The elevated pitch of his voice betrayed his feelings.

She avoided his eyes. "Yeah... in lockup at the precinct currently. He couldn't be bothered to spend the night in jail in San Francisco, so his lawyer, in her infinite wisdom, arranged for a surrender tomorrow morning instead. I got stuck with him."

"All right, then, rain check," he replied, painfully aware he was grinding his teeth. "I'll be here when you're ready."

The glance she threw him seemed filled with regret and something else he couldn't read, an intensity of sorts, something that tugged at his heart. But she stood that very moment, ready to go, and he lost the opportunity to find out.

That smug son of a bitch couldn't be gone fast enough.

TWENTY-ONE
SOUTHBOUND

Unnerving déjà vu.

With so very few changes and so minute, it felt surreal.

Leaving the precinct the next morning with Brian Hanlin in tow. Having an argument by the SUV about him riding in the back. Stopping at Katse to pick up a phone order of coffee and croissants, delivered to the parking lot by the owner.

This time, Tommy MacPherson didn't dare look inside the vehicle and didn't make any comments about Kay's passenger.

Then driving south on a highway crowded with tractor trailers loaded with produce.

"At least, let's stop at a gas station so I can clean up," Brian pleaded, running his hand over his stubble and looking disgusted. "You don't know how people judge you these days if they see your scruff. Idiots believe they can get away with unkempt beards and man buns and shit, but it's their generation that had to invent the word incel."

She didn't reply. The last thing she wanted was a thirty-minute stop at some Chevron in the middle of nowhere, so he could shop for toiletries, then spend forever preening. She was pretty sure they'd lock him in jail just as well unshaven.

"You know, involuntary celibate?" he insisted, resting his forearm on the back of her seat. She bit her lip to not snap at him. "I'm due in court today, for goodness' sake. It's bad enough if I show up in yesterday's clothes and stinking of rural lockup, but I can't show up in court like this. No woman—"

"Are you serious right now, Brian?" she snapped. "You're going to court to pick up women on your arraignment? That's your concern?"

He breathed heavily, visibly angered by her remarks. "Judges can be women too, you know. And if the judge is a man, it's even worse, unless he happens to be a Jason Momoa fan."

He had a point. With a long sigh, she checked the GPS display on her media screen. It showed they'd arrive at eight-fifteen, forty-five minutes before their appointment time. Maybe they could spare ten minutes. At least he'd smell of whatever cheap aftershave they sold in gas stations, not the Dolce & Gabbana that still stirred up memories she wanted to forget.

"I'm pretty sure if I show up for arraignment looking like a thug, the bail will be double. You'd do that to me, Kay? When I'm not sure I can pay anything as it is?"

"All right," she said, squeezing the steering wheel until her joints hurt. "We'll stop so you can shave."

Lightning fast, he placed a kiss on her cheek. "You're the best."

"Do that again, and I'll book you for assaulting a cop," she said, her voice low, loaded with rage. It was just like him, to grab what he couldn't get, to pound and insist until exhausted and sick of it all, she'd cave.

"Can a cop be busted for assaulting another cop?" he asked serenely, grinning widely as Kay pulled in at a gas station and stopped at the pump. It was a large one, newly built on the outskirts of Redding.

"You have twenty minutes," she said sternly. "After which,

I'll drag you out of there in cuffs, and I won't care if you're half-shaved."

He'd already left, slamming the door behind him, but waved at her as he entered the station. She fueled the Interceptor and then waited, looking at the watch impatiently.

Eighteen minutes later, he emerged wearing a fresh shirt he'd probably bought inside, a new tie, cleanly shaved and smelling of Old Spice. Not his fragrance, but it worked. As if his state of cleanliness had instilled self-confidence, he walked with a spring in his step, yesterday's clothes rolled under his arm in a transparent shopping bag bearing the gas station's logo.

"Well?" He posed for her until she pointed at the SUV with a firm gesture. "What do you think?"

She hated to admit but the stop had made a difference. "Yeah, it's better."

Starting the engine, she drove away, fastening her seatbelt as she accelerated. "You don't strike me as a parent," she said after a mile or two driven in silence.

"Yeah, well, my lifestyle caught up with me, I guess."

"Are you really a father to Rachel's daughter?" Kay asked, already knowing the answer.

"I send alimony checks on time, if that's what you're asking."

"That's not what I'm asking." She paused for a while, thinking about what it was that had tugged at her gut. "Your kid has just lost her mother, and you seem fine with her being with her grandmother."

He shrugged. "I'm a wanted felon, Kay. I'd be an idiot to drag an innocent eight-year-old girl with me into this. My daughter is better off where she is." He cleared his throat. "I bet there's a squad car parked in front of Mrs. Epling's house, just waiting for me to be that stupid."

Traffic turned dense as they approached the city. Worried,

Kay kept her eye on the GPS while weaving through with the flashers on.

"But you were going to make it right? Marry Rachel, give your daughter a family?"

"Yes." He buried his face in the palm of his hand.

"Why now, Brian? After all these years, what changed?"

He pulled away. "It was Holly, really. She grew up, started asking questions, and, um, she didn't deserve to worry about me, about us."

Hearing him speak, she realized she didn't have to ask; he probably hadn't been more faithful to Rachel than he'd been to her. He'd probably loved Rachel as much as he was able to love someone in his own deeply selfish and narcissistic way.

Still, there was something that bugged her: the deal Rachel had struck so quickly with the ADA about WITSEC. No one gave those deals to people who only had the description of a vehicle, a car tag, or something like that. Had it been a particular, known-to-police tag she'd recognized? An official vehicle of sorts? A celebrity?

"We have about twenty-five minutes left, and I have more questions." She checked the mirror and saw he was leaning against the back seat with his eyes closed.

"Could we skip them, please? I need to get ready for what's coming."

"What did she really see that night? Just the vehicle? Or did she recognize the driver?"

He opened his eyes and glared at her through the mirror. "She didn't tell me. Possibly because I didn't ask." He raised his voice more and more as he spoke. "I was too busy giving her shit for speaking to the cops in the first place."

"When did the shooting happen? The one she witnessed?"

"Thursday night," he replied with a frustrated sigh. He'd told her that before.

"What did you see?"

"Jeez... you drive me insane with these questions." He groaned, but then he spoke slowly, patiently. "By the time I arrived, she was hysterical and had made a statement already. I didn't hear what she said, and all I could think about was making that statement go away. I begged the cop who'd taken it to just let it go, but he'd called it into the DA's office already."

"And you have no idea what she saw?"

"None!" The syllable snapped like a whip in the tense air inside the vehicle.

"All right," she replied in a pacifying tone. He told the same story no matter how many times she asked or how she twisted her questions. "And they suspect you because..." She let her words trail off, hoping he'd pick up and continue what could only be speculation at that point.

"I'd say I'm being framed, so it's corruption, essentially." He ran his hand over his face as if to tear a veil that covered it with the specter of fear. "It could also be sloppy police work, personal vendettas, anything really." He looked out the window for a moment, absent-minded. The familiar cityscape of San Francisco in the early morning, when the sun started to burn through the dense fog of night, appeared to the left of Golden Gate Bridge, adorned with the gold reflections of the bay. "Look, all I know is I didn't kill Rachel. And without you, I don't stand a chance. If you can't—" His voice broke, and his words trailed. He covered his face with his hands to hide a shattered breath. "I can't believe she's gone. I keep wanting to go back to her house, imagining she's still there, alive, smiling. But she's gone." A stifled sob choked him. "And I can't erase the memory of her body lying in a pool of blood on the—"

"Be quiet, Brian," she whispered. Something else had caught her attention in the rearview mirror, other than the scrunched face of her ex. Since they'd reached the city, a black Chevy Suburban with no tags on the front bumper had been following them, staying behind about thirty yards. Traffic was heavy; that Chevy should've tailed her closely.

"What's up?" he asked, turning to look behind. "How long has that car been trailing us?"

"Since we got off the bridge."

In tense silence, Kay took a few right turns, testing to see if the SUV was indeed following them. When she turned again on Van Ness Avenue to continue to the SFPD Northern District Police Station, the Chevy turned after her.

She'd turned a complete loop. Now she had her answer.

With a frown, she checked the GPS screen. They were still twelve minutes away from the station. "Call your lawyer," she said, turning on the siren. "Tell her we're being followed."

He'd just finished wrapping up the thirty-second call when the black Chevy opened fire. The bullets, slamming into the Interceptor's body, sounded like large hail during a storm, only louder.

Deadlier.

Behind them, traffic turned into pure chaos on both sides of the road. Drivers, panicked or just distracted by the sight of a police vehicle being shot at, smashed their cars into heaps of twisted metal, blocking the access on both lanes. One rammed a school bus, pushing it onto the shrub-covered median. It landed on its belly, front wheels still spinning in the air. Another crashed into a sidewalk lamppost, tilting it to the side.

A bullet slammed against the SUV's body. The sound of plastic breaking told Kay it must've smashed one of her taillights.

"Give me your gun," Brian shouted, reaching out with an open hand. "Give it already, and lower the back windows."

Her hesitation lasted until another bullet smashed the light-bar, mere inches above her head. She pulled the SIG from the holster and handed it to Brian. "Don't make me regret this," she said, lurching forward when the vehicle in front of her climbed on the sidewalk to let her pass.

Through the passenger door window, Brian started shooting at the Chevy, keeping it at bay. He might've hit someone inside, perhaps the driver; Kay wasn't sure. Its windshield exploded in a million bits of tempered glass, and the SUV took an abrupt turn right, disappearing from view.

TWENTY-TWO
FORENSICS

At almost nine, Elliot pulled into the coroner's office parking lot. It was chilly, close to freezing. Traces of ground frost still clung to the grass where sun rays hadn't reached yet. Only two other vehicles were there, Dr. Whitmore's blue Acura and his assistant's sedan.

Elliot breathed in a lungful of fresh mountain air, steeling himself for the smell of human decay and formaldehyde awaiting him inside the morgue. He'd never overcome his reluctance to visit the ME's fiefdom; he probably never would. Something about looking at the bodies of the dead, exposed on the exam tables under powerful lights, sent shivers down his spine.

It was much worse when the victim was someone as young and innocent as Taylor Lorentz. The unfairness of her fate weighed heavily on his chest, filling him with a sense of powerlessness he deeply hated. But it wasn't going to last long, that sense of powerlessness, only until he'd find out who'd ended her life.

He entered the morgue with a determined step, taking his hat off when the door closed behind him. The reception area was deserted; he proceeded straight to the morgue, using the right swinging door to enter. Dropping his hat on a nearby chair, he approached Dr. Whitmore.

"Good morning, Doc," he said. The doctor didn't lift his eyes from the microscope; he only waved his hand a little, acknowledging his presence. Keeping his eyes on the doctor's hunched back, Elliot shifted his weight from one foot to another, waiting patiently. To his side, he glanced at Taylor's body lying bare on cold stainless steel and underneath a white sheet, then quickly looked away, feeling as if his scrutiny was nothing but shameless prying.

"All right," Doc Whitmore said, standing and pushing aside the four-legged stool. It hit the autopsy table with a clang and stopped in place. "I have a few things for you," he said, peeling off his gloves and dumping them into a trash can marked with the symbol of hazardous waste. "The time of death, we know; I can confirm it matches the timestamp of the emergency alert sent by her watch. Cause of death, again, no challenge. Gunshot wound to the chest." He groaned and propped one hand on his thigh toward the back, struggling somewhat to straighten his spine. Probably a lifetime of hunching over dead bodies in all kinds of weather, then over autopsy tables and lab equipment, had taken a toll. "Both bullets hit her heart; she died instantly."

"Small miracles, right, Doc?" Elliot asked, struggling to find some trace of solace in the fact that she didn't suffer and failing. She shouldn't have been there to begin with. At nineteen, her life was just beginning.

Apparently, the doctor felt the same because he didn't reply; he just shook his head silently, his lips tightly pressed together in a gesture of disappointment.

"Such senseless loss," he muttered. "I hope I can give you what you need to do your job quickly and effectively," he said, directing his attention to the wall-mounted TV. Clicking the remote, he displayed a few images. Taylor's phone, the one that had stopped the third bullet from piercing her chest. The same bullet, extracted and lying neatly on a lab tray. Then, a partial fingerprint shown in magnification, with a straight line running across the ridges, whorls, and loops and ending in a rugged smudge of sorts.

He drew closer to the TV and squinted.

"Most people don't realize they leave fingerprints on bullets and cartridges when loading their magazines. Maybe they just don't think about it, or they don't expect the bullets they load the gun with to be dusted for prints. Only contract killers know to use gloves when loading their magazines. They also police their brass." He paused for a moment, searching Elliot's eyes with an unspoken question. "If the bullet hits the mark, the friction against the victim's body and the blood it soaks in will destroy all prints." He pointed at the bullet's tip, protruding from the phone's cracked housing. "In this case, the tip of the bullet cracked the casing. Shards and sharp edges didn't damage the print much."

"Oh, is this what this line is? A shard or something that scratched through the print?"

"No, that's a scar," Dr. Whitmore smiled mischievously. "A highly recognizable scar our perp has, most likely on the tip of his thumb on his dominant hand." He clicked the remote and displayed a cartridge, covered in fingerprint dust and showing a usable print with the same line running across the whorls. "This is where that came from."

"What's this?" Elliot asked. They'd searched the day before and hadn't found any spent brass in the thick grasses by the side of the road.

"Deputy Novack went there early this morning with his son's metal detector and found this right by the bloodstain, in the ditch."

Elliot nodded, grinning. "Go, Novack! He's got a bright future, that young man. Despite his looks," he couldn't help adding, laughing. It was relief and gratitude that fueled his laughter and a touch of pride.

"It's uncanny how much he resembles that sheriff on TV," Dr. Whitmore said. "I watched a few episodes just because everyone was talking about it. The TV show isn't bad either. In any case, he found us a casing chock-full of prints. Well, only a partial, a four-point partial, but highly distinctive. Apparently, the shooter found his other two casings and policed them. The third was deeply hidden at the root of some thicket; he must've given up searching for it. Novack can tell you more."

"Aren't fingerprints destroyed by the heat the bullet is exposed to during the discharge?"

Doc Whitmore nodded with a hint of a smile on his lips. "Great question. Only in some cases, largely depending on a number of factors. Chemical composition of the fingerprint itself and the manner it had reacted—or not—with the shell casing material. Age of the fingerprint. Other conditions such as environmental humidity, the temperature reached during—"

He held his hands in the air. "All right, Doc, I've got it. Any match in AFIS yet?"

"No. The search finished running, and there's no match. That means the perp doesn't have a record, is not a federal employee or applicant, hasn't served in the military, and isn't an alien who has applied for temporary or permanent residence since 2003." A brief pause while he scratched his forehead. "That's if I remember the date correctly. It might've been 2002 when Homeland Security started collecting fingerprints from all foreign nationals upon entry in the United States. Soon after 9/11 anyway."

"How about the bullet? Any ballistics match?"

"I would've told you if I had a match, son." Dr. Whitmore's voice had turned a bit grim. "Now let's talk about Taylor," he said, turning toward the autopsy table.

Elliot followed the ME reluctantly, keeping his respectful distance from the table. "I'm listening."

"Livor mortis confirmed she was dragged and dumped immediately after death." Dr. Whitmore lifted the girl's arm and showed him the purplish staining discoloring the back of her arm near the shoulder. "Tox screen came back clean. No recent sexual activity, and by recent, I mean in the last forty-eight hours. There are a couple of unexpected findings, though." He lifted her right wrist into the air. "A spiral fracture here..." He pointed with his finger above the wrist, drawing lines in the air next to the skin. "Healed, I'd say recently. Two months ago, maybe more, perhaps just a little less." He drew a breath of air while deep ridges settled across his brow. "She was also eight weeks pregnant."

"Pregnant?" Elliot said. "I didn't expect that. Her father said she wasn't seeing—"

"Well, parents don't always learn of these things so early in the pregnancy, especially when the girl is young and unmarried. And you don't have to ask—fetal DNA is running."

Elliot took a moment to think. The ME had mentioned a spiral fracture two months ago and pregnancy on a similar timeline. "Do you think they're connected?"

Doc Whitmore looked at him with kind, tired eyes. "That's your job to figure out. I can only state facts and evidence. But I find the ulnar fracture and the time of the impregnation close enough to warrant some investigative attention from you. Something happened to this girl two months ago, violent enough to break bone."

The medical examiner clicked the remote, sifting through the images until he located Taylor's wrist and forearm X-rays. Then he pointed at the pale white shapes on the screen. "See here? This happens when a person's hand is twisted like this," he demonstrated on his other hand, "to subdue them or pin them down."

"So, it couldn't've been an accident of sorts? She was physically active."

"Accidents rarely cause spiral fractures in the wrist and forearm, although it could happen. In the leg, it happens with skiers and snowboarders when their limb is twisted by being stuck in the boot. Football players too. But in the wrist and forearm, as we see in Taylor, I'd be willing to bet it wasn't accidental."

Elliot looked at the girl's face as if her pale lips could share the secrets of her demise. She'd spoken already, through the voice of Dr. Whitmore.

"A few more things," Dr. Whitmore added. "The hair tie you retrieved from the scene." He clicked the remote until the brown scrunchie came into view. "I should say, this synthetic velour fabric is sticky for hair fibers, almost as badly as Velcro. It had all sorts of hairs on it, not all belonging to the victim. There's a shorter, darker hair that still had the follicle attached. It's running now. And there were multiple feline and canine hairs on her clothing, different breeds, different colors."

"Her father mentioned something about pet-sitting when we stopped by their house." Elliot checked his notes. "One more question, Doc. Were you able to confirm the distance the shots were fired from?"

"Ah, yes," he said, turning toward his computer. "I knew I forgot something. Distance depends largely on the handgun used. The longer the barrel, the more penetrative power. But I closely examined the phone bullet striations and narrowed it down to several potential weapons. You know, I hate guessing or venturing into any sort of estimation, instead of an actual test result. That sort of comparative ballistic test could take—"

Elliot smiled. The ME was nothing if not rigorous in his approach. "Just your gut, Doc, that's all I need for now."

Doc Whitmore sighed. "All right, but don't quote me on it. I'd say it was fired from twelve to fifteen yards away. Oh, and there was trace GSR on her shoulder and her nape, probably a transfer from the shooter when he dragged her body through the woods."

Elliot thanked the medical examiner and left. Stepping outside into the breezy chill of the December morning, he breathed the cold air, welcoming the fir-scented freshness. He had ballistics, fingerprints, and DNA; the case should be easy enough to close.

But murder cases rarely are.

TWENTY-THREE
HIT

After driving the rest of the way to the precinct without any incident, Kay pulled into the station's parking lot and cut off the siren. The second call Brian had made to his lawyer had proven effective. SFPD Northern District was ready for their arrival.

Several officers had taken positions behind the open doors of their vehicles, their backs against the building, ready for a shooting match with any potential attackers. Two SWAT vans were placed at the corners of the building, flanking it strategically. On the roof, several snipers were in prone position, ready to fire.

Kay stopped in the middle of the lot, the nose of her SUV facing the building, then cut the engine. She remained still, watching carefully for a signal from the SFPD units. A few parking spots over to the left, Carly Hosking's Beemer was stopped in the shade of a big redwood, by the chicken-wire fence. She wasn't behind the wheel; she must've already entered the single-story building. Smart woman.

"What now?" Brian asked. He sounded irritated with the entire situation, but Kay suspected this was a form of bravado to hide how scared he was.

Unfortunately, he'd been right. Whoever killed Rachel was now coming after him. They were tying up loose ends.

"Now we wait," Kay replied, whispering, "make like a mouse when the cat's in the house. Sit still, don't make a sound."

When Brian's phone rang in the heavy silence of their space, they both jumped out of their skin.

He cursed in a low voice, then said, "It's Carly."

"Take it on speaker."

He obliged.

"Brian, I have Mr. Diaz, the chief of detectives, here with me." Carly's voice sounded a bit shaky. Some muffled noises ensued as the attorney passed the phone to Diaz.

"Detective Hanlin." A man's assertive voice came across the call with the faintest of Spanish accents and a tinge of concern.

"Yes, sir," Brian replied. "I have Detective Sharp of Franklin County with me. Tell us how you'd like this to play out."

"We've had you on camera since you passed Van Ness and Greenwich. You weren't followed anymore."

"Good to know. Are we cleared to enter the building?"

A moment of silence, then some whispers Kay didn't catch. "Yes, please proceed. Slowly. Some rookie might flinch with the finger on the trigger."

"Copy that," Brian replied. "Proceeding with caution."

Kay opened the door, waited a few seconds, then exited the SUV. She looked around her carefully but didn't see anything out of place, except two dozen SFPD cops and SWAT prepared for World War III. She held her breath and listened: perfect silence in her proximity, against a backdrop of distant traffic noises coming from the city. The section of Van Ness well ahead of and past Turk Street had been roadblocked and secured. Turk Street ran one way from Van Ness, westbound. It was deserted.

And still, something felt off. Hairs tingled at the back of her head where they stood on end. Perhaps from hypervigilance or instinct, but she couldn't think of what could go wrong. Moving slowly so as to not startle someone into pulling the trigger, she closed the front door gently, then opened the back door to let Brian out.

Just as slowly, he got out, holding his hands up in the air for good measure. For another few seconds, they waited in place while Kay closed the back door and studied the surroundings again, then they started walking toward the precinct.

She heard the bullet zipping through the air and wanted to shout at Brian to get down, but it tore into her flesh before she could open her mouth, catching the breath inside her lungs. The bullet's momentum made her twist in place and lose her balance. She grabbed Brian's arm to bring him down, but he resisted, still standing, holding her up instead.

In a split second, she realized she hadn't heard a gunshot. Just the whooshing of the incoming round splitting air.

Sniper.

Then she heard the second bullet ripping through as it approached. Brian screamed and lunged at her, bringing her down under the weight of his body. He shielded her head with his arms, their faces touching.

Gunshots erupted all around. Someone shouted, "Sniper!" but it didn't stop the shooting. They must've seen what they were shooting at. Although the sniper could've been over a mile out, firing from some distant rooftop where any handgun-fired round wouldn't reach. At least they were offering cover fire for them, buying them precious time.

Her left arm throbbing in pain, Kay wriggled free from under Brian's body and looked at his face. He was panting hard, wincing in pain; he was alive and conscious. She started crawling toward the front of the Interceptor for cover, only a few feet away. "How badly are you hit?"

"They got me in the leg," he groaned. Blood trickled

between his fingers where he kept his hand pressed tightly against his right thigh. The bullet had torn through his flesh, through and through, leaving two bloody holes in the smooth fabric of his pants.

"You'll live," she announced, tugging at his jacket. "If you move your ass out of the line of fire."

"Where's it coming from?"

She pointed west. "Over there," she said, leaning against the Ford's front bumper. They were shielded by the SUV, safe for the moment but pinned down. She peeked her head over the hood to look toward Turk Street, where she believed the bullets had come from. She checked every rooftop she could see past the crowns of redwoods lining the parking lot. "I don't see anything."

Brian sat right next to her, panting. "Aren't you glad you're with me?"

She chuckled. "Not in the least."

The shriek of tires peeling off a few hundred yards away caught her attention. She sprang to her feet and ran to the street.

"Stay down over there," she heard Diaz shouting. "Hold your fire," he ordered his people with urgency in his voice. A couple of bullets still popped after he gave the command. "Hold your fire, damn it!"

Standing on her toes at the edge of Turk Street, partially shielded behind the body of a delivery van, she caught a glimpse of a large, black SUV taking the corner so fast it almost flipped on its side.

Within moments, several SFPD vehicles peeled off to pursue it in a riot of sirens, leaving marks on the parking lot asphalt and the smell of burned rubber in the air.

They'd probably never catch that sniper.

So far, he'd been two steps ahead of them the entire time.

TWENTY-FOUR
A LIFE

It wasn't the first time Elliot visited the Lorentz home. He'd been there the day before with Mr. Lorentz to collect his insulin and an item of clothing for the K-9 dog.

An old, small farmhouse, visibly fallen into disarray as of recently, the house wasn't unlike Elliot's. Single story and placed relatively close to the road, the house had been built with thick brick walls and large windows overlooking the meadows behind. The front lawn was overtaken by weeds but trimmed down to a couple of inches. The fence, rotted in places, was crooked to the side, a few planks loosened, soon to fall under the force of wintry gusts.

He knocked on the door. The doorbell was rusted and cracked, and Elliot didn't even try to see if it was working. A weak voice he barely recognized said, "Come in. It's open."

The door squeaked as Elliot pushed it open slowly. The place smelled of stale cigarette smoke, the air bluish and thick. He entered but left the door open behind him. A bit of fresh air wasn't going to do any harm.

Mr. Lorentz was lying on the couch, his swollen legs hanging over the edge. He was dressed in the same clothes he'd worn the day before, stained by dirt and grass where he'd searched the woods for his daughter. A framed photo was facing down on his chest, his hand holding it in place, heaving with every breath.

On the side table, an empty pack of cigarettes and an ashtray filled to the brim with butts and ash told the story of how he'd spent his night. An empty bottle of cheap bourbon told another side of it, the smell of stale alcohol and boozy sweat barely noticeable under the thick layer of smoke that still engulfed everything.

The drapes were closed, leaving very little light to keep him company. Elliot looked, but there wasn't any evidence the man had eaten anything since he'd returned from the hospital. Not a single food wrapper, not a dirty dish in the sink or on the dining room table.

"When did they let you out?"

"Last night," the man replied, closing his eyes. "I didn't want to spend the night. My place is here, with them."

Elliot didn't have to ask. Mr. Lorentz's hand pressed harder on the framed picture against his chest as he spoke.

"I was expecting you to come by and ask more questions." His voice was a raspy, labored whisper. "Different questions than yesterday."

Elliot set his hat on the table and pulled out a chair for himself. "Tell me about Taylor. What was she like? How did she spend her time?"

A tear rolled on the man's pale face. He kept his eyes closed as if reality had stopped being bearable. "My wife passed last year... I think I might've mentioned that."

"Yes, you did. My deepest sympathies. I can't begin to imagine how you must feel."

A weak gesture with a trembling hand thanked Elliot.

"Taylor struggled with grief after her mom's passing. She didn't say anything, but I knew." A shattered breath left his chest. "I changed my job to be home every night, even though that meant taking a pay cut. No more eighteen-wheelers cross-country; now I'm doing local deliveries with a flatbed for less than half the pay. But I wasn't going to leave my baby alone to deal with her mother's loss."

Elliot stood and walked over to the kitchen sink, found a clean glass, and filled it with water. Then he placed it on the coffee table, within the man's reach. He didn't touch it; he didn't even open his eyes hearing Elliot walk around.

"She finished high school with honors and got accepted into college. She studied nights, tears streaming down her face, just saying she wanted to make her mother proud." Another tear escaped the corner of his closed eye. "That's who my little girl was, Detective. An angel. A good kid."

His words made it even more difficult for Elliot to say what he was about to. He didn't have a choice. "What I'm about to say will probably come as a surprise," he said. His hesitation made Lorentz open his bloodshot, watery eyes and look straight at him. "Taylor was pregnant."

The man sat up, leaning against the sofa cushions, pushing himself upright. "I don't believe this. I would've known. My little girl would've told me."

"The pregnancy was in its early stages," Elliot said. There wouldn't be much harm if he'd omit certain details. "It's possible she wasn't aware of it."

"Oh." He closed his eyes for a long moment. "But she wasn't seeing anyone."

"No boyfriend?"

"No." The answer came decisively fast. "She was busy studying. Talk with her science teacher, Frank Livingston. He's been mentoring her to follow in his footsteps, become a teacher when she graduates." He covered his mouth with his hand as if to stifle a sob. "Can't talk about her in past tense. Just can't."

"How about in the evenings? Was she going out anywhere? Hanging out with friends?"

"She kept this house going, with me working and sick and all. In the evenings, she worked as a pet sitter and a house sitter, whatever she could find for extra work, even mowing people's lawns, my little girl would take it to help out. My income has been low. I've been sick, taking time off, but not because I wanted it. They make me stay home if my blood sugar is too high."

"Is it okay if I see her bedroom?"

Mr. Lorentz nodded, gesturing toward the back of the house. "It's the last room through there. She liked waking up to the sight of the woods in the morning."

Elliot's bootheels clacked against the barren, scratched hardwood that lined the hallway. Taylor's room was tidy and almost monastical, devoid of almost all décor that would've indicated a teenager had lived there. The bed was made and covered with a worn blanket with a native motif. The minimalistic furniture was reduced to a small desk with three drawers in old, discolored, and scratched wood and a wooden chair with a straight back shaped like stairway balusters. It used to be lacquered, but the seat and the edges had worn past lacquer to the wood fiber.

A laptop, closed, was placed on the desk's surface amid neatly organized papers, notebooks, and textbooks on psychics, chemistry, and math. Several writing implements were scattered as well, although some were collected in an old ceramic mug with a broken handle. It was white and imprinted with a cartoon of a cat scratching the surface of the mug and the words, "MADE FROM SCRATCH" in black, bold type. The mug seemed to have been a cherished object, perhaps a gift from someone she'd loved.

Elliot opened the drawers quietly and found the usual treasures of a young woman struggling with life. Several pieces of jewelry, all dollar-store quality, made of cheap metal or plastic. School supplies took the big center drawer. The last drawer contained a few photos that Elliot took and looked at. Taylor and her mother in front of the chairlift terminal on Mount Chester. The entire family, when Taylor was about nine, on a beach somewhere. Taylor and a scrawny young man with long hair and thin-rimmed glasses, smiling. His arm was wrapped around the girl's shoulder, and she was leaning into him, enjoying the closeness.

Elliot took the photo with the unknown man and the laptop, and walked back into the living room. Mr. Lorentz was just as he'd left him, showing no awareness of his presence.

The air had cleared a little, and now the house was chilly. Elliot closed the front door, then went over to the sofa.

"Mr. Lorentz, could you please look at this photo? Do you know who this man is?"

He opened his eyes and looked at the picture. "That's a former classmate of Taylor's. I don't remember his name; I haven't seen him in a while." He frowned as if racking his memory. "Walter? Wally? Something like that."

"All right. How about this?" He held the laptop in the air. "Do I have your permission to take this with me? It would help us shed some light—"

"Of course," he whispered. He seemed weak, wasting away. "There's no password on it; house rules." He smiled weakly. "I can give you access to her call log for her phone."

Elliot took the information he provided, writing down usernames and passwords for the phone accounts and Taylor's social media accounts.

"Who killed my baby, Detective?" he asked when they were finished. "You must have some idea by now."

"I don't," Elliot replied honestly. "But I can tell you this: we're going to get him and make him pay dearly for what he's done." Their eyes locked in an unspoken promise.

Then Mr. Lorentz closed his eyes again.

"Close the door behind you when you leave, Detective."

Elliot wished Kay was there to help Lorentz deal with his grief. He didn't know how to handle it, not with her finesse. But he knew one thing for sure. If he didn't say anything, he was going to regret it. Maybe not right then, perhaps in a day or two when the nine-one-one call would come in for his address, and the EMTs would find the man deceased from hypoglycemic shock.

"I need something from you, Mr. Lorentz," he said sternly. "Get up from that couch and fix yourself something to eat. Get a shower. Live."

A sob rattled the man's shoulders. Slowly, he turned the framed photo he was holding to his chest toward Elliot. It showed his late wife sitting on a picnic blanket and young Taylor with her arms wrapped around her mother's neck, their cheeks together, their smiles filled with joy. Clear blue sky and the silhouette of Mount Chester served as a backdrop for that photo.

"They were my reason for living," he sobbed. "I have nothing left."

"Yes, you do," Elliot said firmly, drawing closer to the man and extending a hand. "You want to be there when I bring your daughter's killer to justice."

TWENTY-FIVE
STITCHES

"Sorry, Detective," the young EMT said, probably seeing her wince. "A couple of pokes, and you won't feel me stitching you." She was an athletic Black woman in her late twenties, with a mane of curly, black hair tied in a loose ponytail. Her name tag read Nia.

Kay clenched her jaw, attempting to keep a straight face. The anesthetic smarted like hell. It wasn't too painful, just irritating, grating the nerves it hit before numbing them.

"You should come to the hospital, Detective," the EMT said, finally pulling that needle out of her flesh. "This wound is deep and bleeding profusely."

"I can't come to the hospital," Kay muttered for the third time. "Just patch it up with a couple of butterfly Band-Aids, and I'll be fine." *And don't bloody mention that hospital again,* she thought but kept quiet, not willing to aggravate the woman who played with sharp surgical implements near her open wound.

"That isn't going to happen," Nia replied. "I have to clean this wound and give you about eight or nine stitches." She kept a serious face, her dark eyes focused on Kay's bleeding shoulder.

"It cut straight through your deltoid here. If you want to raise your arm again, I can do this right."

"Thanks." She breathed, grateful for the disappearing pain in her arm. The anesthetic was starting to kick in. "I'm actually surprised you're able to suture wounds on-site."

"We're not," she smiled tensely for a brief moment. "My coworker and I were trained as remote medics and have the necessary certifications to intubate and stitch wounds in the field, but most EMTs can't. You might've noticed..." She paused for a moment, focusing intently on her work. "My coworker, Danny, went over to the other bus to stitch your, um, whatever. The other guy." She laughed, a little embarrassed.

By now, even the EMTs knew who she was to Brian.

"Thanks." Kay kept her eyes forward, a better option than to look at her bleeding flesh being sewn. "We're in a difficult situation, otherwise I would've taken you up on that hospital offer. I appreciate the exception you're making for us."

"The chief of detectives pulled some strings," Nia replied. "We're really not allowed to do this. Wounds could get infected, there's dust everywhere, this stupid wind is blowing it all over everything." She scowled at a fallen oak leaf that had landed on her lap. "I wish you'd let me take you inside, at least we could close these damn doors." She cut the thread after tying it in a neat knot. "But I guess they didn't catch the guy who's out to get you, and that's why we're improvising?"

"Yeah, he got away. He could be anywhere; he could follow us to the hospital to finish the job and risk the lives of everyone there," Kay replied, taking the opportunity to shift a little when Nia wasn't running a needle through her skin. She was sitting on the rear bumper of the ambulance, where she could keep her head on a swivel and see him coming. Maybe. Unless she heard another bullet ripping through the air, and then nothing. The end.

She was being paranoid. The ambulances had been parked

facing away from the precinct, and the SWAT vehicles added more cover on the sides. He had to be one hell of a sniper to try again, under those circumstances. Still, she'd refused to be stitched up inside the precinct or inside the ambulance with the doors closed. As if she'd suddenly developed claustrophobia, she wanted to feel the open air around her, to have some illusion she could sense him coming.

She looked to the left, where the other EMT, Danny, was working on Brian's leg. Her ex was lying on the stretcher, his fists under his chin, looking miserable and in pain. They'd cut a section of his pantleg, exposing a laceration in his thigh about an inch or two deep.

"Detective Sharp, is it? Or is it Doctor Sharp?"

She recognized the voice of the chief of detectives. She shook the man's hand. "Both, actually."

"Gustavo Diaz, chief of Ds," he introduced himself politely, although his eyes were shooting darts at her. He must've been new; she hadn't met him during her years of service as a San Francisco bureau agent. "So, what is it, Detective? Why are you here? As Brian Hanlin's ex-wife? As his doctor?"

Kay burst into laughter, imagining Brian seeing her as a psychologist, lying back on a sofa, talking about his inmost fears. That could never happen. The world would stop spinning the moment her ex sought help for personal growth.

"Stand still, please," Nia admonished her. Kay froze, remembering the curved needle that kept pinching and pulling at her skin.

"I'm not here as Brian's doctor, just as a friend."

Diaz propped his hands on his hips. He was a thin, bony man with a firm jawline and receding hair on the sides. "We don't need you here, Detective. You brought him in, and that's great. Now it's time for you to climb behind the wheel of your Interceptor and go back to your corner of the boonies."

"Oh, wow," she whispered, amazed at the level of hostility. "Are you afraid I might ask some uncomfortable questions?"

Her comment brought a wave of dark redness to the man's face. "You have no jurisdiction here." He took a step closer and towered over her, drilling into her with fiery eyes. "If you so much as ask for directions the wrong way before you leave my city, I will have your badge. Is that clear?"

Kay sustained his glare with a candid look and smiled. "Crystal. I'm here to see that he surrenders as discussed, that his lawyer is present, and his rights are not being messed with." The smile fluttered a little, then waned into an expression of calm determination. "Then I'll go visit the mother of a good friend. She's recently lost her daughter. The visit is personal, not professional; I'll be paying my respects."

"You're done," Nia announced proudly after taping a bandage over the wound. "Have that seen by a doctor at the earliest. They'll probably prescribe some antibiotics."

She thanked Nia and walked past Diaz, not caring she was dressed in a sports bra in the chilly weather. Her shirt was torn and bloodied, littering the ambulance floor.

Walking quickly and feeling Diaz right behind her, she stopped by Brian's stretcher. "Which ADA interviewed Rachel after the shooting?"

"Detective," Diaz shouted before Brian could answer. "This is your last warning. Get going already, or you'll be writing parking tickets for the rest of your career."

"She won't listen," Brian mumbled for Diaz's benefit. He had a spark in his eyes. "She used to be a fed, one of the best the regional bureau had; it got to her head. They're begging her to come back, but she's a bit stubborn."

Great, Brian, Kay thought. *Pour gasoline over the fire.*

But Diaz's change in attitude showed Brian knew what he was doing. His rage decreased a notch. "Fed or not, it's time for your missus to go home."

"I'm not his missus and you know that. Stop embarrassing yourself. I need to speak with the US Marshal assigned to Rachel's case," Kay said, feeling the wound on her shoulder through the thick bandage. It didn't hurt much.

"What the hell for?" Diaz snapped.

"Rachel's daughter might be in danger, her mother too. They need to be placed in protective custody immediately."

"Oh, God," Brian muttered, burying his face in his hands. "You don't think they'd come after my little girl? She wouldn't know anything. Neither would Mrs. Epling."

Kay put a reassuring hand on his shoulder. "We can't take chances with these people, Brian. I'll take care of it."

"You'll take care of going straight home, Detective. You have no business being here, messing with my case. We take care of our own, and we sure as hell don't need you."

"Which one is your case, Chief?" she asked slowly, enjoying seeing him flustered and enraged. The man was a stubborn fool, or maybe a dirty cop who played one. "Which case do you really give a damn about? Rachel's murder? Or the street corner shooting she witnessed?"

His jaw slacked and his eyes lit up with rage. "This is your last warning, Detective. Then I'll start making calls."

She grinned widely. "I'm not breaking any laws. Make all the calls you wish. I'm not here to do your job either, Chief."

"You think you can waltz in here and poke around, and boom, the charges against your hubby get dropped? You must think we're idiots!"

"I didn't say that," she replied serenely. "You did." She paused for a moment to let that sink in. "I'm just doing my job as a family friend with legitimate concerns about their well-being. We almost got killed here today, Chief. If that doesn't tell you something's amiss with your carefully constructed case against my ex, then nothing will. I'm not going to waste another moment trying to convince you."

"Good!" Diaz slapped his hands together, then rubbed them in a gesture of mock enthusiasm. Deep ridges ruffled his brow. "Then you can go home right now, or I'll have you arrested."

He took a step toward her menacingly. She didn't flinch.

"On what charge?" she asked with a hint of a smile.

"Running an investigation without jurisdiction."

"Nah," she let that smile bloom and touch her eyes. "I'm a simple citizen who wants to speak with local LEOs about a potential crime involving the safety of an eight-year-old girl. Are you sure you want to stop me?" She tilted her head provocatively. "Imagine that headline... It's a career killer."

Diaz groaned and clenched his fists inches away from her face, but then lowered his arms. "Then I'll send Detective Brockett with you. You know, for your own safety." Diaz grinned wickedly. He knew how to play the game just as well as she did.

"Not unless I'm under arrest, Chief."

Detective Brockett approached Brian when he stood up, wincing as he put weight on his leg. Carly Hosking was click-clacking a few feet behind him, struggling to keep up with the large stride of the former Marine.

"You're good from here?" Kay asked, squeezing Brian's forearm.

"As I'll ever be," he replied. He was pale and shivered in the brisk wind. "Take care of my daughter, Kay. I'll be all right. And Kay?"

"Yeah?"

"The ADA's name is Leonetti. Palmer Leonetti. He handles organized crime, mostly."

"Got it."

Detective Brockett started reading Brian his rights. Kay could swear he was enjoying it. His voice betrayed him. She studied Brockett for a moment. A tall and well-built man of about sixty, fit and fierce-looking, with a buzz cut that did little to hide thinning gray hair. Rimless glasses made his eyes appear a bit larger than they were. A mustache covered his upper lip, salt-and-pepper, stained yellow by cigarette smoke.

He wasn't going to share any details about the case and why he was proceeding with the arrest after that morning's shooting. He didn't seem like someone Kay could reason with.

He was an old bulldog.

TWENTY-SIX
BOYFRIEND

The admissions secretary at Franklin High, a pudgy little woman with beady eyes and a lascivious smile, had no difficulties recognizing Taylor's boyfriend from the photo Elliot placed in front of her.

"Oh, I know him," she said, smiling crookedly and shooting Elliot a glance above the rims of her glasses. "What's he done?"

"Nothing that I know of," Elliot replied. Excitement made room for disappointment on the woman's face. Sadly, there wasn't going to be much gossip material in the detective's visit to the school. "All I need is his name and an address if you've got it."

"I've got that for you, Detective, and much, much more," she said, batting her eyelashes and lowering her gaze, openly flirting with him. He was uncomfortable being the center of female attention, especially when the female wasn't someone he'd ask out.

She typed something with perfectly red and shiny fingernails, looking at the screen, then turned her attention back to Elliot. "Walter Edward Finley is his name." She gave him the address, then added in a low, conspiratial whisper, "I heard he was working as a lumberjack up on the mountain, where they're cutting down trees for the new hotel parking lot. He's not exactly college material, if you catch my drift."

The drive to the Winter Lodge Hotel was about twenty minutes, but Elliot managed it in fifteen. He found the land clearing crew easily; he could hear the noise of chainsaws and tree trunks falling from several miles away.

A foreman pointed at a skinny kid with long legs and locks of sweaty, curly hair coming out from underneath a white hard hat. About three days' worth of youthful, soft stubble gave the man a thick shadow on his upper lip but failed to make him seem more mature than his almost twenty years of age.

He was busy cutting branches off tree trunks, getting them ready to be loaded onto the platform farther downhill. His chainsaw, wielded skillfully, filled the air with the scent of fresh-cut pine and sawdust.

A pat on the shoulder got the young man's attention. The chainsaw stopped whirring and was abandoned on the ground.

"Detective Elliot Young, Franklin County Sheriff's Office," he introduced himself, flashing his badge for a brief moment. "Walter Finley?"

The man held his gaze unfazed. "Yeah. What's up?"

"I need to ask you a few questions about Taylor Lorentz," he said.

Finley took off his hard hat and wiped the sweat off his forehead with the back of his hand. "Oh? Why is that?"

"I'm sorry to have to tell you this, but Taylor was found dead yesterday morning."

The hard hat rattled onto the ground. The man's jaw slacked a little and his chin trembled slightly. His eyes, instantly filled with sorrow, looked away for a moment, then at his steel toe boots. "That was her, down there by Frozen Falls yesterday? I had no idea." He clasped his hands together at his chest as if praying.

"What can you tell me about her?"

"How did she die?" He put his hand on his forehead, still shocked about what he'd heard.

"Quickly," Elliot replied, refusing to give too much detail at first. "She was shot in the chest."

"I haven't seen her in about six months." He bit his lip nervously. "We broke it off when school ended. She went her way, I went mine."

"Why? It's not like you lived hundreds of miles apart."

"Not that kind of separate ways, sir." Seemingly embarrassed, he shifted his weight from one foot to the other. "It's what she chose to do."

"What, go to college?" Elliot asked derisively.

The young man sighed bitterly. "She was strippin', if you have to know," he said, lowering his voice although no one could hear them. The nearest lumber worker was at least twenty yards away and worked a chainsaw twice as big as Finley's.

"Stripping? Like in a club, dancing?"

"If that's what you wanna call it, sure."

"Her father said she was pet-sitting, house-sitting, that sort of thing. And going to college."

Finley studied his grimy fingernails with interest. "That part she did, the college thing. And she babysat some, enough to get away with *dancing* four nights a week." He accented the word as if he was doing Elliot a personal favor by not call it stripping. "Don't get me wrong," he added quickly, clasping his hands together and twisting and turning his fingers as if he wanted them broken. "I know why she was doing it. They were doing badly for money. Her mom died of cancer after wiping out everything they had in medical bills. Her dad is sick, can't afford his insulin much. He can't work when his sugar's high, 'cause he gets dizzy and can faint and all that. They won't let him drive no more. Poor Taylor couldn't wait to be done with school, so she'd start bringing home some dough."

"When did she start, um, stripping? And where?"

The guy seemed lost in the story he was telling, kicking dirt on occasion with the tip of his steel toe boot. "I offered to help; this here pays well, almost thirty an hour and benefits. She could've moved in with me, kept to real pet-sitting and college, helped her father get by. But she lied and went behind my back, started working there, in that forsaken place."

"Where?"

"At the, um, the Velvet Puss." He lowered his eyes and blushed, embarrassed when he spoke the name of the club. "I couldn't take it... all those men, some I work with, touching her body, laying their slimy eyeballs on her like that. I just went my own way, that's all."

"No one's judging you," Elliot said, seeing the turmoil the young man was going through. He probably blamed himself for her death too. "Did she continue to do babysitting this entire time?"

"We haven't spoken in a while. She used to, or at least that's what she told me. She lied to me, and she lied to her father too." He scratched the roots of his sweaty hair and looked toward the peak of the mountain, covered in fresh, white snow, picture perfect against the blue sky. "I might be the biggest idiot in this town, but I've always respected her for what she was doing. Never despised her... I respected her."

"How come?"

"She did what she had to do to take care of her family, that's why. Never complained, never cried, just did it. Taylor was stronger than most men here on this mountain. She had guts."

"Did you know she was pregnant?" Elliot asked.

Finley stared at him in disbelief. "No... how would I know? We haven't spoken since June or so."

"Are you sure about that?" Elliot pressed, although he didn't see the young man as the one who'd impregnated Taylor, maybe breaking her bones at the same time by pinning her down.

A grimace of contempt curled the man's lip for a moment. He pulled a few hairs out of his head with a quick gesture and held them in the air. "Here. Take it. Rule me out. I know about DNA and stuff. Don't want you wasting time on me instead of getting Taylor's killer."

Elliot took out an evidence pouch and sealed the hair fibers inside. "Thank you, Mr. Finley."

"Mr. Finley is my dad. I'm Walter."

"Walter. I'm really sorry for your loss." He shook the young man's hand and turned to leave.

"I lost her a long time ago," he said, but sadness frayed his voice, contradicting his words. "I suggest you ask the strip joint's manager some questions. Maybe check their surveillance video. Word is they're doing way more in there than just *dancing*."

He picked up his hard hat and put it on his head, then started the chainsaw and resumed cutting tree branches, one after the other, methodically.

When Elliot reached his car, he looked toward Walter Finley once more. He'd abandoned his chainsaw and sat on the downed tree trunk, sobbing.

Fighting a strong sense of doom, Elliot started the engine and was about to drive off when a text message from Lizzie chimed, getting his attention.

Kay's been shot, but she's okay. Nothing to worry about.

He floored the gas pedal taking off from the lumber site, throwing a cloud of pebbles and dust in the air. "Be damned that slick son of a bitch, slicker than a boiled onion," he muttered. "I knew he was trouble."

In over fifteen years of being a cop, he'd put countless perps behind those very same bars, yellowish paint scratched and dented, stinking of human waste and desolation. Now Brian flinched when the door clanged shut, locking him in, pushed closed by a deputy he knew well.

"It's just until they put you with your attorney, Detective," the young deputy said apologetically.

He sat on the cot with a groan, pressing on his thigh to keep the bandage in place as if it was going to slip loose without him holding it. The pain subsided as soon as he took the weight off his wounded leg, but he was restless, anxious. Leaning into his hand for support, he stood again and started pacing the small cell with a limp, holding on to the cold bars at times.

Another detective stopped by a few minutes later with a Hershey chocolate bar and a Coke. He slipped them between the steel bars, looking left and right first as if he were breaking the law by feeding him. Brian understood; any contact with him was career kryptonite for a cop who wanted to stay on the good side of the powers that be, Diaz and his minions.

None of those guys cared about evidence. He'd asked twice

of Diaz to be granted the courtesy to know what they had against him, to be told why he was arrested.

"Why did you run if you're innocent?" Diaz had asked, while Brockett, that brown-nosed piece of scum, snickered.

"I didn't run," Brian had replied. "When I learned there was a warrant out for my arrest, I chose to surrender in a precinct where cops are honest. Do you have a problem with that?"

Diaz had grinned, a smug grin he'd wanted to wipe off his face with a well-landed punch.

"Well, you should, if you don't," Brian had continued recklessly. Seeing Diaz angered soothed his nerves somehow. He hoped Diaz might make a mistake if enraged enough, and his carefully constructed castle of crooked cards would fall apart. "You should clean up your house, Chief, starting at the top."

Diaz had laughed and left without a word. That happened almost an hour earlier. Since then, he'd been fingerprinted and processed, and his clothes replaced by an orange jumpsuit that stank of bleach while Carly Hosking was trying to reschedule his arraignment. Initially scheduled for noon, the morning shooting incident had delayed their plans by several hours. Word was out there that the judge had a problem with cases that didn't show up for their appointed time and date and was unwilling to reschedule it for the same day.

Another young detective swung by and discreetly placed a rolled magazine in his hand. "Good luck," he'd whispered before disappearing.

But he couldn't read. The light was dim in lockup, and his mind was elsewhere.

"We got it." Carly's chipper voice caught him by surprise. "Today, at three."

His mind had wandered off for a while, trying to piece together what he'd heard from Brockett and Diaz in the past few days that could explain his warrant. He was obsessing over that incessantly, although he realized it was madness. He probably wouldn't find out until Carly received the evidence disclosure package, maybe not even then.

"Let's go," she said, waiting for a deputy to unlock the cell door. "I have some questions I need to ask you before then."

Limping behind her perfectly swaying hips, hugged tightly by a skirt that told him she was wearing a thong or perhaps nothing underneath the dark blue fabric, he entered one of the interrogation rooms and refused to sit.

The room was small and painted a faded shade of beige. Obscenities had been scratched on one of the walls, some of them complete with graphic representations of male organs and naming several other cops. Every week or so, the janitors stayed late and tried to cover them up with fresh paint, but indentations still remained.

Carly checked the camera and gave the two-way mirror a distrusting glare.

"Cameras, microphones off," she instructed the deputy in a firm voice. "Or it's your badge and your supervisor's hide for violating my client's constitutional rights." The deputy nodded, flustered, then left, closing the door behind him.

She pulled over a chair and positioned it so she'd have her back turned to the camera and the mirror. Then she invited Brian to pull over the other chair by her side, not across the table from her as protocol dictated.

"Let's talk plea," she said, cutting straight to the chase in her typical manner. "Not guilty, I presume?"

Brian scoffed. "Of course." He checked the time. They had almost two hours left to kill before the arraignment.

"How about bail?" she asked, checking notes on her phone. "Can you manage half a million?"

He whistled. "Like it's growing on trees, Carly. What the hell? Better bring it down from there. A hundred, maybe one-fifty I can pull off, but five hundred? No way in hell."

"Any friends or family I should call?" She shot him a quick, supportive glance.

"No." He clasped his hands together, wringing them every now and then. "Better get me out, Carly. I can't do time. They'll kill me in there."

She breathed deeply and looked at him sternly. "The surrender and the arraignment, Brian. That's what we discussed. That's what we agreed on."

"Carly, I can't—"

"I can't take your case, and you know why." She pressed her lips together for a moment, then said, lowering her voice, "The people I usually represent won't take too kindly to me defending a cop. I can't risk it. I have two kids." She squeezed his hand for encouragement. "But I'll recommend some good attorneys who need the exposure and might take you pro bono."

He scoffed. "Exposure, huh? That's my trading chip these days?"

She pulled away. "Well, don't imagine this won't make headlines, either way it goes."

He didn't react; head hung and shoulders hunched, he stared at his hands, wondering how many years he'd wear chains. She didn't care. She had no problem walking out on him, leaving him there caged like an animal, while she went back to her thousand-an-hour billing of San Francisco's finest career criminals.

"What's on your mind?" she asked, pasting a professional smile on her lips.

"My daughter. I need to know she's safe."

"Oh," she said, her smile waning. Her cold hand found his and squeezed gently. "Isn't your ex looking into this?"

"I'm worried about her," Brian replied, ignoring the attorney's question. "I thought we were okay, me, Holly, Kay..." His words trailed off as his voice broke. "But Kay and I almost died today, Carly. It's a miracle we didn't. I can't assume they won't go after Holly. I can't take that chance."

"What are you saying?"

He looked at her intently. "Whoever these people are, they've killed before, and they won't hesitate to do it again." He swallowed hard. "Maybe it's for the best that you won't represent me, Carly. They'll come after me and everyone else who might be involved, again and again until the job's done."

TWENTY-EIGHT

ORGANIZATION

The San Francisco District Attorney's Office was a short drive from the precinct. Her only stop was a clothing store that sold her a new, white shirt and a blue zippered sweatshirt. Kay breathed with ease when she entered the building after briefly considering a stop for a fresh cup of coffee. Starbucks was on the other corner of the block, tempting and convenient.

She'd given that up eventually; the earlier shooting incident had frayed her nerves more than she cared to admit, making her wary and jumpy and eager to check every rooftop and every black SUV that drove by.

Once inside the gray, grim-looking building, she was taken to ADA Leonetti's office after being told a couple of times that he was busy and probably couldn't see her without an appointment.

He probably was, but that didn't keep her from knocking on his open door. Leonetti was seated behind a large desk covered with stacks of file folders and papers. He'd rolled up the sleeves of his pinstripe shirt and had loosened his tie, seemingly immersed in reading from a case file. Kay vaguely recognized him; their paths must've crossed on some courthouse corridor sometime.

The office was large and had a window he kept with the blinds almost entirely closed, shielding his workspace from the sun. A yellowish light came from a desk lamp. It was old and weathered; he must've inherited it with the rest of the furniture. On the back wall, by the window, the ADA had hung a large whiteboard. It was filled with pasted images and scribbled notes, arranged neatly in what seemed to be the hierarchy of a crime organization.

Standing in the doorway, she waited for a moment, then knocked again. Leonetti lifted his gaze from the file. "Oh," he said, abandoning the file and standing quickly. "It's you." He invited her in and shook her hand. "We were just talking about you and Hanlin and the shooting. It's all over the news."

"On the news? They have our names?" She thought of Elliot, how he'd react if he heard she'd been shot.

"You can't keep a secret in this town, remember?" The tall, dark-haired man smiled, gesturing toward the two leather armchairs in front of his desk. He must've noticed she was intrigued by his familiarity because he added, "You might not remember, but I prosecuted a couple of the cases you worked on as a fed. They were very well documented and supported with evidence. Easy peasy to convict on your collars."

"Ah, that explains why you look familiar," she replied, a little embarrassed she didn't remember him better. "I'm sorry—"

"Don't worry, Detective. I was a rookie back then, sitting second bench." He folded his hands neatly on the desk. "What can I do for you?"

"You heard about what happened this morning with the shooting," Kay said, feeling as if she had to walk on eggshells. "Look, I have no jurisdiction here, and I'm not here to cause any trouble for you or anyone else." He nodded his silent agreement. His intelligent eyes remained focused, interested. "I just want to know what Rachel said the night of the shooting or the next morning." She paused, giving him a moment to reply, but he'd creased his tall forehead and pressed his lips together tightly. "It's a big ask, I know that, but—"

"Let me show you something, Detective," he said, standing and pointing at the whiteboard by his desk. "This is who we're dealing with." He tapped against the board with the tip of his fingers. "La Vida Sangrienta. Remember them?"

The name of the feared San Francisco gang sounded familiar to anyone who'd worked in law enforcement in the city in the past decade. Yet she felt the need to explain her superficial knowledge of the criminal organization. "I worked in a different division, in Behavioral Analysis."

"Yes, I remember," he replied. "You dealt mostly with serial killers. These are psychopaths who get off on money and blood and killing people with street drugs." He tapped against the board again, closer to the top of the hierarchy. A rectangle had been drawn in red marker, with a question mark inside. Above, the name BARRACUDA was written in block letters. "This man is their boss. No one's been able to put a name or a face to the leader of La Vida Sangrienta. We offered deals to every gangbanger we caught. We tried to coerce information, even buy it. Nothing... just the understanding that these people fear the Barracuda more than they fear us." He paused for a moment. "We do know that this man, the Barracuda, has instigated the fight between two other gangs, weakening them and then taking over, uniting whatever was left under his reign."

Kay looked at the board with keen interest. Right underneath the Barracuda's rectangle, another, also empty, linked straight down from it, with the word CIGUATERA and a question mark after the block letters, another question mark inside, where the man's photo should've been.

A third row had a mix of photos, all identified. The first man, Edmundo Buendia, had two photos, one being a closeup of his face tattoo, four teardrops scattered under the corner of his left eye, on the cheekbone and below. Definitely prison ink. The dates below his name confirmed the times he'd been locked up. The second man was Jose DeFranco, nicknamed Big J, an overweight Latino dressed in orange prison garb and posing for his mugshot several years ago. The third was another Latino, Trinidad Cuadrado, nicknamed The Square.

A fourth row held a combination of portraits and empty boxes. Red or black writing above each one stated their names. Two were cut with a diagonal red line, and their death dates were noted below their names. Others were booking photos, and the respective writing indicated the date of their arrests and the places where they were being incarcerated.

The hierarchy continued on two more rows, each box either a photo with a name or a question mark, but most had been identified. Boxes were connected to other boxes on other rows with black marker lines, some of the lines adorned with comments regarding cases, events, or related case numbers.

Seeing the whiteboard brought back memories. She used to have one just like it in her office at the FBI; she used to call it the crazy wall. Mostly because she could go crazy staring at it trying to connect victims with unsubs and their signatures.

"Wow," she whispered, studying the ADA's crazy wall. "I can't believe how many are still unknown." She turned her eyes toward the ADA. "Do you think WITSEC was compromised? Someone leaked Rachel's identity as a witness in the shooting last week?"

He lowered his head. "I don't know." He sounded sincere. "I've been asking myself that since it happened. It could've been someone in the SFPD Northern District, or even someone here, in my own office." He raised his eyes and kept them on the whiteboard, the look of frustration on his face unmistakable. "I thought of giving everyone a mandatory lie detector test, but what good would that do? Those tests aren't admissible in court for a reason; they're not reliable."

"I'm afraid they might come after Rachel's daughter and her mother. We have to do something to protect them. I don't believe the people who shot at us today are done cleaning up."

"Thanks to the media, they know their job's not done," he grumbled. "Make no mistake, Detective, they'll be back. And now you're on their kill list just because you were with Brian Hanlin in the same car."

Just what she needed, to be on some gang's hit list, courtesy of her ex, for something she knew nothing about.

"What can we do for Rachel's family?" She paused, giving him time to think. His brow was creased by a permanent frown, and tension lined his jaw, but he didn't speak. "To be honest, I was surprised you offered Rachel relocation in the program so quickly. Did she sign anything? A statement, something that would point me in the right direction, unofficially?"

Kay believed they'd already related somehow; they'd bonded over past cases and mutual interests. She held her breath, waiting for the answer that could very well be an invitation to leave the office preceded by a lecture on jurisdictions and the promise of a formal complaint filed with the US Department of Justice. But Leonetti stared at the whiteboard with an unusual intensity as if debating what to do. As if figuring out if she could be trusted.

"She must've told you something," she insisted, keeping her voice soft, reassuring.

He tapped on one of the faces pasted on the lowest row of his crazy wall. It had a red diagonal line across it and a date of death marked below his name. "Oliver 'Ollie' Galaz was the victim of the shooting Rachel Epling witnessed last week. Very low in the Vida Sangrienta food chain. He was a street dealer who'd climbed up the ranks and got promoted to be neighborhood lead. Rumor was he was seen talking to a cop just the day before. My investigator reached out to the precincts, and, yes, he was giving some information about a missing prostitute working the same streets. The next day, he was shot. The message is clear: no one in La Vida Sangrienta can talk to any cops."

Kay frowned. "Not sure I understand how Rachel played a part in all this."

He propped his hands on his thighs and examined the carpet pattern for a while. "I'm going to trust you with this, Detective." He made eye contact briefly, and she nodded. "Rachel came into my office Friday morning, prepared to make a statement. WITSEC wasn't on the table at that point. But she did exactly what you did when you first arrived. She stared at the whiteboard for a while. I could see she was turning pale, shaking. I thought she was going to faint." He chuckled quietly. "Instead, she pointed straight at the Barracuda's name and said, 'I believe I know who he is. It was him I saw last night, the shooter who killed that boy.'"

"Whoa... I don't know what to say." How would Rachel know the man she'd seen that night was the gang leader? The girl she once knew and loved was a soft-spoken, fun-loving, psych major. Lightning scared her and sudden knocks on her dorm room. Dark alleys and cabbies who didn't shave daily. She was a scaredy-cat. She wouldn't even come close to knowing gangbangers by their names.

Leonetti shook his head. "Then she pointed at this," he tapped on the single, empty box on the second row, "and said, 'Ciguatera is not a person. It's what happens if you cross the Barracuda. It's the poison that will kill you, and there's no escape.' You see, she'd already given the cops the description of the vehicle involved in the shooting, and it matched what we had on file as one of Barracuda's vehicles of choice."

"But it makes no sense," Kay said, still shocked by what she'd heard. "Why would the head of such a powerful organization risk it all by shooting a two-bit drug dealer? I'm sure the head of La Vida Sangrienta has dozens of lieutenants eager to carry out his orders."

Leonetti shrugged. "Maybe it's a statement he wanted to make."

"Now I understand why you reached for the drawer and pulled out WITSEC documents."

"That's exactly what I did. I called a US Marshal and had her sit in. But it had the opposite effect. Instead of reassuring Rachel Epling that we would protect her, she got scared. She must've realized what she was about to do. She started backing away, recanting, but we pressed on. Then she eventually agreed to tell us what we needed to know and started signing the documents. That's when Brian Hanlin arrived, and we stopped asking questions." He clenched his fists and shoved them in his pockets. "I didn't want to expose her to one more person, although I'm sure he knows everything already, but he won't talk." He chuckled with bitterness in his voice. "I don't blame him; I probably wouldn't talk either. WITSEC is no cakewalk. It's life-changing and not for the better."

"Then you let Rachel go?" Kay couldn't believe he'd made such a rookie mistake.

"She insisted." He cleared his voice and then added, "No. She *blackmailed* us into letting her go and have a few more hours to wrap up her life, as she called it, before the US Marshal went to pick up her and her daughter. Those were her terms for agreeing to testify. She wanted to call a friend who's a fed. I'm assuming—?"

Kay pointed at herself. "She left me a voicemail. I was in interrogation and couldn't take her call. Later I called her back, but it was too late."

"Did she say anything we could use?"

Kay played Rachel's voicemail. Leonetti had earned that. He listened, visibly intrigued by the regrets Rachel had expressed in the message, but then seemed to realize what the issue was about.

"I didn't realize it until now; Hanlin used to be your husband, and she used to be your college friend. They said it on the news. Was Rachel Epling—" he started to ask but then stopped.

Kay's throat went dry. "It's okay. Ancient history." She gave the crazy wall another look. "So, you never learned what she wanted to tell you? Who the Barracuda is?"

"No. All she really gave us, on a signed statement, was the make and model of that vehicle and a couple of numbers off its tag. It was a black Chevy Suburban. La Vida Sangrienta uses them a lot."

So that's who the sniper was. Brian was right; they'd never stop until they were all dead. Brian, Holly, Rachel's mom. Even herself.

"One more thing she said," Leonetti added, "something about seeing a red flicker when the shooter had put his hand out the window to fire the weapon. I suggested it might've been a laser spot, but she said no, it was something else, something closer to the car, not the victim. We didn't know what to make of it, and she didn't seem to either. Maybe it was the reflection of another car's stoplights, who knows."

"Thank you for trusting me with this," Kay said, feeling a weariness in her bones. The day had been challenging, and it wasn't over yet. "Could you please tell me how I can find the US Marshal who—"

"Say no more," Leonetti replied, then pushed a button on his phone. When his assistant picked up, he said, "Send Debra in here."

"What happens now?" Kay asked while they were waiting.

Leonetti struggled to hide a disappointed sigh. "There's no one left to testify. If we put Rachel's family in the program, there's no foreseeable end to it. It could be years... And we have a mole we can't identify, either here or in the Northern District precinct. Procedurally, we're in a bind."

A quick rap against the door, and Leonetti beckoned in the US Marshal, a woman of about thirty years of age, dressed in black tactical gear and wearing a khaki vest with the insignia of her service. She shook Kay's hand firmly, speaking her name. "Debra Buscher."

Kay studied her for a brief moment. The woman held her gaze openly. "I believe Rachel Epling's mother and daughter are in danger. I need your assistance…"

"Go," Leonetti said, when Debra looked at him for approval.

Within moments, they were on their way to the Epling residence.

Kay hoped they weren't going to be too late.

TWENTY-NINE
VELVET

Elliot had called Kay a dozen times, each time getting her voicemail. He couldn't think of anything to say in a message on a machine when he wanted to hear her voice, to find out if she was okay.

Driving off the mountain, he battled with himself for a while. Should he put Novack in charge of the investigation and head down to San Francisco to have Kay's back? She'd specifically told him to stay put. But what if things had changed since and she needed him?

When the phone rang, he pressed the steering wheel button without looking at the media screen.

"Elliot?" Kay's voice filled the silence in his vehicle. She sounded worried, tense, but it was her. Alive.

He breathed, the sense of relief exhilarating. "Kay." He paused for a moment, at a loss for words. "I was just—"

"I tried to call you earlier, but things here have been a mess. I got caught up, and—"

"I heard you were shot. Are you okay?"

"Yeah, it's superficial. Nothing to worry about."

"I'm about to put Novack on the case and buy me a day off from Logan. I'll be there in three hours at the most."

"No, Elliot, don't." She sounded almost panicked, desperate. "I'll be leaving soon," she added, the rushed hesitation in her voice a dead giveaway of something she wasn't saying. Others, she might've fooled with that, but not him.

She just didn't want him there and wasn't going to be honest about it.

"Where are you going?" he asked, letting air out of his lungs slowly like a deflating balloon after a party.

"I meant, I'm almost ready to come home."

"You're done there already?" He tried to hide how relieved her words made him feel but failed. His voice sounded chipper, like a teenager about to head out on a date.

A moment of silence. "I'm going to Rachel's mother to put her and her granddaughter in protective custody. I have a US Marshal with me."

"She's there, in the car with you?"

"No," Kay laughed. "She's following me in her own vehicle. She'll take Holly and Mrs. Epling, and then I'll probably head home right after Brian's arraignment. There's not much I can do here."

"Are they still charging him?"

"Yes." She sounded tense again, the moment of laughter gone. "If they don't see today's shooting for what it was, I don't know what would make them think differently." She stopped talking, the silence between them loaded with unspoken questions. "Once he's out on bail today, he'll be free to figure things out on his own. There's no reason for you to come down here."

He didn't believe a word she was saying. Maybe the details of what she'd said were true, the arraignment, Mr. Totally Wrong getting out on bail and all that, but she didn't want him there for a different reason. That reason colored her voice with shades of fear.

"If that changes, I'll be in my car heading south fast enough to catch yesterday. You know that, right?"

He thought he heard her sniffle. "Yes, I know," she whispered. "Talk soon, all right?"

"Take care of yourself, partner," he replied, but she'd hung up already, leaving him to wonder what in the world had happened to put tears in Kay Sharp's voice.

He was still wondering what she was hiding when he reached town. A few minutes later, he pulled into the Velvet Puss parking lot. The place opened at six every evening, but several cars were parked there, one of them a blue Audi Q7, the owner's car.

Larry Melby had crossed Elliot's path before. A slimy fifty-year-old with a weight problem and spiky, oily hair, he'd been arrested a couple of times. He'd managed to dodge the most recent charge that would've been his third, claiming he didn't know people were dealing drugs in his club. Novack had collared him, but he'd later cut a deal with the DA, giving some small-time dealer names in return for all charges dropped.

The door was locked. Elliot had to pound against it with his fist until he finally got someone's attention, a young man who worked there as a bar back. The man didn't open the door; he scowled at Elliot's badge, then rushed to the back of the building. Shortly after that, Melby appeared.

Dressed in a pair of Levi's with suspenders and a white, sleeveless T-shirt, he stared at Elliot through the glass door with a look of contempt on his face.

"Open up, Melby," Elliot said. "Ain't got time to waste on your fussing."

Elliot's comment only increased the look of disdain in the man's bloodshot eyes, but he opened the door. "This is about Taylor, huh?"

"You know about her?"

"Not through any police courtesy, I don't." He spat on the

concrete, missing Elliot's boot by a couple of inches. "Some of my customers were talking last night when she didn't show. They'd seen it on the news."

Damned news people. Gave scum like Melby time to prepare, discard evidence, and rehearse whatever string of lies he was about to start reciting.

Melby got out of the way, and Elliot stepped inside. The club was lit *a giorno* with white fluorescent lights, and several people scrubbed the floors, the tables, and counters, everything. They used buckets with water so dirty it almost seemed black, and didn't put much effort into their work. The result was a layer of wet sheen added to years' worth of layered grime.

The place stank of stale sweat and smoke and filth. There was a faint halo around the ceiling lamps reserved for the club's maintenance hours. The building's crappy ventilation system probably couldn't handle the smoke delivered by its patrons during the night. One of the very few places in the area that still allowed smoking indoors, the club had gained popularity when the state of California had imposed its ban on lighting up in restaurants and bars. Over time, smoke had stained the walls and ceiling, giving the club a weathered, decrepit feel.

"Trust me, it looks better when the music's on, and the girls are up there, wiggling their tight little butts," Melby said, laughing hard and keeping a hand pressed on his bouncing abdomen as if to steady it down. "I'm sure they have places like this in Texas, don't they, Detective? No need to crinkle your nose at mine."

Elliot let his comment go unanswered. "When's the last time you saw Taylor?"

He scratched his blotchy goatee with pudgy fingers. "The day before yesterday. We're only closed on Mondays."

"Did you notice anyone picking on her, giving her a hard time?"

He rolled his eyes. "Every now and then, some dude doesn't

know the house rules, but I've got bouncers for that. I take care of my girls. Talent like Taylor is hard to find in this area. She'll be missed." A lewd smirk blossomed on his thick lips.

"What exactly did she do for you?" Elliot examined the ceiling above the stage inch by inch until he found what he was looking for.

"She danced. What the hell else?" Melby scoffed, probably thinking Elliot was some kind of bonehead.

"How about you show me some video?" Elliot asked, pointing at the camera trained on the stainless-steel pole at the center of the stage. "With Taylor, I mean?"

Melby stared at him with squinting, venom-filled eyes, probably weighing his chances if he refused. Then he beckoned Elliot to follow him as he faltered toward the back. Elliot studied the layout of the area for a moment, taking in the placement of all video cameras until an employee found the recording and cued it on Melby's computer.

"Here," Melby called Elliot's attention with a raspy, bawdy voice. "Regale yourself with a free show."

It took all of Elliot's willpower not to slam his fist into Melby's filthy mouth. He watched the video, silently fuming, promising himself he'd put Melby behind bars someday. The man had been toeing the line carefully, but that didn't change who he was. One day, when he'd slip ever so slightly, Elliot would be there to collar his big ass. And the third time's a charm; he wasn't going to skate so easily when that third charge happened.

The computer screen bore greasy fingerprints where Melby must've touched it numerous times, but it was large enough for Elliot to catch what was happening on the screen in detail. Taylor danced and stripped lasciviously, apparently indifferent to the catcalling, cheering, and hollering. Every now and then, someone reached toward her with dollar bills in their hand, and she drew near, swaying her hips and allowing the man to slide the bills under the edge of her bikini.

Another dancer performed about six feet to her left, barely visible on the screen. She was just as young as Taylor, barely eighteen. Elliot sped through the recording until he noticed several of the men had grouped into two teams, two of them on Taylor's side, three in the other dancer's corner. Both teams shouted loudly, holding wads of cash up in the air. The rest of the crowd seemed on fire, cheering for one of the teams as if they were watching football.

Melby grew increasingly anxious, his eyes riveted to the screen. "Seen enough? I have a business to run."

"What's going on here?" Elliot asked, pointing at the two groups of men.

"That? It's nothing." He made a dismissive gesture with his hand. "Come on, let's go."

"Humor me," Elliot said in a low, menacing voice.

"Son of a bitch," Melby muttered, barely audible. "It's for private lap dances," he eventually said. "If customers want a private lap dance, they have to bid for it." He pressed his lips together in anger. "Nothing illegal; I asked my lawyer. My girls only do one per night, each."

Elliot felt his blood start to boil. "Are those really lap dances? Or should I book you for pimping these girls to the highest bidder? I'm pretty sure the DA would have a field day with this; sex slave auctions are considered human trafficking." He stared at Elliot, seemingly confused. "That's twenty years, Melby. You'll need diapers by the time you get out."

Melby held his hand out as if to stop Elliot. "No, no, Detective, I swear they're just lap dances, all right? Nothing else."

"I want to see a video of that private dance. Now."

He shook his head so forcefully that his jowls bounced. "No, sirree. What happens behind closed doors is none of my business. That's what the customers pay for: a private dance with the girl of their choice."

Elliot stared at Melby for a moment. It would take a couple of phone calls and some warrants, but he was going to rip this place to shreds until he got to the truth.

There was no way a slimy piece of manure like Melby respected anyone's privacy.

Elliot pointed at the screen. "I want to speak with this girl. What's her name?"

THIRTY

HOLLY

Driving on Ciara Epling's street brought back memories, some sweet, some painful. The Thanksgiving party eight years ago where Kay had learned about Rachel's pregnancy had taken place there, in the cozy bungalow with lemongrass bunches and citrus trees planted by the edge of the single-car driveway. But before that, countless Sunday dinners, holidays, or just evenings when Rachel and she had craved a homecooked meal had been happy and serene and cherished.

Kay's heart thumped in her chest, worrying they were too late. As she approached, she saw a deputy vehicle bearing the signage of SFPD Northern District parked in front of the house and breathed with ease. Chief Diaz had meant it when he'd said, "We take care of our own."

She pulled over at the curb, then waited for Debra to catch up. "I'll go inside and get things started with Ciara," Kay said. "Feel free to come along, but know she's a dear friend I haven't seen in a while. Not just some grab-and-go case."

Debra was a woman of few words. She nodded, then waited for Kay to lead the way.

She rang the doorbell, a little anxious at the thought of

seeing Ciara again. She'd missed the woman whose kindness and hospitality she'd enjoyed in college. Her falling out with Rachel had taken a heavy toll, including on her relationship with Ciara. Although she cared deeply for her, Kay thought it best to just disappear from her life after the divorce. It would've been awkward to not do so.

Ciara opened the door. Her face lit up when she recognized Kay. "My sweet girl," she said, opening her arms. Quite unexpectedly, Kay was wrapped in a familiar hug she'd missed terribly over the years.

"Ciara, I'm so sorry about Rachel," she whispered as she pulled away.

Sadness washed over the woman's face like a heavy cloud before the rain. "I know," she said softly. "I was hoping you'd come by." She stepped out of the way, inviting Kay and Debra inside. Seeming slightly confused, she threw Debra's tactical attire a quizzical look.

"Ciara, this is US Marshal Debra Buscher." Kay introduced them as she closed the door behind her.

Ciara shook Debra's hand with a look of concern in her eyes. "What's going on?"

"Come, let's sit," Kay asked, hesitant to drop upsetting news on the poor woman so abruptly. She'd been through a lot; her drawn face and dark circles under her eyes were evidence of her struggle with grief.

Ciara was dressed in black and wore no jewelry other than a small crucifix on a silver chain. She'd added a few pounds since Kay had seen her last and moved around slowly as if battling arthritis. Her fiery red hair had tamed to a softer shade because of numerous white strands. Once she found herself in the living room Kay remembered well, she sat in her usual armchair and gestured toward the couch. "Sit down and tell me what's wrong."

Kay didn't take her seat right away. Instead, she walked

over to the small fireplace. The narrow, marble mantle was covered in framed pictures. Rachel and her mother on her birthday, the year before Kay's wedding. Rachel with Kay, dressed for a party, colorful streamers in their hair. Rachel with a red-haired girl with sparking blue eyes and freckles on her nose, laughing.

She picked up that picture and studied it closely, noticing similarities between mother and daughter. They had the same smile, the same dimple in their chins, the same cheerfulness in their eyes.

"That's Holly Flynn Epling," Ciara said. "The light of my life."

"Flynn?" Kay laughed. "That's an unusual name for a girl, isn't it?"

"It is, but shouldn't be. It's Irish for 'the descendant of the red-haired one,'" she clarified, making air quotes with her fingers. "Can be either gender."

"She's beautiful," Kay said, a tug at her heart making her wonder what her life would've been if she'd had Brian's child and a normal marriage. She looked at the little girl's face again and failed to notice any resemblance to Brian, as if the child was only her mother's. "I'm looking forward to meeting her."

Ciara nodded and smiled shyly. "My daughter was always sorry for what she did to you," she whispered, her voice heavy with sorrow. "I wanted to call you, to ask you to not be a stranger, but I thought maybe it was too painful for you to speak to me."

Kay walked over and crouched by Ciara's armchair, squeezing her hand. "I missed you too."

"Have you forgiven my daughter for breaking up your marriage?" Ciara's voice was soft, unassuming. "I wouldn't blame you if you haven't."

"I have, a long time ago," Kay replied. "I don't believe it was her fault, really."

"You're too kind, my dear. You were always kind. Are you remarried?"

"No." Kay turned her gaze away. "I don't believe marriage is for me. My job, and the life I live, with its risks, I don't think—"

Ciara's hand touched Kay's face, then smoothed Kay's hair gently. "Don't let that heartbreak define who you are, Kay Sharp. You deserve to be happy. You deserve a family." A tear beaded on Ciara's face. She wiped it with her hand and forced herself to smile. "She never wanted you to suffer. She told me that many times whenever she asked me how to live with what she'd done. That entire affair ruined her just as much as it ruined you, my dear. Some men are like that." A sob shattered her breath. "If she were here today, she'd beg you for your forgiveness, and she'd pray for your healing."

"I know," Kay replied, leaning her face into the woman's warm hand. Tears burned her eyes, threatening to break the floodgates open. "If only she would've spoken to me about Brian back then, about what was happening in her life now. Maybe I could've done something—"

"Don't blame yourself, Kay. It was God's will to take her, and nothing you could've done would've mattered. But I miss my baby so much," she whispered. "I don't know how to live in a world where she's not."

For a moment, Kay shared Ciara's tear-filled silence. She seemed to have forgotten about Debra, and Kay was dreading the moment she'd have to uproot the woman and her grand-daughter and throw them into the whirling maelstrom of witness protection.

"Brian, um, he was cheating on Rachel." Ciara's soft voice gained a vein of bitterness. "Just like he cheated on you. I tried to warn Rachel about it ever since she told me she was pregnant with his child. I was appalled, heartbroken for you, and scared for my baby's happiness. He wasn't going to change; no man ever does."

"It's over now," Kay replied quietly. "It doesn't matter. I know Brian loved her very much. In his own way, which didn't always include faithfulness, he loved her nevertheless." Ciara's skeptical glance found Kay's eyes. "Otherwise, he wouldn't've been engaged to her."

"I wasn't happy about that one bit." Ciara crossed her arms at her chest, pouting. "He's not an honest man and I knew he would make her suffer, just like he did with you. But it was long past time he made an honest woman out of my daughter."

Kay bit her lip, frowning. "Brian said they were getting married in December, on Christmas Day."

Ciara crossed her arms at her chest. "I know he's my grand-child's father, but I don't know about him. A cheating man can never be trusted, not even when he recites the Gospels. I only approved because of Holly. Good or bad, he is the girl's father."

"What do you know about the circumstances surrounding Rachel's death? What did they tell you?"

"Brian told me someone got into her house and shot her." Ciara's voice broke. "That's all I know." She looked at Kay with pleading eyes. "Do you know more?" Then she glanced quickly at Debra, who sat impatiently on the edge of the sofa, quietly bouncing the heel of her boot against the Persian rug. "Please tell me what you know. All of it. Please."

Kay filled her lungs with air and squeezed Ciara's hand. "Rachel witnessed a drug-related shooting last week. She spoke with the cops about what she saw. She was willing to testify, and I believe they killed her for that."

"Oh, my goodness." Her hand covered her agape mouth, but the sobs still came out. "She told me about what she saw the night it happened. She came here right after that, still shaking like a leaf. She was brave, my little girl."

"Yes, she was." Kay remembered how she used to be in college, before life interrupted their friendship, before Brian happened to both of them. Brave when it came to the important things in life, and scared out of her mind by the tiniest noise. "Brian has been charged with her murder," she added gently.

Ciara stared at her in disbelief. "Brian? Why? If you say it was that drug-shooting thing she witnessed, why him?"

"I'm sure he'll be cleared soon, don't worry."

The woman stared into thin air for a while, thinking, her shoulders heaving from panting breaths. "He's a cheat, and I'm no fan of Brian Hanlin, but I can't imagine him killing my baby. I just can't."

"Ciara, there's more," Kay said, a gentle squeeze on the woman's hand forcing her to focus. Fear was written in her eyes, fear of what Kay had yet to say. "We have to put you into protective custody. There's a police car outside, ensuring your safety, but we have to go now."

"Why me?"

Kay swallowed and squeezed her hand, hoping her gesture would instill courage and strength into the woman's heart. "There was another shooting today. The same people who killed Rachel came after Brian and me. We both got shot, but we were lucky."

Ciara gasped. "You're hurt? Why didn't you tell me?"

"It's okay. It's just a scratch," Kay said, putting her hand on her shoulder where the bandage lumped through the fabric of her sweatshirt. "Brian was hit in the leg, but he'll be fine too."

Veering her eyes toward Debra, Ciara whispered, "Oh, dear. You think they could come here?" Her shaking hand covered her mouth.

"There's a police car in front of your house, and Debra is here too. She'll take you and Holly—"

Her jaw dropped, and her eyes opened wide with a sheer look of panic dilating her pupils. "What do you mean, Holly? She isn't here!"

Her high-pitched words sent icicles through Kay's blood. Debra sprang to her feet, ready to fight an invisible enemy.

"She isn't?" Kay swallowed hard, feeling her throat dry. "Didn't Rachel come here after the shooting she'd witnessed?"

"Yes, to say goodbye. She was going into the witness program with Holly. I thought the US Marshals had her," she sobbed, bent forward on the armchair as if her backbone could not support her anymore. She grabbed and pulled at her collar as if she was choking, unable to breathe. "Oh, God, no... I thought she was safe. My poor little girl... Oh, Lord, have mercy."

"We'll find her," Kay said, shooting Debra a worried look. Six days had passed since Holly had vanished, and no one seemed to know anything about it. But why didn't anyone know she was missing? "Who notified you of Rachel's death?"

"Brian," she whispered. "He told me they got to Rachel before he got home, and—"

Kay recalled Brian had said that after the shooting, Rachel had taken Holly to her mother's. That's where he thought Holly was. "Did he ask to speak to his daughter?" Ciara shook her head. Tears fell from her eyes, staining her black blouse. "Did you ask him about Holly that night after he told you Rachel was gone?"

"I—I don't remember," she whimpered, wringing her hands desperately. "I was in shock... I must have asked... I don't know." She wiped her eyes with her hands. "Rachel told me she and Holly would be safe, and that there was a female US Marshal..." Her voice trailed as she realized who Debra was. "That's you, isn't it?"

"Yes, ma'am," Debra replied. "I'm so sorry for your loss."

"I thought Holly was with you. Rachel called me around three on the day she died. Told me Holly was safe, and I shouldn't worry. She told me for a while we wouldn't be able to talk, not even on the phone. I didn't think..."

"That's correct," Debra stated simply. "The program

doesn't allow phone calls to family or friends. Phone calls can be traced."

Ciara closed her eyes tightly as if refusing her reality. "I should've asked Brian about Holly. I just—maybe I did, I don't know." A pained sob escaped her chest.

"We'll find her," Kay said, taking her hand and helping her up. "But now we have to go. Pack a small suitcase with the bare necessities, some clothes, your medications, one or two personal items, and Debra will take you someplace safe."

Ciara stood and looked at Kay, a quiver in her chin telling her she was barely holding back tears. "Promise me you'll find Holly. She's all I have left."

"I promise." She gave Ciara a tight hug. Then she watched her pick up the framed photo of Rachel and Holly as the first of several items she was gathering.

As soon as she went into her bedroom to pack, Kay called the Northern District precinct and asked for Detective Brockett.

"This is Brockett," the man's raspy voice said. "Who's this?"

"This is Kay Sharp, Brian Hanlin's ex."

"Ah, the gift that keeps on giving," he grumbled.

Kay ignored his comment. "We have a serious problem, and I need you to keep it to yourself until after Brian's arraignment."

"You *need* me to?" He laughed heartily. "Well, if you *need* me to, that's what I'll do. Goodbye, Detective. Get a life in your own ZIP Code."

"Wait, don't hang up," Kay said quickly. "Did you know Rachel's daughter is missing?"

The long, confounded silence that followed gave Kay her answer.

THIRTY-ONE

PLAN

There was a place by the barren hearth where Holly could hear what the grownups argued about. They never just talked; they only argued, every conversation ending in shouting and cursing and lots of words she didn't understand.

The moment the woman left her room and locked the door, Holly jumped out of bed and went there, placing her ear against the wall. For a while, she didn't hear anything but the woman's heavy footfalls departing, fading up the stairs and into the distance.

Patiently, she waited, her bare feet frozen from the contact with the cold, concrete floor.

Another day had passed, another time the small window where the snail lived had lost sunlight. The woman had brought her food twice today, the first time in the morning, some stale bread with peanut butter and jam. She didn't eat much, just enough to not have her yell at her. She'd asked her lots of questions, like before, but she didn't say anything. The rules were the rules, and she didn't break them.

But Mommy hadn't come to get her yet. She believed with all her strength, just like Mommy had said she should, and still nothing. The entire day had passed like that, waiting for Mommy to come, fighting her fear, trying not to shake and cry. She had to be brave.

Then the woman returned when the light started to dim in the room. She brought a bowl of hot soup and a lot of questions. She was angry this time.

"*Basta de esta mierda,*" she'd shouted as soon as she opened the door. "You're going to tell me what I want to know, or else I'll beat you with this belt." She'd tugged at her waistband, where a wide leather belt snaked through the loops of her dirty jeans. "When did you last see your mother?"

Holly trembled, hugging her knees and hiding her face from the ugly scowl on the woman's face. She must've hated that because she reached and grabbed a handful of Holly's red hair and forced her to look her in the eye.

"Tell me what I need to know, you little bitch. Did you see who shot your mother?"

Holly squeezed her eyes shut and started crying loudly, her chest heaving with spasms. "No, it isn't true," she shouted after her sobs receded somewhat. "Mommy is coming to get me. Just wait and see."

"*Tu madre* is dead," she said, letting go of Holly's hair and shoving her hard. She fell on her back, panting, then writhed away from her until she reached the wall.

"No," she shouted, her tears gone. "It's not true." The woman was mean. She wasn't going to touch her soup.

"She's dead, *estúpida,* and you'll stay locked in here until you remember everything that happened."

Holly sent the bowl of soup rattling on the floor with a kick and shouted, "No!"

The woman's hand landed hard across her face. She fell on her side, seeing stars, sobbing, although she'd promised herself she wasn't going to cry anymore.

The woman lifted her by her hair and showed her the

spilled liquid on the floor. "You're going to lick this clean, you fucking pig." Then she shoved her down so hard her knees bled.

Holly didn't dare look at her or stand up. Panting hard, she waited for another blow, but it didn't come. After a while, she withdrew to the back of the room and climbed on the bed. The floor was too cold.

Then she looked up.

The woman was staring at her, a deep frown on her face, a look of hatred in her eyes like Holly had never seen. Then she turned and left the room, muttering words Holly didn't understand.

As soon as she heard the lock being turned, Holly went by the fireplace to hear what the witch was going to say. She was going to tell on her, that she'd spilled the soup on purpose.

She heard nothing at all for a while, then some faint footsteps. Then, a man's voice asked, "Does she know anything or not?"

"The little bitch knows something, but she isn't saying. She doesn't trust me, and I'm wasting my time with her. She's stubborn. Tomorrow, I'll smack her around, and I'll get her to talk. You know what she did?"

"*Hija de perra*," the man replied. He sounded angry. Holly shivered, whimpering faintly. "Don't care what she did. Only what she saw."

"I don't know, all right?" she shouted. Now she was mad too, madder than she'd been about the spilled soup.

"You know what needs to happen."

"Please, Edmundo, she's just a kid." Some heavy footfalls coming and going told Holly the woman was pacing the floor upstairs. "Even if she's seen anything, it's not like she can pick people from a lineup or testify. You shouldn't worry about it."

"Do you want me dead?" The man had raised his voice so much it sounded as if he were just outside the door, startling Holly. "Is that it? You want me killed on the side of some road or here, in this house, in the dead of night?" Silence was all she heard for a moment. "Then deal with it or I will. Put one round in her head. Here, use my piece. It's got a silencer."

She listened some more, but nothing happened. Not another word from upstairs, not a whisper or a curse. Her heart thumping in her chest, Holly climbed into bed and curled on her side, trembling, her frozen hands tucked between her knees to stay warm.

"Mommy is coming to get me," she whispered to herself for courage.

In her voice and in the many thoughts rushing through her mind, the tiniest hint of doubt started spreading icicles through her blood.

What if she isn't?

THIRTY-TWO

NAME

"How the hell is she missing?" Brockett's voice came through angrily, ripping through the silence in Kay's SUV. "How come no one knew about it?"

"That's a very good question, Detective." She started the engine and drove off. She was already late for the arraignment. "As far as I know, Brian thought Rachel had left the child with her mother on the day of the shooting she witnessed. And Mrs. Epling believed the girl was already in protective custody. Apparently, Rachel had called her mother the day she died, at about three in the afternoon, and told her Holly was safe, in WITSEC already."

She heard clacking of keys on a keyboard on the other end of the call. "Wait a second, I can check that. I have the vic's phone records," Brockett mumbled. "Yeah, that three o'clock phone call actually happened. But why the hell did she lie about her daughter?"

"Maybe she wanted her mother not to worry about the little girl." Kay exited the peaceful neighborhood, headed for the Bay Bridge. At almost three in the afternoon, it was going to be hell to cross it, even with flashers and siren on. In the distance, the San Francisco cityscape was shrouded in the gold tinge of the afternoon sun, tall skyscrapers starting to light up in bright spots reflected in the calm bay waters. "At this point, I can only speculate, Detective, and that won't help."

"Damn right, it won't. Your job's done. The moment you notified me, you're done here. Go home, Miss Sharp."

"It's Doctor Sharp or Detective, and nope, not yet. I'm going to Brian's arraignment. Please don't tell him that his daughter's missing. Let him focus on his release first."

A long moment of silence, then a frustrated groan. "He left already, but all right. You tell him. While at it, ask him how come he didn't have the curiosity or the interest to speak to his kid for six days after her mom was killed. How does he explain that?"

Her thoughts exactly but she had an inkling of an idea. "He's not exactly father-of-the-year material, Detective. As far as I could gather, he wasn't closely involved with Holly as a parent. I was married to the guy long enough to learn that, for Brian Hanlin, there's only one person who matters in the entire world, and that's—"

"Brian Hanlin, I get it."

"Are you getting the feds involved?" Kay asked, turning onto the interstate ramp. "Want me to make that call?"

"Not your job. If you learn anything new about this, keep me posted," he added, speaking in a low, pained voice as if saying the words cut into his flesh and made him bleed, "Don't go anywhere other than the courthouse; don't investigate this for a single moment. Is that clear?"

She grinned silently at the man's territoriality, albeit justi-fied. "Sure."

The call ended without warning. She could imagine Brockett slamming the receiver down in its cradle, a therapeutic luxury mobile phones didn't offer. She turned on the siren and wove through traffic the remainder of the way to the Criminal Justice Court of San Francisco.

When she entered the courtroom, the hearing had already started. Brian, dressed in a suit she hadn't seen before, with a white shirt and a matching tie, had been invited to stand. The judge, a man in his sixties with an aquiline nose and eyes like a vulture, stared at him through the thick lenses of his glasses. They must've been loose at the temple or too wide for him because every few seconds, he pushed the frame's bridge up his nose with a quick gesture.

The judge changed his focus to Carly Hosking. She stood by her client, waiting patiently. "Miss Hosking, is your client ready to enter a plea at this time?"

"Yes, Your Honor."

The vulturine stare shifted to the left. "Well, Mr. Hanlin, how do you plead?"

"Not guilty, Your Honor." Brian's voice sounded strong, determined, innocent.

"So entered," the judge acknowledged. "Bail, counselors?"

The ADA was the first to speak. Kay recognized the ambitious, up-and-coming Donna McCollister from her years with the San Francisco FBI. She was fiercely intelligent yet unscrupulous, looking only to win and show a great conviction record when the time would come to advance her career and run for the district attorney seat for the state. Justice was a second thought to her, if even.

"The people are seeking remand, Your Honor. The defendant is charged with the brutal murder of a young woman he was involved with romantically. He has the means to flee and the knowledge and skill to avoid capture."

The judge pushed his glasses up his nose. "Defense?"

"We're asking for release on his own recognizance, Your Honor. My client is a tenured detective with the San Francisco Police Department and has an impeccable record. He's not a flight risk. After hearing of the warrant for his arrest, my client turned himself in voluntarily. Furthermore, this morning's shooting substantiates the fact that the murder he's accused of is, in fact, a gang-related—"

"We're not hearing the case now, Counselor. Just bail recommendations. And I've heard enough."

Hosking pressed her lips together for a brief moment under the judge's stare. "Yes, Your Honor."

"Bail is set at six hundred thousand." The gavel fell. Moments later, the judge left the courtroom. It seemed Brian's arraignment was the last one on the docket.

A look of consternation descended on Brian's face. "Sixty grand? I'm not sitting on that kind of cash," he told Carly. He seemed unaware of Kay's presence. "Help me here, Carly."

"Brian," Kay said, touching his arm to get his attention.

He turned and lit up when he saw her. "Good, you're here. Got any money I could borrow until I get home?"

It was just like him to ask. He should've been grateful he only had to come up with ten percent of that for the bond. "No, Brian, I don't. You'll have to figure something out. I'm a country cop now, making next to nothing."

A flicker of an arrogant smile flashed briefly on Carly's lips. Her pantsuit was probably worth what Kay made in a month, if not more. "I'll take care of this," the attorney said, squeezing Brian's hand a moment too long. "You pay me back when you get home."

Kay's eyebrow raised, but her questions were for a different time and place.

Two bailiffs were approaching, ready to take Brian back into lockup. Out of time, Kay rushed into their path and said, "Did you know Holly's missing?"

His hand covered his mouth while his eyes, open wide, stared at her in disbelief. "Since when? They got to her?" he shouted, getting everyone's attention. "You promised, Kay, you said she'd be fine."

"She's been missing since Friday, Brian, there's nothing I could've done. Brockett is looking into it. Feds will get involved."

He stared at her as if he couldn't process what he'd heard.

"Brockett's dirty. He's the one setting me up. He won't find Holly. He'll get her killed." He grabbed her forearm and squeezed hard, looking at her with eyes wide in panic. "I can't lose her too."

He wasn't being rational, but she couldn't blame him. "The feds are involved. They're good at this."

He scoffed. His burning glare was filled with contempt. "*I* should be out there, looking for her. Not Brockett, not the damn feds."

"How come you never called her since Rachel died?"

Brian looked at her as if he didn't understand the question. "You mean Holly? Why didn't I call her? Is that what you're asking?" He ran his hands over his face almost frantically. "Jeez, Kay!"

Kay nodded. "I would've expected you to call your daughter, and Ciara, to spend some time with them after Rachel's death. People who grieve often come together."

He shook his head forcefully. "Not me. I was freaking out, Kay. I was the one who found her, remember?" He limped in place restlessly, confined to the small space next to the defense table. "And what difference does it make? The old woman hates me, that was never a secret. She hates me because of you. Of what happened to you. And Holly... we don't speak that often. I don't really know how to be a good parent, but I'm trying. I was hoping when we'd live together, we'd have a stronger bond, Holly and I." He grabbed Kay's shoulders, squeezing hard, sending shards of pain through her wound. "Got to get me out of here, Kay, please. I have to find my kid. I know where to look for her."

She winced and pulled away, and he let go quickly, whispering a rushed apology, his eyes desperately drilling into hers, pleading still. A bailiff reached out for his arm, but he pulled himself free. "Let me go," he said, looking around as if he was looking for a way out. "They've taken my daughter."

The bailiffs didn't care. With expert movements, they immobilized his hands behind his back and cinched on a pair of handcuffs. Then they started hauling him away, holding him by his arms while he was kicking and screaming.

"Kay," he shouted when they were almost at the door. "Get me out of here! I know who has my little girl."

For a moment, she wondered if he really knew who had Holly. Did he have a suspect in mind? Or just the La Vida Sangrienta organization as a whole? She couldn't wait for his release, not when that sweet little girl had been gone for six days.

When the door closed behind the two bailiffs hauling Brian back to lockup, Kay and Carly were the only ones left in the courtroom.

"What happens next?" Kay asked.

The attorney collected all her things and took out her checkbook. Then she wrote a check for sixty thousand dollars and tore it along the dotted line with expertly manicured fingers. "Now we deposit this. It will take about an hour to process it, then they'll let him go."

Not a moment to waste. Kay smiled and looked at Carly as if she were the hero of the day. "That's absolutely wonderful. You're a true friend, exactly what Brian needs right now. Could I ask you to drop him off when he gets out? There's something I need to do first, then I'll call him."

She left before the bewildered attorney could say no. When she got to her car, she called Brockett's number.

THIRTY-THREE
CARMELA

The girl, barely eighteen, turned pale when she saw Elliot's badge. With eyes filled with fear, she took an instinctive step back, holding her hand raised as if to stop him from coming any closer.

She wore a black, sleeveless sequin top, a tiny black bikini, and white stockings with black stripes, the kind a schoolgirl would, only much higher, all the way up to her midthigh. Ridiculously high platforms with transparent heels and straps gave the illusion she walked on air. Elliot wondered how she managed to stroll or dance on those contraptions without breaking her neck.

"Nothing to worry about," Elliot said. "I have some questions about Taylor, that's all." The girl seemed relieved.

Melby sat at his desk, watching the interaction with a menacing grimace.

"Melby, give us the room, please," Elliot asked, then walked over to the office door and held it open, inviting him out with more than his words.

"She's my employee," the man pushed back. "I have a right to—"

"—remain silent?" Elliot asked, the threat made clear in his tone of voice and the slight tilt of his head. Melby understood and left the office hurriedly, slamming the door behind him.

"Whew," Elliot said, leaning against Melby's desk. "The air is cleaner somewhat, isn't it?"

The girl smiled. "A lot cleaner, yes." She had a nice smile and long, brown hair with the bottom half of some strands bleached blonde.

"Will you help me find out what happened to Taylor?"

The girl looked around as if to see whether she was safe to talk. "He's got cameras everywhere."

"I don't think he'd bug his own office, do you?" He'd checked earlier and found nothing, but he wanted to make sure. "We'll play music, and we'll talk in a low voice. That way, it won't matter. You okay with that?"

She hesitated, still scared. "I—I don't know." Anxious, she bit her lip. "I've seen what his cameras can do. Music is loud in the club, and still, he can get the words of people talking." She gave the walls one more suspicious look. "This place is a dump, but his tech is super expensive."

Strange. What Elliot had seen so far didn't seem like top-shelf video equipment. More like twenty-dollar cameras bought on eBay straight from China. What the hell was Melby trying to record, to be worth the investment? Who cared what those girls talked about among themselves?

"Let's go outside, then." He would've gladly taken her to the safety of the precinct, but he didn't want to leave Melby's office before the warrants and the deputies arrived to take ownership of all the evidence, all the recordings he'd made. He didn't trust Melby wouldn't destroy whatever evidence was left regarding Taylor's activities at the club.

Elliot started toward the door, but the girl stopped him. She went behind Melby's desk, where several darkened windows were hidden behind a hideous curtain, a dark blue fabric patterned with mudflap girls in strident, fluorescent shades of red, yellow, green, and magenta. She pulled the curtains and opened one of the large windows with some difficulty, just as Elliot was about to lend some of his strength.

Daylight tore through the semi-obscurity of the office. The smoke and dust suspended in the thick air whirled, thinning by the second. It was as if they'd opened a tomb that hadn't seen the light in thousands of years.

The girl beckoned Elliot to follow suit as she threw her leg over the windowsill and stepped outside, holding on to the edge until her high-heeled sandal gained solid footing. The window backed into a lightly wooded area behind the building. Carefully choosing where she stepped, she walked a good twenty yards away from the building before she said, "I'm Carmela." She smiled awkwardly and held out a thin hand with long fingers and multicolored acrylic fingernails. "Now we can talk."

"Thank you. Were you and Taylor close?"

She shrugged, her thin, bony shoulders poking through the sequined fabric of her top. In the daylight, Elliot noticed her clothing was worn out, sequins missing here and there, the fabric thinned and torn in places. "We're the only dancers here, and she was kind, not like some bitches I've worked with in the past."

"How old are you?" he asked, surprised by her comment. She'd spoken like a veteran of the business.

Carmela blushed under the heavy makeup. "Almost nineteen."

"How long have you been doing this?"

Fear clouded her gaze. "Please, don't make me," she whispered. "I don't want any trouble."

Elliot decided to let it go. It didn't come as a surprise that Melby hired underage girls as dancers. He held his hands up in the air to put Carmela's fears at ease. "It's all right. Only tell me what you're comfortable with." She nodded with a grateful smile. "I've seen a video of Taylor dancing, and I noticed groups of men bidding for lap dances. Is that what happens?"

Seemingly embarrassed, she looked away. "Yeah," she muttered. "Melby makes them bid. In other clubs, they'd just tip us more, and we'd do the lap dance for them, right there, in the main club room."

"How does it work?" Elliot asked gently. Carmela was wringing her hands, every now and then looking around as if expecting to be caught and punished for speaking with Elliot.

She bit her lip and seemed to think about what to say. "He advertises in the local media. He's sneaky about it too. The ads sound like, 'Go head-on for the girl of your dreams, only tonight.' It only happens once or twice a week."

"Not every day?"

The girl laughed bitterly. "We wouldn't last long if it happened every day. We can barely take it as it is."

Her words confused Elliot. Melby had painted a different picture. "Then what happens?"

Her head hung low. She tucked a long strand of hair behind her ear with trembling fingers. A tear fell from her eyelashes, messing up her makeup a little. "By the time they get here for the auction, they're already drunk or high, ready to get at one another's throats for some action." She glanced at Elliot quickly, then looked away, visibly ashamed. "Then they bid. The winner gets the girl of their choice, the runner-up gets the other girl." She paced, a little unstable on her heels on the soft ground covered with fir needles and cones. "Then we dance." She pressed her lips together and looked at Elliot for a moment, her gaze filled with unspeakable pain.

"What happens in those rooms, Carmela?"

She sniffled and looked away, hesitant to speak. "Most customers are okay. They just watch, sometimes have weird, sickening demands or a happy ending, but they mostly never touch us. Others are terrible. Violent, out of control." She fought hard not to cry and breathed a few times deeply, blinking fast. "Melby doesn't care if they rough us up as long as they pay for what they do. He takes the money and closes the door, and for twenty minutes, we're alone in there with them to do as they please. There's no bouncer, no way out. Even if we scream, the music is loud enough in the club to cover it."

Elliot clenched his fists and plunged them into his pocket. Melby was going down for this. He felt the urge to run back into the club and slap handcuffs on him, but he had a few more questions for Carmela. Melby wasn't going anywhere.

"Did you know Taylor was pregnant?"

Carmela shook her head, then touched her eye gently with her finger, where a fresh tear threatened to smudge her eyeliner.

"About two months ago, she broke her wrist. Does that ring a bell?"

The girl looked toward the parking lot, where early patrons were starting to arrive. It wasn't six yet; there was still some light, but shadows had grown longer.

A shiver rattled her thin body. "An auction dance went really bad a couple of months ago," she said, staring at the ground. "Taylor cried for days after that night, didn't come to work. Melby didn't fire her, which was weird. Usually, if you don't show up once, you're gone." She clasped her hands together for a moment, then crossed her arms at her chest, shivering. It was chilly, almost freezing, and she was dressed only in that thin, sleeveless top.

Elliot took off his denim jacket and wrapped it around the girl's shoulders. She gave him a tiny smile of gratitude. "Want to go inside?" he asked.

She shook her head. Her long earrings clinked. "When she came back, her wrist was wrapped in an elastic bandage, and her makeup was heavy, hiding bruises on her face, her thighs, her wrists, everywhere. I think she was raped that night." Carmela breathed away a sob. "There was one man that night, a regular. Melby paid Taylor off not to report the incident, as he called it. He promised her he wouldn't let the man inside the club again. I was there. I heard him make that promise. I know he paid her off, and I know how much." She shot Elliot an apologetic glance as if any of that was her fault. "Melby made it sound like she was lucky she was assaulted because that's how we make the really big bucks."

"Who was he, Carmela?"

"I don't know," she replied, her voice filled with sadness. "Melby swore he wouldn't set foot inside the club again, but he's been back. He hasn't bid on a girl again, but he just sits there in the crowd, silent, staring at Taylor weirdly, like a psychopath. No cheering, no tipping, no coming near her." She turned toward the club. "I can show him to you on the video you were watching. He was there Tuesday night."

They walked back, and before she could climb over the windowsill back into Melby's office, Elliot offered his hand for support. She took it and thanked him. Then she stopped in front of the monitor and hit the play button. A few moments later, she paused the video and pointed at a man's face in the crowd surrounding the dance stage.

He sat on a chair, leaning back against the backrest, his eyes riveted on the young girl. Elliot played the video and watched the man stare, completely motionless, for the entire dance duration. He didn't light up a cigarette, didn't take a sip of his drink. Nothing. He just stared at her.

Elliot took out his phone and snapped a screenshot with the man's face at the center.

"Here, thanks," Carmela said, handing him back his jacket.

"You know we're taking Melby down, right?" He put the jacket on. It smelled of jasmine and makeup and body lotion. "Tonight. You can go home if you wish."

Carmela nodded, wrapping herself in a hug. "I'll be out of work." She sighed and shrugged. "I need the money. But I can't do the lap dances anymore. Not after what happened to Taylor."

"You'll be fine, Carmela," he said, offering his business card. "You have what it takes to survive. If you remember anything or you need help, don't hesitate."

"Thanks, Detective. You're a kind man. One day, you'll make a lucky woman very happy." She left the office, clacking her heels toward the back of the building.

He walked toward Melby just as Novack and two other deputies entered the club with papers in their hands. Elliot laid a heavy hand on the man's shoulder. "You're under arrest for sex trafficking. Deputy Novack, please read him his rights."

Melby's jaw slacked. "You promised," he mumbled, flailing for a moment until the deputy locked his arms tightly and cuffed him. "You son of a bitch, you promised," he shouted as they took him to Novack's Interceptor.

The parking lot was almost empty. All the patrons had vanished at first sight of a police car. After Novack slammed the door, locking Melby in the back seat, he turned to Elliot. "What now, Detective?"

"Tear this place apart. Find every camera and secure every minute of footage and every hard disk you can find. Check the back rooms thoroughly."

"Copy that, Detective," Novack said, then directed the other two deputies to secure the premises and start the search.

Elliot was about to head back to the precinct when he thought of a faster way to identify his suspect. Approaching Novack's Interceptor, he opened the back door and held out the phone in front of Melby's bulging eyes. "I want his name."

Melby scoffed. "What do I get?"

Elliot grabbed Melby's lapels and squeezed until he choked. "You get to keep the charges list shorter. I'll drop the sex trafficking charge."

"And I'm supposed to trust you?" He spat on Elliot's boots. "You're a lying sack of pig shit."

"Or I can start adding charges to the list and recommend they'd be served consecutively."

"Motherfucker," Melby mumbled.

"All right, have a nice twenty-to-life," Elliot said, turning to leave.

"Darrell Bates," Melby shouted. "That's his name. He's some hot-shot businessman; that's all I know. And you better make good on that promise."

The door slammed shut in his face.

THIRTY-FOUR
BROCKETT

The SFPD Northern District precinct was just a few blocks west of the courthouse. Kay drove there as fast as she could and pulled into the precinct parking lot as Brockett was leaving the building, headed toward his vehicle.

She cut the engine and rushed to intercept him, the vigorous movement reminding her of her shoulder wound with rhythmic throbs of pain. "Detective," she called and waved to get his attention.

He closed the distance with a brisk step that seemed out of place for someone of his age and bulky build. He stopped squarely in front of her and propped his hands on his thighs. "What now?"

Kay noticed he was wearing a bulletproof vest under his old-style checkered jacket in shades of brown. "Have you released the crime scene yet?"

"Rachel Epling's house?"

She nodded.

"No, it's still sealed. Forensics needs more time. There are questions about the timing of certain fingerprints."

"I need access." Her words instantly lit his anger ablaze.

She could see his eyes glinting with rage. "You're going after Holly, right? To talk to people on the streets, your informers, right?"

"What do you want, Doctor Sharp? You've done enough. Now you need to go."

She clasped her hands together in a pleading gesture. "Listen, I know them both very well. One was my best friend and the other was my husband. I might see things you missed, things only I would pick up on or understand."

Brockett let out a frustrated groan. "Yeah, because us San Francisco cops are fucking idiots who don't know how to do our jobs. Good thing you came by, Doctor." His voice was dipped in venom. "You're wasting my time, and that little girl can't afford the time you waste," he threw over his shoulder, departing quickly.

"Last time you were there, you weren't looking for a missing child," she shouted, rushing to catch up with him.

He froze in place, then turned slowly to face her. "What are you saying?" He scowled at her, visibly impatient.

"I'm saying that's not just the crime scene for Rachel's murder. I believe that's the abduction scene for Holly's kidnapping. No one knew she was gone. Let me look for evidence of who might've taken her."

"We processed everything. Tire tracks, fingerprints, blood spatter. We didn't miss anything. Contrary to your opinion, we're not idiots."

"I never said you were, Detective. I'm just saying, if we want to understand who took her and why, we need to revisit that scene. And you have better things to do, to speak with those informants. While I don't have much of an agenda at the moment."

"How convenient." The sarcasm in his voice was unmistakable.

"I can't wrap my head around why they didn't kill Holly

too," she confessed. The question had been bothering her since she'd learned that the little girl was missing. "This is the first I've heard of a hit put on a capital case witness that leaves loose ends hanging."

His frown eased up a bit. "Go on."

"Grabbing a kid is no easy feat. They scream, they kick, they raise hell. Everyone's DNA is hard-coded to respond to children's cries for help. I know you think differently, Detective, and you believe Brian Hanlin shot Rachel, but I look at the evidence, and I see gangbangers cleaning up loose ends after that drug dealer's shooting last week."

"And?"

"Run this scenario with me. Let's assume there's a gang-banger involved who was sent to eliminate the witness to last week's shooting. Can you think of any scenario, no matter how far-fetched, in which he would kidnap the little girl instead of shooting her at the scene?"

He broke eye contact and stomped his foot angrily. "He developed a conscience? Has some personal code of ethics that prevents him from killing kids?"

"And took her without being seen or heard? To do what with her?" The silence was uninterrupted for a moment.

"Then what else?"

"Maybe she fled, hid away somewhere, and is afraid to come out. Or her mother gave her to a close friend to be taken care of until she was ready to enter WITSEC. Until Debra was coming to pick her up."

"Debra, huh? My, my, how well you've immersed yourself into this case. You know everything." He rubbed his mustache with the tips of his fingers. "I could've sworn you were warned to stay out of this."

"Yeah, whatever, I'll sign the disclaimer saying I've been dutifully warned. But listen to me, I can go there and figure out if there's anything at the scene we can use to understand why she was taken instead of killed."

"All right, Detective, I have to admit your ex looks less and less guilty," Brockett replied, calling her Detective for the first time.

Kay breathed. "Why did you suspect him in the first place?"

Brocket scratched his buzz-cut scalp and looked away, probably wishing he didn't have to answer that question. "There have been rumors that Hanlin's dirty. Nothing proven, not ever. I know for sure Diaz had him under surveillance for a while." He looked at her intently for a moment as if to get her to acknowledge his vote of confidence. "I'm trusting you with information I probably shouldn't. I hope you know how to keep a lid on it."

Kay nodded. "Count on it."

"But he lives above his means, not enough to warrant an official questioning, just enough to raise suspicion. Expensive suits, that sports car of his."

She shrugged. "His house is paid for. Inherited from his parents before we were married. In this area, free housing is a life changer."

Brockett whistled. "What do you know? If we had questioned him, we would've looked like idiots." He sighed and pulled out a pack of smokes. He lit up a cigarette and inhaled hungrily as if his lungs couldn't take one more moment without the nicotine. "But that wasn't the only reason Diaz and I suspected him. Ninety percent of the time, in these cases, it's the spouse, right? Or the boyfriend." He blew the smoke forcefully, then took another drag. "He didn't have an alibi. Did you know he 'found the body'?" he asked, making air quotes with his fingers. "I was on the scene within minutes. He wasn't there... he'd fled the scene."

"Wait... what?" Kay asked. That wasn't how Brian had

described the sequence of events that night. "What do you mean, he fled the scene?"

"What I usually mean when I say that," he replied, giving her a long, curious stare. "I got there; he was gone. He came back in a few minutes, gave me a reason why he'd fled—"

"What did he say?"

"He said he wanted to see if he could catch the killer." He scoffed, his voice filled with contempt. "As if he could know which way the killer had gone after he left their cul-de-sac."

"True." Questions crowded Kay's mind, but Brian wasn't there to answer any of them.

"His demeanor was off," Brockett added, sounding less and less convinced.

"And that was enough to issue an arrest warrant on a fellow detective?" At best, they'd rushed the job and called it done, but Kay was surprised the DA had signed off on such a sloppy job. Even a pro bono attorney would have the charges dismissed for lack of conclusive evidence.

"He had blood on his hands, trace GSR on his clothes, and his fingerprints were all over the place."

"Yeah, 'cause he lives there," Kay replied, sounding a little harsher than she'd intended.

Brockett's brow furrowed. "Don't insult me, Detective. I've put twenty-five years into this job and done it well. He seemed guilty to me." He inhaled one last time before flicking the butt over by the trash can. "I have to say... I don't know anymore. I might've been wrong. They came after him today."

"Who else could've killed Rachel?" Kay asked. "Did you have other suspects you were looking at?"

"Honestly, no. He was there, acted weird, didn't have an alibi, and left the scene. It was enough to issue the warrant. No one knew about his little girl."

"There's a leak somewhere," Kay said prudently. "Maybe someone in the DA's office, spilling info to La Vida Sangrienta?"

"Could be," he said, still shaking his head. It was clearly visible he had his doubts about the case. Every good cop has doubts; only stubborn, arrogant ones don't.

"What's with this gang? Are they new? I hadn't heard much about them before I left San Francisco."

"They're the worst scum that's crawled onto this part of the land. Relatively newly organized, from remnants of other gangs. Maybe you remember when gangs used to shoot one another in the streets a few years back?"

Kay nodded. She vaguely remembered; it seemed like a lifetime ago.

"Some of these guys are former Street Kings, others are Norteños, but they're crazier than any other gangbangers we've dealt with."

"How so?"

He sighed and stared at his feet for a moment. "They kill quickly and effectively, without leaving a trace of evidence. They execute their own members just as quickly for the tiniest of mistakes." He shrugged. "There's always more young people out there, ready to sign up and join *the bloody life*." He looked at her with visible concern. "If these guys took Brian's kid, I don't think we'll find her alive."

THIRTY-FIVE
BATES

It was completely dark when Elliot left the club. The chill in the air had turned into near-freezing gusts of wind that cut through his denim and put vapor clouds in the air with every breath. The sky was clear, the stars sparkling brightly, the way they do on clear winter nights.

A quick search on his laptop while seated behind the wheel of his SUV, blowing into his hands and rubbing them together, revealed the address for Darrell Bates. By the time he finished reviewing the man's background, the Ford's vents were blowing warm air, and he could unzip his jacket.

Bates was forty-four years old and had a spotless record. Not even a parking ticket had been issued to him in his entire life; he was, at least on paper, a model citizen. The internet had many articles about him, showcasing his career as a promising vice president for a major bank.

"Banker," Elliot muttered. "Ain't no bigger liar on this green earth." He pulled out of the Velvet Puss parking lot and drove toward the mountain again. Mr. Bates lived in one of the over-size, modern cottages near the foot of the ski slopes. It must've set him back a couple of million dollars. They were built a year ago, a gated community dedicated to San Francisco's posh skiers who wanted to escape over the weekend and catch some time on the snow.

His thoughts wandered to Kay. It was almost seven-thirty, and she hadn't called him back. Was she on her way home? Mr. City Slicker's arraignment must've been done by now. A grin blossomed on his lips at the thought that he might've been remanded. Innocent or not, Elliot didn't want that man anywhere near Kay.

The police code worked seamlessly at the gate. A wide section of wrought iron fence drew to the side on rollers, opening silently. A minute later, Elliot stopped in front of Darrell Bates's house. It was well-lit with blue projectors, enhancing its contemporary modern design. It sprawled on at least three thousand square feet, surrounded by carefully archi-tected landscaping on several acres, including park-like alleys with benches. Yet Mr. Bates lived there alone, and only part of the week, when he wasn't robbing people blind in his day job.

Elliot rang the bell and waited. A sequence of soft chimes announced his presence. A moment later, the door opened, and Mr. Bates gave his badge a disgruntled look.

"What is this about?" He wore a light gray tracksuit over a white T-shirt. He zipped up quickly after the first gust of wind.

"Detective Young with Franklin County Sheriff's Office," Elliot introduced himself. "I have some questions. May I come in?"

Bates gave a quick, hearty burst of laughter. "Hell, no. I'll call my lawyer."

"Here? Or at the station?" Elliot asked calmly.

Bates didn't flinch, didn't bat an eye over Elliot's veiled threat.

"Here is fine. I'll make the call. You go ahead and wait in the car until he gets here."

Elliot took two steps toward the vehicle, then stopped.

"He'd better make it in fifteen minutes. If he can't, we'll move this little show to the precinct instead."

Bates didn't reply; he just gestured with his hand, which could've largely been interpreted as *whatever*.

Elliot watched him close the massive door while on the phone. As soon as the door was shut, Elliot climbed inside the Interceptor. Then he took out his phone and called Kay.

"Hey, partner," she answered. Her voice sounded tired against the whooshing of traffic and tires on asphalt in the background. She was driving.

"Kay," he said, then stopped, realizing he was about to sound like an anxious husband. "How's it going?"

"You mean, am I on my way back yet?" They laughed together.

"Yeah, that's exactly what I mean," he replied, grateful she wasn't there to see him turn redder than a beet. How did she manage to know what he was thinking from all the way south of the Golden Gate?

She sighed loudly, seemingly lighthearted but failing to make it believable. "Well, I'm not, Elliot. I can't come home yet." He waited patiently for a silent moment. "Rachel's eight-year-old daughter is missing. I have to—"

"Remember what Logan said," he interrupted. But he knew Kay well enough to know she would never favor her career over the fate of a missing child. She'd risk anything to find her.

"Yeah, I remember." He could hear the smile in her voice. "I'm just going to look at some things and come back. How are things going on your end?"

"I'm about to interview a suspect, then I'm headed down there. You need to eat, right? We'll find a place that stays open late."

"No." Kay's voice sounded almost scared, the urgency in it unmistakable. "Elliot, I can't," she added, a bit more her normal self now. "This girl's been missing since last Friday. I can't spare a moment until she's found. Actually, I gotta go. Talk later, all right?"

She ended the call before Elliot could reply. The fear he'd sensed in her voice in that imperative, almost panicked *no* wasn't something Elliot could easily forget.

The powerful headlights of a Lincoln disrupted his thoughts. The Lincoln pulled up at the curb in front of his vehicle, and a man climbed out, panting heavily and carrying a small briefcase. It was Ackerman, an attorney Elliot had crossed paths with in recent past, there to represent Bates.

"Come on, Detective, I haven't got all night to waste on this nonsense," Ackerman said, rushing toward the door. "I was about to watch the game with my son."

Bates opened the door quickly and invited them in. The foyer was huge, two stories high, and decorated solely with a modern chandelier. Bates invited them into the living room with a hand gesture. Elliot followed and took a seat at a twelve-seat dining room table, across from Bates and his attorney.

"All right, Detective, what do you want to know?" Bates asked. He'd changed into whitewashed jeans and a black shirt, buttoned up almost all the way to the collar.

"Do you know this young woman?" Elliot said, pushing his phone across the table where the two men could see. The screen displayed Taylor's photo.

"What's this about?" Ackerman asked.

Lawyers always made things difficult. "She was found dead yesterday morning at Frozen Falls." He paused, watching for reactions in the two men. Bates frowned and shielded his eyes with his hand, casually leaning his forehead into his palm as he stared at the phone. Ackerman didn't react in any way other than to lean over and whisper something into his client's ear.

"I don't know anything about this," Bates replied. Ackerman nodded slightly as if to approve his client's statement.

"Did you know her, Mr. Bates?"

"N—no," he stammered, shooting a glance at his attorney.

"Mr. Ackerman, please remind your client about the consequences of making a false statement to the police."

Ackerman scowled but leaned over and whispered some more, raising his hand to cover the movement of his lips. Then Bates muttered something back, and Ackerman nodded.

"I don't know her personally," Bates said. "I don't know her name. I have never socialized with her, never called her."

"Then, how do you know her?"

Some more whispers. "She might've been a dancer at a club I sometimes patronize. I can't be sure."

Elliot repressed a groan. Couldn't be sure? If that wasn't a lie, he'd never seen a liar in his entire life. "Does the name Taylor Lorentz mean anything to you?"

He shook his head a little too enthusiastically. "No."

"Where were you yesterday morning between five and eight?"

He seemed relieved, visibly so. Mr. Bates was afraid of something else, not the girl's murder. "I was here, sleeping. I don't get up so early when I don't have to drive into town." Ackerman's hand landed on Bates's forearm as if to tell him to keep his answers short.

"Can anyone vouch for that?"

He shrugged. "I live alone, Detective. But there's video surveillance in this house, and I'm certain some location information could be obtained from my phone's—"

"My client has answered your question," Ackerman intervened and stood, ready to leave. "I believe we're done here?"

Elliot shook his head slowly, feigning regret. "Unfortunately, without a verifiable alibi, your client will have to come with me. We'll detain him—"

"Just for watching a girl strip in a club? I don't see a judge willing to sign *that* warrant."

"I'm not arresting him yet," Elliot said, watching Bates's

anxiety grow. "I can detain him for a while until we sort things out. Come on, Mr. Bates, let's go. Your attorney has a game to watch with his son."

Bates turned to his lawyer desperately. "Ackerman, do something, for Pete's sake. I'm paying you enough."

"Detective, you're about to make the mistake of your career. No judge will sign that arrest warrant, and my client will sue for harassment."

Elliot shrugged and sighed with pretend indifference. "Just doing my job." He took out his handcuffs, watching Bates's pupils dilate.

He sprang from his chair and took a few steps back, distancing himself from Elliot.

"See there, Mr. Ackerman?" Elliot said. "That's exactly why I'm detaining your client. He's skittish, and he could bolt. He's got the means to disappear. Don't want to be chasing him all over the country when I could have him wait in lockup for a day or two." He paused for effect. "Three, at the most."

"Detective, you're being ridiculous."

Bates pressed his hands on his temples, pacing furiously like a caged animal. "This isn't happening."

Elliot played with the handcuffs, making them jingle. "There is another way, but you probably won't consider it."

Bates approached the table quickly and leaned over it, hands placed flat on its glossy surface. "What other way?"

"We have found DNA evidence at the scene. You could give us a sample for elimination."

Ackerman held his hand up in the air. "Mr. Bates, I strongly advise you don't provide any DNA without a warrant."

"The hell with it, Ackerman!" Bates shouted. "I didn't kill that girl, and I'm sure as hell not going to spend my night in jail if I can avoid it." Then he turned to Elliot. "What do you want? Hair?"

Elliot put the handcuffs back in his back pocket and extracted a swab. "Saliva will do."

Ackerman grabbed his client's forearm, holding him back. "Mr. Bates, don't—"

"Enough. You can't make this go away, fine. I'll do it." Bates opened his mouth and let Elliot swab the inside of his cheek, holding his rage in check and his breath inside his lungs.

Elliot sealed the vial in an evidence pouch and slipped it into his pocket. "Don't leave town for the next few days."

"I have to go to work," Bates said, frustration boiling in his high-pitched voice.

Elliot stopped in the doorway. "Call in sick, Mr. Bates. Don't make me come after you."

A moment later, Elliot drove off, headed for the ME's office. Bates might've seemed relieved when he heard the questions about Taylor's murder, but he probably wasn't thinking about her assault.

He patted the pocket where he'd slid the DNA vial and muttered, satisfied, "Works every time." There was nothing as effective as the threat of a few nights spent in jail to turn even the most stubborn of people into a model of collaboration and helpfulness.

Now all he had to figure out was whether he should make a run for San Francisco.

THIRTY-SIX

RACHEL'S HOUSE

Rachel's house was small, even smaller than her mother's, and in the same style. A brick bungalow of not more than fourteen hundred square feet with a single car garage and potted plants on the front porch seemed the perfect fit with what she remembered Rachel liked. The front door was secured with a police seal, barring entry for any unauthorized persons.

Kay looked carefully around her, expecting at any time to be stopped by an angry SFPD cop or shot at from some nearby roof. On the driveway, wide tire tracks were still visible among a multitude of narrower, standard-size ones. One of the wide tires had left a mark on the lawn, where it missed the pavement. Kay took photos, although Brockett had been thorough and the print showed blue traces of silicone, the substance forensic teams used to take tire track molds.

She was willing to bet the wide tire belonged to a Chevy Suburban, late model, like the one the sniper used.

Ready to go inside, she pulled out a small switchblade knife from her pocket and exposed the blade. Then she cut the seal neatly exactly where the door touched the jamb. In doing so, she made sure when she was inside, and the door closed, the seal would appear intact to anyone checking from a few feet away, like an SFPD cruiser on patrol.

Her Ford Interceptor parked on the street was a dead give-away of her presence, but it didn't bear the insignia of Franklin County; it was just an unmarked, black SUV with flashers embedded in the grille and in the rear bumper. Most San Francisco detectives drove identical units.

She slipped on a pair of fresh gloves before entering. Although the crime scene had been processed, she didn't want to risk contaminating a scene that had not been released yet. Once inside, she closed the door behind her and locked it, just in case.

The house was eerily silent. Kay turned on the lights, and breath caught in her chest. It was just as she'd imagined Rachel's home would be. She remembered her friend liked Oriental rugs; one was now in front of the leather couch paired up with two armchairs and a small coffee table. Two cases filled with books because she loved how a novel felt in her hands and had been reluctant to adopt an e-reader. And everywhere Kay looked, the color blue, Rachel's favorite. Blue drapes at the windows. A blue throw on the side of the couch. Blue pillows with cheesy messages, like she used to have in the old dorm room. The one pillow she'd bought for Rachel on her birthday, with "Live, Laugh, Love," written in cursive blue lettering, a bit stained and faded, but still there, at the center of her sofa. She'd kept it.

The photos on the walls and on the narrow fake fireplace mantle were of Rachel and Holly, Ciara in a couple. No Brian anywhere. Perhaps Rachel had decided not to display photos of him, knowing Ciara's aversion to the man she loved.

Kay took everything in, every detail, every swirl of fingerprint dust still visible on doorknobs and flat surfaces, even on the TV remote. The living room showed no signs of struggle, and the front door lock was intact, not jimmied. A trifold pamphlet caught her eye on a small table by the window. It was published by the American Heart Association and titled "Living With Your Pacemaker." Kay frowned, slipping it into her pocket. Rachel didn't use to have a heart condition as far as she knew. Who had the pacemaker? Was it Ciara? Or Holly?

The impression that Brian didn't stay there too often was reinforced as she went through the bedrooms. In the large one, there was a king-size bed, neatly made with clean sheets. All the dressers had been dusted for prints, and Kay opened several drawers, looking for Brian's things. There weren't too many. A small drawer with a few changes of underwear and socks. A single change of clothes in the main closet and a pair of running shoes. In the bathroom, a couple of travel toothbrushes still sealed in their wrappers, and an electric razor near a can of shaving foam, Brian's favorite brand, that smelled exactly as she remembered. The can had been dusted for prints. She took it in her hand and weighed it. It was almost full, and the sprayer head was completely clean. Unused.

Everything Brian kept at Rachel's place were "just in case" items. It explained why he wasn't too attached to Holly. The father and daughter lived separate lives in separate places. It didn't explain why Brian was marrying Rachel. She'd kept on living in her own house with her daughter when she could've moved in with Brian if he was that serious about her.

Then Kay remembered who he was: the chronic cheater, the ever-wandering hound. He needed space for his countless affairs. Why marry her then? But then again, why had he married Kay eight years ago?

It was the same thing. Same logic or lack thereof. Or maybe it was more this time.

She remembered how Brian looked when he talked about Rachel, about her death. He was upset, genuinely so. Maybe Rachel had endured through his many affairs and had learned to take him the way he was, and that had made her unique, the

woman who could become his wife but not expect much faithfulness. Perhaps she'd put up with him for Holly's sake, so her
little girl could have a father.

With a sigh, Kay admitted to herself she knew very little
about Brian's relationship with Rachel. When Kay withdrew
from their lives eight years ago, Rachel was pregnant with Holly
and desperately in love with Brian. Maybe things had stayed the
same... maybe not.

The kitchen came next. Brightly lit by sunshine coming in
through the window, the floor was visibly smeared in shades of
crimson. She cringed. "Oh, Rachel," she whispered. The
remnant of a bloodstain was visible where she'd fallen. The
crime scene cleanup crew had done a rushed job, not bothering
to remove the stain completely.

The small table was set for one, with a place mat and a
clean plate and silverware. The only other objects on the table
were a grate, the type used to set hot casseroles on, and an oven
mitt. Kay made a note to ask Brockett if she could see some
crime scene photos. Maybe there had been something else on
that table, something that was no longer there, something the
cleaning crew might've removed.

Either way, Kay was certain that Rachel would've never
eaten alone with full ceremony, the way she used to call it. If
she'd been alone, she would've grabbed a couple of crackers
smeared with peanut butter and munched while standing in
front of the open fridge door. In that respect, Kay and Rachel
could've been sisters.

The knife holder on the counter, blackened by fingerprint
dust, was missing the largest knife. Kay searched for it in the
drawers, but it wasn't anywhere. Perhaps it was never there to
begin with, broken and discarded who knows how long ago.
The stove was clean and so was the oven.

The dishwasher door was closed. Kay grabbed the handle
and pulled, but it wouldn't open more than a couple of inches.

It rattled and resisted, no matter how hard Kay tried. Glaring at the dishwasher as if it might make a difference, Kay knelt on the floor, careful not to touch the bloodstain. Reaching under the dishwasher, she felt around for the object that was blocking the door from opening. There was something under there, stuck. She lowered her head until she could look under, shining the flashlight to see better.

A knife. Stuck a few inches deep, probably pushed in deeper when someone had tried to open the dishwasher. Kay grabbed a skimmer from one of the drawers, then reached under the dishwasher with its handle, pulling and sliding that knife until she could grab it out.

There was no visible trace of blood on the knife and no fingerprint dust either. She sealed it in an evidence bag she retrieved from her SUV and set it on the table. Then she finally opened the dishwasher.

A plastic place mat, a perfect match to the one on the table, unfolded when the door opened, releasing a knife and a fork. The two pieces of silverware clinked as they fell to the bottom of the dishwasher. A plate, perfectly clean, was lying flat on the lower shelf, not vertical as one would place it for washing.

Taking another evidence bag, she sealed the plate and the cutlery she found inside the dishwasher. Then, as she was about to close the dishwasher door, another object caught her eye, fallen at the bottom of the dishwasher. Rachel's phone.

She picked it up carefully and looked at the screen. It was dark. She touched it, expecting it to stay dark, but it lit up barely, showing a one percent remaining charge. She rushed into the master bedroom, looking for the charger she'd noticed on Rachel's night table, then returned and plugged in the phone, holding her breath until she heard the chime.

The passcode she used to have in college didn't work anymore. Kay tried her birthday and failed for a second time, leaving her with only one attempt. Holly's birthday was

December 30. She tried that, and the phone unlocked its secrets.

A quick review of her email and text messages didn't reveal anything relevant. Another evidence bag sealed the phone and its charger; maybe the SFPD would have more luck with it.

Kay placed the sealed bag on the table and studied the objects with a raised eyebrow. The only possible explanation was that Rachel wasn't about to dine alone when she was shot, but she had desperately tried to hide she had company. She'd done so in a terrible rush, throwing everything into the dishwasher and hoping the unexpected visitor wouldn't look.

She was protecting someone.

Holly.

Kay started to visualize the scene. Rachel must've known the killer was coming. She hid her table accoutrements, then sent Holly to hide... Where? Outside, in the backyard. Then she'd bravely fought the unsub with a kitchen knife against a gun.

Knowing she'd lose the battle, but giving Holly the time to run and hide.

Squinting in the sun, Kay opened the door and went outside. The yard was small, part of it a wooden deck with built-in benches. A narrow, concrete slab pathway led to a small shed in the back. Beside it, to the left, a tall cedar with low-hanging branches.

On the way to the shed, she found a little footprint where Holly had stepped on the moist ground, barefoot. A couple of yards farther, there was a dragged partial print of an adult-size sneaker. Only the front part of it was visible as if someone had walked on their tiptoes. Or as if a child wore her mother's shoes, dragging her feet to keep the shoes on.

The door to the shed was ajar. Kay looked inside and found nothing out of place. The shed was home to a lawn tractor and some gardening tools. No signs of struggle, no discernible footprints.

Back outside, she checked the rest of the yard for clues as to where Holly could've hidden. She found several fallen branches under the tall cedar. Stepping back toward the house, she could follow, in her mind's eye, the little girl as she ran out of the house to hide in the shed, probably because Rachel had told her to do so. But then she must've sneaked out; Kay had found the shed door open just a tiny bit, enough to let an eight-year-old girl sneak through. SFPD had not dusted it for prints; they'd had no reason to.

Then the little girl must've climbed up the tree to look inside the house. From there, she could've easily seen what was going on through the kitchen window. Then she must've fallen, perhaps startled by the gunshots. The fallen branches at the cedar's root told that story clearly, yet without an ending.

Then what happened?

Had neighbors heard the gunshots? From what she knew from Brian and, implicitly, from Brockett, no one had heard a thing. How come?

Probably a suppressor was used. Not surprising for a gang hit.

Groaning, Kay went inside the house, ready to leave. She had nothing to help her find Holly, and only one incomplete, speculative scenario for her abduction.

The only viable explanation was the little girl had yelped or cried when she took the fall, and the killer must've heard her. That simple. One snapped tree branch, and Holly had become a loose end.

Then, why wasn't she dead, her body in the morgue, and a bloodstain just like the one in the kitchen marking the place where she'd been killed?

Collecting the evidence she'd bagged, Kay almost made it through the door when she realized she needed one more bit of information. Abandoning the evidence bags by the door, she started rummaging through the drawers in the kitchen and bathroom, through cabinets, until she found what she was looking for.

A small orange pill box with a white label containing prescription medication for arrhythmia. It was under Holly's name.

Now she had her answer. The little girl had the pacemaker.

THIRTY-SEVEN
COFFEE

In a clear case of déjà vu, Elliot arrived at Dr. Whitmore's office early in the morning, just like the day before. Ground frost was thicker, the air colder, the wind angrier than yesterday, and the differences didn't stop there. Yesterday he hadn't come to visit the morgue after tossing and turning an entire night, thinking of Kay Sharp and the reason she didn't want him anywhere near San Francisco.

Perhaps it had something to do with her shooting. The thought froze his blood faster than the gust of wind that nearly blew his hat off when he got out of the car. Was she still at risk of being shot? What was she not saying?

He rushed to the door and, holding two large coffee cups with one hand, opened it with the other enough to slide through, hat and all. Once inside, he took his hat off and walked briskly toward the autopsy room, where the lights were on, and low-key chatter came through the hinged, swinging doors.

He pushed one door open with his elbow and stepped in. The bright lights were on at blinding intensity, although no hapless corpse was lying on either of the stainless-steel tables.

The low-key chatter was coming from the wall-mounted TV that Dr. Whitmore used to display autopsy information and imaging, not the latest rerun of *Grey's Anatomy*. The medical examiner was toiling at the large microscope, seated on a four-legged stool and hunched over the ocular, mumbling something Elliot didn't catch.

"I smell a good morning," Dr. Whitmore said, standing and meeting Elliot halfway, taking the offering of fresh-brewed java with both hands. A grateful smile bloomed on his face. "My wife would faint if she heard me, but I love the Katse brew way more than her homemade concoction. There's something they add to it to give it this intense flavor." He took a sip and savored it. "Ground eggshells, I heard someone say."

"That's a new one on me, Doc." Elliot scratched his head. "Glad you like it. I don't believe I've seen you smile in a while."

"It's not just the coffee that's put a grin on my face today, my young friend." He took another sip, then abandoned the paper cup with the Katse emblem on the table by the microscope. "I'm thrilled to give you good news. We have a match."

"For the DNA I left with you last night? Darrell Bates's sample?"

"Yes. It ran all night, and this morning it sang for me."

Elliot stared at him, confused.

"The 'match found' computer chime," he clarified. "Darrell Bates is the man who impregnated Taylor Lorentz; there's no doubt about that."

"I'll be damned," Elliot muttered, then patted Doc Whitmore on the shoulder. "You made my day."

"For the murder investigation, it doesn't do anything. Forensically, we can't place him at the scene. His car didn't leave the gated community until eleven that day. My assistant took some time last night to check community cameras. Now she's working the GPS location of his phone, but it doesn't look good. We left the home surveillance system for last; his attorney had a change of heart and is demanding a subpoena for that."

Elliot wasn't surprised; Bates had been too relieved to hear the question about Taylor's murder; he wasn't guilty. But for the crime he'd thought he got away with, he didn't.

"Paternity doesn't prove assault," Doc Whitmore said as if reading Elliot's thoughts. "It's a long shot from here."

Elliot stared at the tip of his boots. He still held on to hope for that to stick. Novack and the other two deputies had brought back loads of confiscated video from the strip club and heaps of high-end video equipment they found hidden in the ceiling above every room. Carmela had been right. Melby didn't spare a coin when he shopped for technology.

"Any news on the confiscated video material yet?" Dr. Whitmore asked, again proving an uncanny ability to read Elliot's mind.

"Not yet." Elliot walked over to the side table and leaned against it, crossing his legs at the ankles. It was the closest he'd ever been to one of the pieces of furniture in the autopsy room. "I'm thinking of calling Bates in for an extended interview."

"And play one of Kay's renowned bait-and-switch interrogations on him?"

Dr. Whitmore's comment caught him off guard. "What? No." He gave it some thought, which the ME probably misinterpreted for hesitation or confusion.

"If you pretend this is about other suspects, and you get him to admit he and Taylor had sex at the club, then..." Dr. Whitmore left the word hanging in the air, the phrase unfinished. "On second thought, I should stick to what I know, like DNA and fingerprints and other such palpable, tangible, and precise things."

Elliot smiled with a hint of sadness. He loved to talk through a stubborn case with someone. With Kay. He missed her wit, her ideas, her unconventional approaches that gave results.

"How is she, by the way?" Dr. Whitmore asked, rummaging through a drawer filled with metallic implements that rattled as he searched.

"Doc, do you read minds?"

He abandoned the search and looked at him briefly. "No, my young friend. But I know people. It's what I do." He gave him an encouraging smile and added, "She'll be fine. I heard her wound was merely a scratch."

"Yeah." Elliot plunged his hands into his pockets. "If there isn't anything else, Doc, I gotta go." He picked up the coffee cup he'd abandoned on the tiled lab table and took a swig. It was almost cold.

"Just a moment." The search inside the drawer ended with Dr. Whitmore extracting a replacement inkjet cartridge. He took out the old one from a small printer, sending it with a swift move straight into the trash can, then peeled off the plastic protections from the new one and plugged it in. "Okay, now we can print." The printer whirred to life. "I don't print that much lately; everything's electronic," he added, probably an apology for the time he took to make the printer work.

"What are you printing?" Coffee cup still in hand, Elliot drew closer.

"The killer's fingerprint wasn't in AFIS," Dr. Whitmore said, "but this thumbprint is so distinctive I think you should have it with you. Who knows, maybe you'll run into someone who will leave a thumbprint on a bottle of Coke or something. I'd like to send you off well prepared."

"You're sure it's a thumb, this partial?" Elliot watched as the printer's head whirred left and right, slowly putting out the printed image. "It's narrow enough to be anything."

"Yes, I'm sure. It was left on the round when the magazine

was loaded. I tried for an hour to load bullets into a magazine using other fingers to push the bullets down, and it doesn't work. This particular man or woman has a scar on their thumb, on their dominant hand. I can vouch for it."

"Thanks, Doc."

"You're welcome. And thank you for the coffee. You saved me a trip around the hill."

Around the hill was where Taylor used to run. That's what Mr. Lorentz had called it.

Elliot frowned, staring at the coffee cup in his hand. A few years ago, Katse had introduced the ridiculous floral design on their paper cups, chain-linked daisies in bloom. One could tell it was a Katse cup from twenty yards away. It was recognizable, unique, making Tommy MacPherson really proud, although people still laughed at how juvenile the design looked. That year, he'd once told Elliot, he'd spent a small fortune redecorating the coffee place, redesigning the cups and logo, getting new furniture, and new kitchen equipment.

And installing security cameras on the summer patio and in the parking lot.

By the road.

Where they could catch the passing traffic, not much, perhaps a tiny sliver of it, but still. How many cars would've driven past Katse two days ago from six-thirty to seven-thirty in the morning? With a little bit of luck, he could see the tag or at least the make and model of passing vehicles at the time of Taylor's death.

One of them could be his suspect. The others could be valuable witnesses who might've seen something. Anything.

He abandoned the coffee cup on the lab table and grabbed his hat, putting it on his head and bolting for the door. "Got to go, Doc."

"It's still printing," Doc Whitmore protested.

Rushed, Elliot turned back and took a photo of the fingerprint image displayed on the screen with his phone. Then he touched the brim of his hat as he departed, leaving the medical examiner slack-jawed.

Before the swinging door swung to a close, he heard Doc Whitmore laugh and say, "I'm such a dinosaur."

THIRTY-EIGHT
SHOWER

Brian sat pouting on the Beemer's passenger seat, arms crossed at his chest over the seatbelt, looking at the courthouse building with a disgusted scowl as they left it behind. The Beemer immersed into the thick traffic on Van Ness in a dissonance of honks and screeching brakes. Impassible, Carly Hosking weaved through traffic with elegance, making good time on her way to drop Brian off at his house.

He couldn't believe he'd had to spend another night behind bars, waiting for a stupid check to clear. But taking it out on Carly didn't make any sense. She deserved his gratitude, every ounce he could muster. Slowly, Brian's scowl vanished, and his innate charisma reemerged.

"Thanks for doing this, Carly. You saved my life. I'm not cut out for life behind bars. And for driving me home... I appreciate it."

"Sure," she smiled. "What are lawyers for, right, Brian?" She shot him a quick glance.

"Right." He chuckled, then looked through the window at the passing traffic. "Are you sure you won't represent me at the trial?"

"I can't, Brian." She reached out and squeezed his hand. "I'm sorry. This could go incredibly wrong for me, and you know that."

"Then I'm so screwed." He checked the time on his phone with nervous fingers and abrupt movements. "And my daughter's missing." He buried his face in his hands. "Who knows if I'll ever see her again. Carly, we can't let that happen. We have to do something. I can't lose my little girl."

"Were you close?"

A moment of silence. "We were becoming close. I wasn't there much when she was a baby, but I tried my best."

"What are you planning to do?"

"I'm going to look for her. I believe I have a pretty clear idea who has her."

"Don't forget you're officially suspended." Carly sighed. "Whatever you do, don't add to your charges. Get Brockett to help. Or Diaz—he'd get involved if you pinpointed a location and asked for support, right?"

"Yeah," he replied, sounding unconvinced. "I don't trust them, Carly. One of these guys is setting me up. And I don't know if it's Brockett, Diaz, or both." Carly pulled to a stop in front of Brian's house. He turned toward her and looked at her intently. "Want to come in for a minute or two?"

A smile fluttered on her lips. "Why not?"

The moment he stepped inside, Brian took off his jacket with an angry gesture and discarded it on the floor. "Screw them," he said, frowning again. "The thugs on my shit list won't know I'm suspended."

Carly's eyebrow popped as if challenging his statement.

"All right, so they'll know because whomever they're paying will have told them already or they've seen it on TV. But the voice of a nine mil speaks the same language, badge or not."

"Unregistered weapon, I hope?" Carly whispered, still standing by the door as if unsure where to go and what to do.

"Of course." He walked over to the bar. "Here, pour us a drink, will you?"

She abandoned her purse on a chair and clacked her heels across the hardwood to the bookcase. Several shelves had mirror backing and were stocked with enough alcohol and glasses to host a fraternity party. "Bourbon?"

He nodded, undoing his tie impatiently. Soon, the silk accessory found the jacket on the floor by the wall.

She fished several ice cubes from the icemaker with long, manicured fingers and let them drop into two glasses. Then she added bourbon generously from a bottle of Woodford Reserve and handed him one glass.

He took it and inhaled the scent of the alcohol. "Thanks, Carly, you're the best." He smiled, his eyes wandering to her full lips for a long moment, then dropping altitude to her cleavage. "Never thought I'd say this to anyone, but thanks for busting me out of jail."

Cut crystal glasses clinked, and they drank, Brian thirstily as if the bourbon were water. Carly took it slowly, savoring it absent-mindedly as if preoccupied with something.

"How about Kay?" she asked, licking her lips. She sat on a large leather armchair and crossed her legs, not overly concerned that her tight skirt was riding up her thigh.

"What about her?"

"She seemed eager to help you. Even get shot with you, which, I have to say, kind of beats the standing record of the worst client surrender I ever had."

Brian scoffed and rolled his eyes. "Kay? She's an angel, but I had to threaten, blackmail, and beg her to leave her cozy mountain resort job and come down here to do some real police work."

"She doesn't have jurisdiction, Brian. You heard Diaz."

A lopsided smile tugged at Brian's lips. "Yes, but she has

such a sense of what's right and wrong she'd kill herself to correct an injustice."

"*Your* injustice?" The innuendo was clear.

"Anyone's." Brian finished the bourbon and set the glass on the table. "That's what makes Kay so special. By the way, let me call her."

"Ah," Carly replied, then leaned against the back of her armchair and played with the ice cubes in her glass, studying them, making them clink with the golden swooshing liquid.

Brian speed-dialed Kay, pacing the living room slowly. The moment she took the call, he said, "It's me. I'm out. Any news of Holly?"

"Where are you?" Kay asked. She sounded a bit out of breath.

"I'm at the house. Our old house."

"Stay there, Brian. I'm coming over. Don't go out there and do anything stupid."

"I don't want to waste any time, Kay. Holly might not have a moment more."

"I'll be there soon, all right? Promise me you won't go anywhere until I get there. People are out to shoot you, Brian. Don't make their job easier for them. Stay put. Drapes closed. Light off. Make like a mouse."

His pacing quickened. "I know who has her, Kay, and we're wasting time. Believe me—"

"I think you have some idea who has her, and we'll follow your leads. When I get there. Is that clear?"

"Fine, whatever. Only don't take your damn sweet time."

He ended the call and dropped the phone on the large walnut table. It clattered and slid over.

"You talk to her like that, and she still helps you?"

He groaned, stopping in front of Carly with his lips pressed firmly together. "I'm an asshole, I know. But she wants me to wait here and do nothing when I could be out there, looking for my kid."

"She's the smarter one, trust me." Carly took another sip of bourbon, watching Brian unbutton his shirt. He peeled it off and sent it to the floor in a heap over the other items.

Her eyes clung to his well-defined pectorals. Brian noticed; he smiled and looked away. "I'll take a shower to get the jail stink off me. Pour yourself another drink if you'd like. Don't wait for me."

He left her sipping her drink by the window and entered the bathroom, his entire body craving the cleansing of a good shower. He dropped the last of his garments on the floor and stepped into the granite enclosure.

Setting the shower head on the strongest jets, he turned on the water, wincing when it reached his leg wound. He endured, watching traces of blood swirling in the water before going down the drain, then slathered generous amounts of Dior Sauvage shower gel on his weary body with energetic hand movements, foregoing the mesh sponge. The clear liquid turned into scented creamy foam under his hands, invigorating his muscles, awakening him.

He felt a whiff of colder air when the door opened, and Carly stepped in, naked. She squeezed a handful of gel into her palm and asked, "Can I do your back?" Her voice was low, sultry, filled with promises.

Grinning, he propped his hands against the tiles and allowed her to play with his body for a while, then turned to face her and pinned her against the wall with her hands above her head. She looked at him intensely, wanton, panting.

"You know, newly released ex-cons have strong urges," he whispered in her ear, kissing her neck and watching her body's reaction to his touch.

She leaned into him, welcoming his skilled fingers, wrapping herself around his body like a vine.

"It's dangerous to let a man fresh out of jail see you naked like this."

THIRTY-NINE
EVIDENCE

Before heading out to Brian's place, Kay met with Brockett in front of the SFPD Northern District precinct. When she'd called him asking to meet, she was expecting to find him out there, interviewing informers about Holly. He claimed he was doing that for a while and had just returned. Seemingly intrigued by her request to meet, he chose the parking lot, then stepped outside, warily looking around. Yesterday's shooting had left everyone a little jumpy.

"Any news?" she asked, although the answer was written all over his face.

His face was tired yet impenetrable. "Nothing. Not a word out there on the streets about this kid."

"That's unusual," Kay muttered, rubbing her forehead. The details of this case refused to make much sense, even after a few hours of sleep caught on the lumpy bed of a Redwood City motel. "What are the feds saying?"

Brockett seemed displeased with her question. "They're looking at other aspects. You should know, they consider the little girl alive until found dead; it's procedure."

"Uh-huh, and?" She failed to see what was wrong with that.

"It's been a week; her chances are really slim. And they're not exactly too forthcoming with information. I'm sure you remember that too."

She nodded, wondering if she should call in a favor or two with some former coworkers and get some information. First things first, she was there to speak with Brockett.

"Any chance I could see some crime scene photos, Detective?"

His shiny scalp creased above his eyebrows. "What do you want to know?"

"If there was anything else found on the kitchen table," she explained with a sigh. She had to explain; it was infuriating, but she had to be patient. "Something the cleaning crew might've disposed of."

"This is relevant, how, exactly?"

"Humor me."

Muttering something unintelligible, he took out his phone and started sifting through images. It would've probably been easier to go back inside and grab the case file, but then he would've risked being seen collaborating with her. A deathly sin in that precinct, or so it seemed.

"There."

She took the device and looked at the photos, squinting and struggling to make anything out in the bright sunshine. She held her breath, seeing Rachel's body in a pool of blood, from multiple angles, under strong crime scene lights and surrounded by numbered yellow markers. Then the kitchen table was photographed several times. On the grate she'd found on the table, there used to be a casserole with an herb-encrusted roast. A sliver of the crust was missing as if someone had used their fingers to peel off a piece of the mouthwatering roast and munch on it. A red plastic mixer bowl with mashed potatoes had also vanished from the table.

Rachel had cooked a Sunday dinner for Holly and herself

and had set the table for them to enjoy a good meal together before entering WITSEC.

Kay handed the phone back to Brockett. "Did you know Holly has a pacemaker?"

He frowned and propped his hand on his thigh. "What? No."

"The brochure was in plain sight, at the scene," she couldn't help mentioning, although it did little good but make the detective bristle. "If it's a modern device, we could trace it. Maybe... if we're lucky. It has to be registered, new enough, and in an area with an unsecured Wi-Fi."

He took out a cigarette and lit it, inhaling thirstily. "I'll get the subpoenas going. One for the hospital to disclose device details. Another one for the device maker to assist with locating the device. It's going to take days, maybe a week."

"Not good enough," Kay snapped. "Not fast enough." Her voice sounded cutting, abrasive, the last thing she wanted.

"If you have another way, Detective, then go ahead, knock yourself out." He filled his lungs with smoke, then exhaled abruptly.

"I'm going to quote you on that," Kay smiled, trying to appease him. It didn't serve any purpose to have the detective's blood boiling each time they spoke.

"Whatever gets you out of this ZIP Code faster," he said, studying the tip of his cigarette. "We done here?"

"Almost." She opened the trunk of her Interceptor with the remote. "I found the missing knife."

He threw the cigarette butt away with a forceful gesture of frustration. "What the hell? Who told you we were missing a knife?"

She tilted her head in disbelief and chuckled. "Wasn't that hard to figure out. Big knife block, one slot empty, the largest. Guess what's missing."

He seemed deflated, staring at the asphalt, hands on his

hips, stomping in place, so visibly eager to leave. Was that man on the take? Was he keen on locking Brian up for Rachel's murder, no matter what the evidence showed? If so, how did he persuade everyone else to follow along? Diaz, the ADA who'd okayed the arrest warrant, everyone in the criminal justice system? They couldn't all be on the take, could they?

Still, his posture, his body language didn't speak of a crooked cop—rather, a tired and discontented one, set in his own archaic ways of investigating crime, burned out to the point of not giving a crap anymore about what was right and what was wrong.

"That's not all I found." She grabbed the evidence bags from her trunk and handed them over. "Rachel's phone, low on battery. I packed the charger too. The passcode is one, two, three, zero."

"How on earth would you know that?" He stared at her in disbelief, but Kay thought she'd caught a flicker of respect in the glint of his brown eyes. "When was the last time you saw her?"

"Eight years ago. The passcode is her daughter's birthday. Not rocket science. Thought I'd save you the time you'd spend trying to unlock it."

"And what's this?" He held up the bag containing the place mat and silverware.

"These were found in the dishwasher, and so was the phone. Rachel tried—"

Brockett scoffed and clapped his hands together once in a gesture of annoyance. "Sure, 'cause that's where people keep their damn phones, in the dishwasher." Visibly embittered for having missed so much evidence at the scene, he lit another cigarette. "Jeez... the world has gone insane."

She waited for him to finish his defensive ranting, then tried to get her message across again. "Rachel hid her daughter's place mat, plate, and silverware in the dishwasher, then faced off her attacker with that knife to give her time to escape. At the time of her death, Holly was there."

A flicker of real interest sparked in his eyes. "We have a timeline now."

"Yes, we do."

"What do you think happened? I walked the scene, but I couldn't tell." Another drag on his second cigarette inflamed the tip. Smoke swirled in the air for mere split seconds before being dissipated by the chilly wind.

"You weren't looking for a kid, Detective." She paused for a moment, letting him take it in. "I could picture what happened. Rachel saw someone was coming. She must've realized that the visitor was trouble, perhaps because she'd realized the risk she'd taken by agreeing to testify, by telling the ADA what she saw the night that kid got shot. Maybe that's why she called her mother and told her Holly was already in protective custody... Just in case they were monitoring her calls, to throw them a curveball and protect her daughter. I'm speculating here; maybe we'll never know."

She stopped for a moment, processing what she'd just said. She shouldn't tell Brockett what she'd learned from Leonetti, not before she could be sure he wasn't on the take. It was better to stick to what she'd learned at the crime scene. "She sent Holly into the backyard, barefoot, then maybe gave Holly her own shoes, I believe, because Rachel's body was found barefoot, and I found footprints in the backyard that speak to the little girl being barefoot and, respectively, wearing her mom's sneakers."

Brockett listened intently, the burning cigarette hanging between his fingers, his head slightly lowered. "Yeah, it had rained earlier that night and has been dry since. Footprints would've lasted."

"Then Rachel must've taken everything that spoke of Holly's presence in the house and shoved it where she could, the dishwasher, to buy her daughter more time to run and hide. Then she went to open the door."

Brockett nodded. "It makes sense."

"It explains why the door wasn't jimmied or broken." She pointed at the evidence bag holding the knife. "And it explains this, and why I found it under the same dishwasher. When Rachel fell, it must've dropped to the floor and slipped underneath." She let out a long sigh, feeling her chest tightening as if gripped by a steel claw.

Fear.

What if Holly was already dead?

"From what I could tell, the little girl climbed up the tree and fell when a branch snapped. It was a pretty high-up branch, about seven feet from the ground. She must've yelped. It doesn't explain why the unsub didn't kill her where he found her or in the house."

Brockett stared at the evidence bags he was holding with a look of pure dismay on his face. "I just had my ass handed to me, by a country cop no less. I must be getting old." He scoffed bitterly. "You're a bit more than just Brian's ex, the troublemaker from the hills. What are you planning to do next?"

"Follow the pacemaker and hope we're not too late. Before I go, tell me about the tire track lifted from Rachel's driveway. Was it the same Suburban model that chased us yesterday?"

He seemed surprised by her question. "That? No. It's from Brian's sports car, an old Chevy Corvette. It was eliminated." He shook her hand, this time vigorously. "Godspeed, Detective. I'll put in for the subpoenas, just in case you need them. And I'll spend a few hours now explaining to my boss and the feds why I didn't find these items the first time around." He gave the evidence bags a quick glare.

Kay climbed behind the wheel and started the engine. Brian would perhaps know something about Holly's pacemaker, although he didn't seem to be close to any real parenting issue regarding his daughter. However, someone else would know every single detail, and Kay didn't have any time to lose.

Driving off toward Brian's house, she called the US Marshal's number. It went straight to voicemail.

"Debra, it's Kay Sharp. We have a development, and I need your help. Ciara would know everything about the pacemaker her granddaughter has. When it was implanted, where, at which hospital, which doctor. I know she can't call me, but I'm hoping you can give me this information. Don't need to tell you time is of the essence."

She'd barely reached the highway when her phone rang. The display showed Debra's number.

"Detective," the US Marshal said somberly, "I thought you knew, I'm so sorry. Mrs. Epling had a stroke on the way to the safe house. She's in the hospital, in a coma."

Holly woke up with a start. The voices upstairs were louder than usual, distant and muffled, but there was something different this time.

The woman's voice was piercing, loaded with tears, sobbing and pleading, and the man's was angry, threatening. Muted thumps that made the floors creak marked every time the man paced toward the part of the house where the stairs were. The sound of a slammed door in rage rattled the walls.

The basement was chilly, although the sun was up, sending slivers of light across the room. Shivering, Holly slipped off the bed and landed on the cold, concrete floor with bare feet. Then she went over by the fireplace and placed her ear against the wall.

"I can't shoot her, Edmundo, *por favor*," the woman was saying. "She's just a kid. She's confused. I don't think she saw much. She would've told me."

"Enough!" A thump, and then something rattled as if the man had slammed his fist against a table filled with dishes and silverware. "We don't have a choice here, Isabela. It's her life or ours. Don't you get that? The boss was clear about it. If she's seen anything, she has to die."

Holly whimpered, her eyes filling with tears as she kept her trembling hand over her mouth to stay quiet.

"*Te lo ruego*, Edmundo," the woman cried. "Just a little girl. Can't we say she escaped and just let her go?"

Hope filled Holly's chest for a brief moment until she heard the sound of a blow, and the woman shrieked, then started sobbing loudly.

"Don't you get any crazy ideas, bitch! I'll end you where you stand."

He paced for a while as the woman kept on sobbing. Then the sobs turned into breathless whimpers. "We're going straight to hell for this," she said.

Her comment made the man burst into laughter. "You've shot people before. What made you think you were going anywhere else?" A few more muted thumps. "We took an oath, *querida,* both of us, to obey all orders. He wants you to shoot her. He probably wants to test you."

"Please, Edmundo, don't make me. Not a little girl like that."

The sound of metal scraping against metal resounded loudly. "We can't risk the little twerp opening her mouth and sending us all to jail. I'm so damn tired of this. I'll do it." A pause, quiet enough for Holly's heart to thump loudly and be the only thing the little girl heard. "I'm disappointed in you, *querida.* I never took you for a coward."

Then a door squeaked as if opened, and Holly froze, fear strangling her, stopping the breath in her chest. Desperate, she looked around but didn't find anywhere to hide. Under the bed, yes, but it would be the first place they'd look.

Footfalls drew nearer as one of them climbed down, probably the man. Out of options, Holly snuck into the fireplace and started climbing up the chimney, her bare feet using the bricks for support, her back against the narrow walls, her hands pushing against the wall to lift herself. She stopped moving when the basement door swung open and held her breath, hoping she'd climbed high enough.

The man entered the room and paced around. "Where the fuck is she?" His voice was high-pitched, confused, enraged. "Isabela?" he called loudly, then punched the wall next to the fireplace. Tiny bits of cinder fell to the hearth, some on Holly's head. "Get down here, woman!"

Heavy, rushed footfalls down the stairs. "What happened?" the woman asked, then shrieked in pain.

"Don't tell me you knew nothing of this," he growled, then the woman's body landed on the floor with a heavy thud. "Where the hell is she, Isabela? Did you let her go?"

"*Te lo juro,* no. I swear on my life. You have to believe me." Whimpering, she crawled away from where Holly could see part of her body. "She was here when I left her this morning."

"Did you think to lock the fucking door?" His voice was a low, threatening whisper.

The woman didn't answer, just whimpered again.

Footsteps rushed up the stairs, probably the man's. Holly heard him call some names, then tell someone, "Find her. She can't be far."

"Yes, boss," someone replied.

Then the woman climbed the stairs, leaving the basement door ajar. Upstairs, the crying resumed, but Holly wasn't paying attention anymore. She couldn't last much longer in that chimney. Her hands and feet were cramping from holding on too long, and she was freezing.

As soon as she dared, she slid down carefully from the chimney and tiptoed over to the bed. She needed to pee badly but didn't dare to use the decrepit toilet, afraid of the noise it would make. Instead, she slid under the bed, where they had looked before and weren't going to look again. And when they finally went away to look for her outside, she'd climb upstairs and run.

Keeping her eyes fixed on the door, she didn't notice the trail of ash and cinder bits she'd left behind on the floor.

FORTY-ONE
STACEY

Tears burned Kay's eyes as she drove to Brian's place. Since she'd arrived yesterday in the city that had been her home for more than ten years, she'd been a disoriented zombie, lost, unable to catch up, out-of-breath, chasing shadows. It sometimes felt like an out-of-body experience or one of those vivid nightmares that feel unnervingly real. She couldn't figure out who she could trust at SFPD. She couldn't trust her instincts anymore, not with Brian, not with anyone else. And she was losing people she cared deeply about, faster than she could handle. First Rachel, now Ciara. At her age, a stroke could be devastating and debilitating, even fatal. She couldn't believe she could've already had her last conversation with Ciara or shared their last hug.

She needed someone she could talk to and trust with all her heart.

Elliot.

She recalled his number on the media center screen and pressed to connect. He took the call almost immediately.

"Kay..." He sounded breathless. "Are you all right?"

"Yes, I'm fine. Why do you ask?" She did her best to hide the tears that overwhelmed her when she heard his voice.

"No, you're not. I can hear it." He paused for a moment while silence filled the air between them. "What happened?"

His voice was strong, warm, his presence on the call a shoulder she could lean on even from a distance. She blinked away fresh tears. "It's Ciara, Rachel's mother. She had a stroke. I'm afraid I'm going to lose her too."

"Come home," he pleaded, the intensity in his voice not something she'd heard before.

"Soon, maybe even tonight. I promise." She wiped her tears with her fingers and muted the mic while she sniffled and cleared her voice.

"I know you don't want me there, Kay. But if you change your mind—"

"I'll be coming home soon. I have a strong lead on Rachel's daughter. If that pans out, it won't take much longer. A few hours at the most. If not... we might never find her."

"Did you get any rest last night?" He knew her too well.

"Yes, I did, actually." She tried to put some cheerfulness in her voice, but it sounded fake to her own ears, forced. The silence grew heavy for a moment. "Brian spent the night in jail, and I visited an old motel I knew by the bay."

"Can you be honest with me for a moment, Kay?"

"What do you mean?" His question surprised and hurt her, although she'd been holding back quite a bit. He was an excellent cop; of course, he'd see through her lies.

"I mean, give me a straight answer to a straight question?"

"All right, shoot." She held her breath.

"Are you still in danger?"

"Of what?" The deflecting question left her lips instinctively before she had a chance to think about it. He'd asked for honesty, and she was avoiding the issue.

"Kay, please."

She forced some air into her lungs. "I honestly don't know. They tried to kill Brian yesterday, not me. I believe I was collateral damage or maybe the wind was blowing too hard, and the sniper missed." She swallowed with difficulty, her throat dry, constricted. "I can't think of a reason why they'd want me dead, but I'll be careful anyway. I promise." A sense of doom unfurled in her gut, knowing she was making promises she couldn't keep.

"A sniper could be a mile away. You'd never see it coming, Kay." A beat. "I can't lose you."

Hearing his words, her heart swelled. For a moment, she couldn't speak, afraid of the tears she was still fighting. "I'll be on my way soon. The moment I find Holly, I'm leaving this place in my rearview mirror."

"And your ex? What about his murder charge?"

"I've done all I could," she said, doubting that statement and herself at the same time. "He's out on bail, and he's a good cop. He has plenty of time to find out who killed his fiancée." A brief silence ensued while Kay waited for Elliot to say something. "Dinner when I get back?"

"You're on." He still sounded tense.

She ended the call, as she turned onto the cul-de-sac she'd called home for a while eight years ago. She loved the street name, Cedarwood Court; she always had. It made her think of Christmases spent on the beach, where the salty sea air brought out the smell of cedar sap.

Brian's house was a brick bungalow with a three-car garage, a rare find in the cramped and overpriced San Francisco Bay Area. It was large by local standards and well maintained, with trimmed shrubs and a clean-swept driveway. Probably he had people doing it; no matter how hard she tried, Kay couldn't envision Brian grooming anything else but himself.

A red 1967 Corvette Stingray was parked in the driveway. "Stacey," Kay muttered as she approached the car. Brian had named his car Stacey after the movie *Gone in 60 Seconds*. He used to be obsessed with that movie and with all the cars in it. He knew all sixty by heart, makes, models, years, and girl nicknames. Then, when they'd just started dating, he'd found the Stingray for sale for a ridiculous amount of money, but he didn't care. He took two lines of credit at two different banks and wiped his savings account clean but "nailed Stacey," in his own words. And there she was, proud and shiny and red. Brian hadn't cheated on Stacey yet.

Remembering the tire tracks she'd seen at Rachel's house, Kay crouched by the car and looked at the rear wheels, comparing them with the picture she'd taken. It was a perfect match. Brockett was right.

She rang the bell twice, eager to get going. With Ciara unable to help, her only hope to follow Holly's pacemaker was Brian. Her strategy made much more sense than busting into gangsters' homes with guns drawn to get information.

He opened the door and smiled the moment he saw her. He smelled of the same shower gel she remembered, and his hair was still moist, falling in black rebel strands on his forehead. He was dressed in slacks and a clean shirt, still buttoning it up. Before she could react, he wrapped her in a hug and pulled her inside like old times, then kicked the door shut. "Oh, Kay, I'm so grateful you're here." He placed a quick kiss on her lips, one she didn't welcome. "I missed you."

"I find that hard to believe." She pulled away, uncomfortable with what the scent of him did to her senses, and angry she was taken for granted, considered a foregone conclusion because no woman ever resisted him. She wouldn't fall back into his life or into bed with him. She realized something about him that moment, watching him let her go with unabated self-confidence, which explained his success with women. Brian was intoxicating to the senses, addictive like heroin, and equally inescapable.

The bedroom door opened and Carly stepped out, wrapped

in a towel and drying her hair with another. Her bare feet left wet footprints on the hardwood. "Should we get some lunch while—" She froze in midsentence when she lifted her eyes and saw Kay. "Oh."

"I'm glad to see you're well represented," Kay said, hiding her initial shock behind sarcasm. "Jeez, Brian, you're incorrigible. But I guess I don't have to worry about your trial anymore."

Carly resumed drying her hair with vigorous moves. She stood tall and unfazed, her perfect body flaunted with arrogant self-confidence. The towel barely covered her buttocks, but she didn't seem to care. "I'm not defending him at trial."

Strange. Kay shrugged, forcing herself to not give a damn. "I didn't see your Beemer in the driveway."

"It's in the garage," Brian replied. "Carly doesn't want dust on it." He stepped away, walking with a slight limp, and grabbed a glass from the table. It still had some remnants of liquor in it, and he downed it with one thirsty gulp. His eyes sparkled with secret enjoyment as if seeing the two women in his living room did something for him, something Kay couldn't grasp. The half-naked lawyer dripping water on his floor didn't make her jealous, but maybe he thought she did.

Carly disappeared into the bedroom without saying another word, walking slowly with a sway in her hips, then closing the door quietly.

"How's your arm?" Brian continued buttoning up his shirt with methodical gestures, then put on his favorite cuff links, the gold ones with five oval rubies mounted to form an X, a cherished gift from his father. She'd seen him put those on countless times, sometimes sitting on the side of the bed, caressing her skin before leaving for work.

"I'm okay." Somewhat hesitant, she walked through the living room that she knew well, trying not to remember all the things she'd willed herself to forget. The places where they'd made love. The leather sofa they'd picked together at Macy's.

The painting of a fluffy white dog they bought from a street vendor by the pier.

Yet some things were new. A late-model Roomba, charging at its station in the corner. An eighty-inch TV on the wall. Original, branded Swarovski cut crystal glasses and bottle. And probably satin sheets on the bed, although Kay didn't care to verify her assumption in person. It seemed as if he lived above his means, but there was no mortgage weighing him down and probably no car payments either.

"How come you kept this house?" Kay asked. "You could've made a fortune selling it. Or renting it." He grinned and handed her a glass she refused to take. "This isn't a social visit."

Brian didn't reply. He looked out the window. Then he pulled out a drawer, extracted a Glock, and slipped the holster clip on his belt. He pulled out the weapon from its holster, checked its ammo, and then put it back.

"I thought you would've lived here with Rachel and her daughter," Kay insisted.

He smiled uneasily. "It used to be ours, yours and mine." His voice was low, melancholy. "I hate the thought of not having it, of having our memories erased, superimposed with another life, with someone else."

Kay's eyebrows raised in surprise, finding herself at a loss for words for a moment. "And where were you and Rachel planning to—"

"Enough about us, let's find Holly. She's all I have left now. I'm ready to go." He walked over to her with determination and urgency in his step. "She has a heart condition. Too much stress could do a lot of damage."

"Tell me about her pacemaker, Brian."

He seemed surprised but contained it well. Kay hadn't told him about her visit to the crime scene.

"Nothing I can tell. I haven't been involved much in her life. I know of it, but very little else." He stared at the floor for a while, seeming embarrassed. "My parental skills were limited to writing alimony checks and buying gifts, and occasionally showing Holly a good time." He sighed and plunged his hands into his pockets. "If we're lucky enough to find her, I guess that will have to change."

"So then, you're not a real father to her." Kay's voice was cutting, cold. "Why am I not surprised?"

"Yeah, I guess you could say that," he replied. A flicker of anger lit his eyes. "You shouldn't judge me. I'm trying. It's not like I ever wanted kids. But once I saw her the first time and I held her in my arms, everything changed. *I* changed. Is it really that hard to believe I love my daughter with all my heart?"

His gaze softened after a while and veered off, then he looked at his watch. Kay checked hers. There were many questions still unanswered, but time was running out.

Carly emerged from the bedroom fully clothed but barefoot. She walked toward the window, where she'd kicked off her shoes by the coffee table and where a lipstick-stained glass still had about a finger of bourbon on the bottom. She downed it unceremoniously while slipping on her heels, then walked out, dangling her car key fob in her hand. "Good luck, Brian," she said, just before the door closed behind her.

Brian didn't react. It was as if she'd never been there. He checked the time again, seemingly nervous, but didn't say anything.

"In court, after your arraignment, you said you knew who has Holly. Tell me what you know."

He looked at her for a long, silent moment as if to figure out if he could trust her. Kay found his hesitation infuriating.

"I know who killed that street punk, Oliver Galaz, in the shooting Rachel witnessed. That's my starting point."

FORTY-TWO
TAGS

Katse Coffee Shop brimmed with chatter, laughter, and the clattering and hissing sounds of a busy café during lunch hour. The smell of strong java and freshly baked pastries enlivened Elliot's stomach, reminding him he hadn't had a bite to eat since the night before when a Hilltop burger washed down with a cold Heineken was all he'd had time for.

Behind the counter, Tommy MacPherson was moving unbelievably fast for his girth, beads of sweat covering his forehead. His face was flushed, constantly exposed to heat coming from the ovens and the coffee makers. When he saw Elliot, a line of worry creased his brow.

"I get lots of attention from cops lately, if you don't mind me saying." He pressed a button on the cappuccino machine, and steam started blowing through a small stainless-steel pipe into a cup of milk, frothing the liquid. "I get some business too, and I appreciate that, but, hey, you know, I still have PTS from my former life."

Elliot chuckled. Tommy MacPherson had straightened his life after serving a couple of years for a slew of minor felonies.

Fresh out of jail, he'd taken the family business to the next level, realizing it was a better alternative than the reckless stunts he'd pulled for money in his misguided youth. His self-deprecating humor was ignited whenever one of the cops came for coffee and, heaven forbid, donuts. When an order of donuts was involved, he went on a roll, and there was no stopping him.

Unlike many ex-cons, Tommy didn't hate cops. He'd grown better than that, the twenty years of hard work he'd put into the coffee shop lending him wisdom and perspective. For instance, he knew well that he should've worn a cap and beard netting while serving food and coffee behind that counter, but he rarely did. In his own words, he looked unattractive enough to need any help in that department.

Tommy's finger released the button, and the hissing stopped. Satisfied, he took the cup of frothed milk and, using a knife, skimmed the top, transferring it into a fresh-brewed cup of coffee. Then he handed it to a middle-aged woman and ran her card.

"What can I get you, Detective?" Seemingly worried, Tommy gazed at the laptop Elliot kept under his arm.

"Coffee, a sandwich, and some of your time."

"Whoa," Tommy feigned fear with amusement in his eyes. "How much time am I doing now?"

Elliot couldn't help but laugh. In a small town like theirs, everyone knew everyone and everything about everyone. Tommy's humorous approach had served him well, putting people's fears about his background at ease. Otherwise, his business could've failed, as not many local residents were willing to take coffee and food from the hands of an ex-con. "Just twenty minutes or so."

"What will you have on that sandwich?"

Elliot shrugged. "Whatever you got ready. I'm pressed for time."

"Cool." He poured him a tall cup of coffee, put the lid on it, then extracted a sandwich packaged in shrink wrap from the fridge. "Ham and cheese okay?"

"Perfect." Elliot gave him his card. Tommy refused to take it at first, then ran it in the usual dance he did every time one of the local cops placed an order. Then he whistled, and a young man wearing a white apron stained with coffee and cocoa powder came out from the back. "Cover for me, all right?"

The young man nodded, then took the order from the next person in line.

"What can I do you for?" Tommy asked, wiping his hands on his apron.

"I need to see your security camera feeds for Wednesday morning."

He scratched behind his ear. "For when Taylor Lorentz was killed? I was wondering when you'd come by looking for that."

Elliot swallowed a curse. It had taken him a while to think of Katse's video surveillance, and only as a last-resort measure. The crime scene, miles away from any camera and situated in pristine woods by Frozen Falls, didn't immediately have him think of video surveillance.

"Yeah, well, let's see if we get lucky," Elliot mumbled, following Tommy to the back of the coffee shop.

The surveillance system was housed on a small table propped against the wall between supplies neatly arranged on steel shelving. Coffee beans in brown burlap bags filled the space with an intense aroma. A monitor, a control unit, and a keyboard with a mouse were placed on the small, crooked table that probably used to be part of the old patio furniture.

Tommy moved the mouse, and the screen lit up with a view of multiple cameras, six trained on the inside of the café, only two showing views from the patio. "Which one do you want?"

One of them caught a slice of highway but from that angle,

he'd only see the cars passing by, perhaps catch a glimpse of the driver's profile and no tags. The second one was aimed at the far side of the patio along the highway and the fence. It barely caught a sliver of highway at a distance, but at the right angle to land on vehicle tags.

"This one," Elliot pointed at the latter. "Let's go back to six in the morning on Wednesday."

Tommy pulled over a rusty, old wrought iron chair and invited Elliot to sit. He remained standing, his curious nature tethering him to what Elliot was doing.

He watched the video for about a minute and saw Taylor's silhouette running past Katse at 6:02 a.m. when the light was so dim, he barely noticed her slim figure against the grainy background. Then nothing. Not a single car passed for a while. "Any way we can speed this up?"

"Sure," Tommy said, demonstrating how. "If you hover over the image, the controls pop up. Just click on the double arrow as many times as you like."

Elliot clicked the double arrow once, increasing the speed at which absolutely nothing happened on the screen, only the time code digits moved faster. Then he clicked again and again. When a car finally passed, it moved so quickly he nearly missed it, a brief streak of red on the pixelated image.

"There," Tommy said excitedly, but Elliot had already stopped the fast forward and was rewinding the feed. He went frame by frame when the car was in view until he caught a glimpse of the tag. Opening his laptop, he brought up the DMV screen and searched for the vehicle owner. The time code read 6:07.

"I know her," Tommy said. "She's the receptionist at the new La Quinta. Miriam something."

The DMV search screen loaded, displaying the driver's license and vehicle registration. Tommy was right.

"This was headed north, right?" Elliot asked, realizing he didn't know the exact orientation of the camera.

"Yeah, she's going to work. Sometimes she stops for coffee."

Of course she did. The entire county stopped for coffee at Katse.

The vehicles going left to right on the screen were driving north; the others were southbound. A lopsided smile tugged at Elliot's lips. The valley didn't have other roads or entry points; Taylor's killer had driven northbound or southbound on that road and had passed in front of Tommy's camera. Unless he'd driven from the north with the purpose of killing Taylor, and had turned around and drove back afterward, when the job was done. Not likely.

He noted down the first vehicle's make and model, time code, and the letter N for direction on a piece of paper borrowed from Tommy, and resumed watching. Not much traffic went into the valley at that early time of day.

The next vehicle was a southbound white Ford sedan, a rental car, at 6:15 a.m. An out-of-state tag was next at 6:21 a.m., probably going home to Washington. It belonged to a Seattle businessman and it was a gray Acura SUV.

Then a white Toyota Tacoma truck zoomed through, headed south. It was a California tag, partially obscured by the rising sun's glare. Elliot couldn't make it out.

"I know that one," Tommy said, pointing at the screen. "It's Roger's new truck." Elliot frowned, unsure who he was talking about. "Roger the plumber? I forgot his business name. Everyone knows him as Roger the plumber." Tommy chuckled. "Just like they know me as Tommy the coffee guy."

Elliot checked the partial digits anyway and found the truck; it was registered to Mount Chester Plumbing.

At 6:43 a.m. a black Chevy Suburban zoomed by, going north fast, probably over the limit. Elliot looked at Tommy, but he shook his head. The DMV database showed the vehicle registered to a business in San Francisco, an LLC.

He'd have to ask Kay to track it down and interview the driver.

Time code 6:49 a.m. gave him a southbound brown Hyundai that Tommy immediately recognized. It belonged to the local high school science teacher, a man by the name of Frank Livingston, the science teacher Mr. Lorentz had mentioned. They had crossed paths before when Elliot and Kay were investigating the Angel Creek murder-kidnapping.

For about eighteen minutes, no one else drove on that stretch of highway. Then a bottled water delivery truck headed north drove past at 7:01 a.m.

"I know this guy," Tommy replied before Elliot could run the DMV search. "He stops by every night at the end of his shift, to get some goodies for the wife and kids. His name is Bob. I'll have him call you tonight."

"Thanks, Tommy." Elliot gave the surveillance video another ten minutes of his time, completing the list of all vehicles that had passed by. At 7:09 a.m., Deputy Leach's vehicle drove northbound. At 7:14 a.m., it drove back up the hill. Some search Leach had performed, not even four full minutes. Elliot stopped the video when Tommy recognized Gabriel Lorentz's car. He knew from the man's statement that he'd found no one at the scene, no stopped cars, no pedestrians, not a soul. By then, the killer had vanished.

Armed with loads of data and images about early morning vehicles and their drivers, Elliot thanked Tommy and shook his hand.

"Glad to help," Tommy said, grinning widely. "But what if the perp drove southbound to Frozen Falls, then turned around and went back north? Then he never reached my place, and he's not on this video."

Elliot put his hat on and opened the door for a rushed

woman carrying four tall coffee cups in a carton. "You'd make an excellent sleuth, Tommy."

Back in his car, he looked at the list of vehicles briefly, but didn't waste much time deciding.

La Quinta was only two miles away.

FORTY-THREE
LAYERS

Kay stared at Brian in disbelief. As always, getting a straight answer out of him was next to impossible. "You know who shot that street dealer, Oliver Galaz?" She stepped closer to him until there were mere inches between their faces. Her eyes were fixed on his pupils. "I thought I'd made myself clear, Brian. No more lies."

"I'm not lying." He stood calmly, allowing her to scrutinize him, unflinching.

"You told me you had no idea what Rachel had witnessed."

"That's correct."

"Then? Which statement should I believe?" She groaned and rolled her eyes. "I'm so tired of your games, Brian. You're about to stand trial for a murder you say you didn't commit. People are out there looking to put a bullet through your skull, and you still withhold information from me? I must be the world's biggest idiot, still wasting my time with you." Her question had turned into a rant that didn't end until she ran out of breath.

"You can believe both because they're both true."

Angry as hell, Kay propped her hand on her hip. "Really?"

"Rachel never told me what she saw. Later, I figured out who killed Oliver Galaz. That simple."

Kay looked at him, wondering what made her lose her sanity whenever talking with Brian. It *was* simple, had she only thought him capable of telling the truth. He had been truthful, yet she'd assumed otherwise. Deep inside, the lies he'd told her about sleeping with Rachel and other women when they were still married colored every statement he made now. She couldn't separate the two worlds, past and present, no matter how hard she tried.

She sighed. "Who did they arrest?"

Brian shrugged. "Nobody, as far as I know." He kept his hands in his pockets and remained standing in front of her calmly. "You don't think I'd repeat Rachel's mistake and start running my big mouth to the ADA, do you?" His voice carried undertones of sarcasm and sorrow. He must've believed Rachel had been killed because she'd been stupid.

The thought of that infuriated Kay. "Some people sacrifice themselves and do the right thing, Brian, and that's something to take pride in, not contempt." She shook her head, realizing she was wasting her time. The narcissist in Brian probably resented Rachel for having put truth and justice ahead of his personal needs. "Tell me where to find Holly."

"I can tell you where to start." He arranged the knot of his tie, then walked over to the bottle and poured some more liquor in his glass, then downed it with one swift move. "From the gang that took out Oliver Galaz."

"Okay, then," Kay said, looking at the time again. "Tell me what you know about the Galaz shooting."

He sat in an armchair with some difficulty, touching his leg where the bullet had ripped through his thigh muscle. "Word on the street is, our friend Galaz was skimming, keeping for himself a part of the proceeds. The organization wanted to make an example out of him." While he spoke, he took out a phone from his pocket and quickly typed something on the screen, then dropped it back into his pocket. A familiar chime confirmed a text message had been sent.

"What organization?" Kay decided to keep for herself the details of her conversation with ADA Leonetti. She wondered how come Brian hadn't asked her about that. Maybe he'd had too much on his mind with the arraignment and now with Holly missing.

"You didn't work organized crime when you were in the FBI, right?" Another chime announced the arrival of a new message on Brian's phone, but he didn't seem interested in checking.

"No, I didn't."

"We had gang wars on these streets for a couple of years. It started sometime after our divorce. The Street Kings battled the Norteños—those names ring a bell?"

"Yeah, keep going."

"A new gang emerged from the bloodied remnants of the two. The killing was the worst in Oakland, not here, and that's where this new gang is centered. They're called La Vida Sangrienta." He looked at Kay for a moment. "I wasn't on the organized crime task force, and everything I learned I pieced together myself after Rachel was killed." He ran his fingers through his hair. "That's why they killed her, for witnessing LVS in action. Then Brockett was quick to point his finger at me, the sad sack of shit. I'm willing to bet he's LVS himself."

Kay was waiting for him to finish, but he stopped talking and looked at his hands folded in his lap. "And?"

"And Galaz was LVS," he added, using the gang's acronym. "So that's who killed him, and that's who's out there, looking to shoot me. Maybe you too. I would've never involved you in this if I knew it would put your life in danger. I'm so sorry, Kay."

Feeling her rage coming back, Kay scoffed. "Don't tell me

the entire organization pulled that trigger. Do you or don't you know the name of the person who killed Galaz?"

"Maybe." She wanted to slap him. "I know a few LVS, and I want us to start banging on doors tonight, work our way up the gangbanger food chain. If Holly's out there, they have her; I'm sure of it."

"Tell me again, why did Brockett pin it on you? What do they have?"

He stood and started pacing the floor angrily with a slight limp. "For the fiftieth time, Kay, my fingerprints are all over that scene."

"You didn't live there, did you?"

"No, but I visited often enough. Sometimes I spent the night."

"And Brockett didn't know Rachel was your fiancée? They must've known; they're your coworkers."

He stopped pacing and lowered his gaze for a moment. "A few of the other cops knew I was, um, cheating on her. They'd seen me out with other women. Brockett said it could've been motive, said we argued over my cheating, and I lost my temper. Stupid."

Kay chuckled bitterly. "Of course, you were cheating on her. What else is new?" She breathed, willing herself to stay calm for the sake of that little girl. But there was something about Brian's words, the way he explained things, that made her think he wasn't telling her everything he knew. "Brockett said you left the scene before he got there. Is that true?"

"I was trying to catch up with the killer." He cruised by the bottle of liquor for another quick fix. "Blood was still gushing from her chest wounds when I found her. She'd been dead maybe a minute or two, maybe five." His voice broke. "I thought I had a chance to catch him. But Brockett didn't believe me. The Ring camera on a neighbor's door caught my Stacey leaving the scene, not anyone else's vehicle."

"Ah, there's video," Kay whispered. Getting the facts from Brian was like peeling an old, yellow onion, layer by layer, to get to the core. And it always ended in tears. "This is the first time I've heard of it."

"It's not like we have video evidence of anything," he shouted, resuming his limp pacing, then stopping squarely in front of her. "Would it kill you to believe me just this once, Kay? Huh? What would happen if you understood I sleep around, but I'm not a murderer? It's not the same thing, you know. Fooling around is not illegal." He walked away from her just as she lowered her gaze, embarrassed.

He'd come to her for help. He'd trusted her with his life. Why would he lie to her?

She breathed a couple of times to steady herself. "Tell me about this Ring camera video."

He stared out the window, leaning his forehead against the glass. Outside, the shadows grew longer. "I don't know why the killer's car doesn't show. Maybe the motherfucker *walked* over to Rachel's. The stupid camera only covers half the road." He raised his voice to the point of shouting, still facing away from her. "I don't know, all right? I wasn't there!" He pounded against the glass with his fist. The window resisted.

"All right, Brian." She drew closer and touched his shoulder. "I believe you."

He turned to face her, visibly distraught. "I kept telling Brockett, hey, I'm a cop. If I want someone dead, I know ways to do it, so no one will know. No one would ever find the body. But Brockett's on the LVS payroll; I'm willing to bet my life on it. That's what's going on here. The Sangrientas are tying up loose ends, and I'm one of them." He took both her hands in his and squeezed, looking at her intently. "Please, let's go. Let's find Holly."

FORTY-FOUR
SUSPECT

The La Quinta Inn & Suites in Mount Chester was about two miles east of Katse, on the winding road that led to the slopes on the southern versant of the mountain. It was new and had already attracted hordes of tourists, filling the parking lot every weekend starting Thursday evening through Sunday. The room rates were more affordable than the Winter Lodge Hotel, appealing to a younger crowd.

A young couple emerged from the reception area through automatic sliding doors as Elliot pulled under the porte cochere and cut the engine. The woman held the leash of a large poodle that took immense interest in Elliot's Ford. She tugged at the leash, but the animal's nose seemed glued to the front wheel of his SUV.

"Sorry," she said, tugging away at the reluctant canine. To her flushed embarrassment, the dog lifted his rear leg and left his mark on the tire, looking straight at Elliot the entire time.

Elliot grinned, waving her concerns away, and walked toward the lobby entrance. As the doors opened, he heard the woman say to her human companion, "He doesn't look it, but I think he's a cop. I saw his badge."

Maybe he didn't really look it. He'd remained faithful to his Texas attire, whitewashed Levi's over cowboy boots and a shirt, a belt buckle large enough to eat dinner from, and one of the wide-brimmed Stetson hats he couldn't leave the house without. He stood out from the typical California crowd, tourists included. To the locals, he'd always been the new cop who looked like a cowboy, or shorter, the cowboy cop. And he'd grown to like it just as much as he liked the mountain air and the early morning horse rides through the misty meadows.

He approached the reception desk and waited until the receptionist finished checking in a customer. The hotel was almost full; it wasn't at all surprising for a Friday afternoon. Up on the Mount Chester slopes, fresh snow had fallen and glittered under the powerful lights of the chairlift, promising tourists an excellent weekend.

The customer took his room key card and left. He advanced to the counter, showing his badge to a thin redhead whose nametag read *Miriam*.

"I have a few questions if you could spare a minute."

She smiled awkwardly. "Just a moment, please." She called a number and whispered into the phone, "I need you to take over." Then she hung up, and her professional smile reappeared. "What can I do for you?" She beckoned him to follow her as she stepped to the side, out of the tourists' earshot.

A bulky man showed up a moment later and started checking customers in. He wore a tag that said *Manager*.

Elliot pulled the image of Miriam's car driving past Katse Coffee Shop on Wednesday morning. "Is this your car?"

She frowned and studied the photo for a moment. "Y— yeah, that's mine. What's wrong?"

"This was taken two days ago at six-oh-seven in the morning as you were driving past Katse." She listened with eyes widened, a mix of angst and curiosity. "Did you see anyone as you drove through the valley?"

Her hand rushed to her chest. "Oh, God... I know what this is about. That poor girl, the jogger, right? She was killed on that stretch of highway. I saw it on the news."

"Did you see anything?" Elliot repeated.

She nodded and swallowed. "Yes. I saw the poor girl running. She was alone, and it was barely light. The day before yesterday wasn't the first time."

"Where was she when you passed her?"

"She'd just started downhill, past Katse."

"Did you see anyone else?"

She shook her head and bit her lip nervously. "Uh-uh, no one."

"Any cars, maybe stopped on the side of the road?"

"No, there wasn't anyone. I would've remembered. I'm always a little afraid when I drive through the valley. There's no phone coverage, and if my jalopy ever breaks down..." Her words trailed off.

"What time did you get to work that morning?"

She threw her manager a quick, worried look, then lowered her voice. "At six-twenty-five. I was late."

"Thank you, Miriam." Elliot took out a business card and slid it over the counter. "In case you remember anything else."

The next stop was in the Angel Creek subdivision, where Frank Livingston lived. On the way over, he called the car rental company that owned the white Ford sedan on the video. It had been leased to a woman traveling with her two children. The car rental employee hesitated somewhat but then shared the woman's phone number with Elliot. But the call didn't bring any usable information; the woman, a vacationing widow from Los Angeles, had seen nothing. Instead, she gave Elliot an earful on the conditions of the roads in California, considering him personally responsible for each and every pothole between Oregon and the Mexican border.

The next call he made was to the local plumber, where a morose employee by the name of Roger Mera reluctantly admitted he drove the truck past Katse two days ago in the morning. He didn't see anything, and no, he didn't know Taylor. He didn't recall seeing her jog, but he rarely paid attention to the scenery. His hostile tone and short, monosyllabic answers triggered Elliot's curiosity. He pulled over and checked the database. Mr. Mera had a criminal record for a B&E almost ten years ago. Elliot thanked him and hung up; something in his otherwise cranky tone of voice told Elliot he probably wasn't guilty of much else other than not paying attention while driving.

Coming down from the mountain, he drove past Katse heading northbound and then turned right into the subdivision, after passing through the valley and then by Frozen Falls. It was about two-thirty when he reached the Livingston residence, but the brown Hyundai was in the driveway. The high school science teacher was home.

He pulled behind it and was almost at the door when Frank Livingston stepped outside with a rake in his hand. Surprised to see Elliot, he abandoned the tool, leaving it leaning against the garage door. "Detective," he greeted Elliot, shaking his hand. "What brings you here?"

"Taylor Lorentz," he replied. The man's smile vanished, replaced by sadness. "Did you know her?"

He nodded, clasping his hands together. "She was my student, one of the best I had in the past years. I knew her family; what a tragedy. Her father wasn't the same after Mrs. Lorentz passed. The poor girl worked hard to earn her degree as quickly as possible."

"So you stayed in touch after her high school graduation?"

"Yes." The sadness on his face intensified. "I was her mentor. She wanted to become a science teacher here, in our hometown, and I was grooming her for that. I'm only a few years from retirement myself. She would've made a wonderful teacher."

Elliot checked his notes. "Video surveillance shows you driving past Katse after passing through the valley at six forty-nine."

He nodded. "Sounds about right."

"Did you see her jogging?"

"Not Wednesday, no. The sun was starting to come up and the road was well lit, but I didn't see her. Not that day."

"Other times you had?"

"Yes, many times. She liked running on that road, although I told her to be smart and run after sunrise. But kids don't always listen."

"Did you see anyone else? A vehicle, maybe?" Elliot looked at the note showing the black Suburban headed north at 6:43 a.m. It must've passed right by Frank's brown Hyundai some-place north of Katse, between the coffee shop and Angel Creek.

The teacher ran his hand through his perfectly white hair, thinking. "I believe so," he said, looking at Elliot with widened eyes. "Oh, my goodness, I didn't think of it until now, but there was a dark SUV, a large one, that was headed north. It seemed odd at the time; I thought I'd seen it stopped at the bottom of the valley, but it took off before I reached it."

"Did you see anything about the driver?"

"The SUV was still far away when I drove past the top of the hill, and it came into view. I thought he was taking a leak or maybe dropping someone off, but why there, in the middle of nowhere?" He sounded apologetic, probably feeling guilty he hadn't stopped to check it out. "I honestly thought he'd stopped to heed nature's call."

"You had no way of knowing what was going on, Mr. Livingston. It's not your fault."

"Thank you. I looked around when I reached the bottom of

the valley, you know. Where I thought the SUV was stopped. But I didn't see anything. That's why—"

"Was that SUV a Chevy Suburban, maybe?"

"I'm pretty sure of it, yes."

"Did you run into anyone else or see anything else?"

"No, I'm sorry. I can't believe I was there when—" His voice broke, and he put a hand to his mouth, then picked up the rake as if trying to keep himself busy with something.

"You've been very helpful, Mr. Livingston."

They shook hands, and Elliot left. Frank Livingston looked after Elliot's Ford with dismay, leaning into the rake, frozen in the middle of his driveway.

Why would a vehicle registered to an LLC in San Francisco travel all the way here to kill an apparently random young girl? Was the driver another one of the Velvet Puss bidders? He felt tempted to pull over and call the number listed for that LLC, but why give the perp a heads-up? They might flee.

It was better to call Kay. She could pay them a visit instead.

A hint of a smile flickered on his lips.

He could drive down to San Francisco himself to question the suspect together with his partner.

FORTY-FIVE
DEVICE

"We should go to Oakland and start banging on Sangrienta doors," Brian said for the fifth time since they'd left his house. "I don't understand what you're trying to do with this hospital business."

Kay rolled her eyes. She'd explained her strategy before, but he was itching to do things his way, to be in control. "Where did Holly have her pacemaker implanted?" She threw him a quick glance via the rearview mirror. He sat in the back seat, leaning forward, holding on to the front seat headrests. His breath touched her face at times, bothering her. She didn't welcome the closeness. He smelled fresh, of shower gel and his favorite aftershave, and she hated everything about it. The memories it brought back. The lasting effect of the scent and how she'd find it tomorrow and, for days after that, stuck to the upholstery like an embarrassing stain.

"It was the university hospital, I believe." The hesitation in his voice was clear.

"You believe? You're not sure where your daughter had life-altering surgery?"

He groaned, pulling away and letting himself drop against the backrest. "It's been a while, all right? And I'm not your typical parent." He shook his head. "It's not like I was living with them."

"Where, Brian? Which university? Stanford? Or UCSF?"

"UCSF Mission Bay," he said, the words blurted out with annoyance on a loud breath.

"Do you recall the name of her doctor? Any other contact, anything we could use?"

"No, I don't. I just paid for it, all right? I wasn't there." He ran his hands through his hair. "Jeez, Kay, you didn't use to be like this, asking me the same thing over and over. What am I, a perp in interrogation you're trying to break?"

"You don't find it remotely intriguing that you, Holly's father, haven't got a clue where your kid had surgery? What am I supposed to believe?"

"I told you the truth! And now, I'm following your lead, chasing wild geese with this hospital business. What are they supposed to be doing for us? We should be out there, collaring Sangrientas and leaning on them, pounding on them until one of them talks."

"You don't have a badge anymore. You've been suspended. And I don't have jurisdiction here."

"How would they know?"

It was a bad case of déjà vu. They'd had that conversation already, at least twice. Thankfully, the large Mission Bay hospital campus came into sight after another turn. She slowed her speed, reading the posted signs and figuring out where to stop and which entrance to use.

Cardiology seemed like a good start.

She parked and dashed to the entrance. Brian kept up with her rushed pace, mumbling something about getting her craziness over with so they could really go after Holly.

She stopped in front of a large reception desk. "We need to see someone who can help us track a pacemaker."

The receptionist, unimpressed with the badge she flashed quickly, seemed overwhelmed by her question. "Track a pacemaker? I wouldn't know about that. Do you have an appointment?"

Kay wanted to scream. "I need to see the head of cardiology right now."

The woman typed something on her computer with rhinestone-encrusted fingernails so long she had to type disturbingly slowly, then called an extension and spoke softly into her phone. "Hey, yeah, it's Shanice at the front desk. I have some cops here who want to speak with Doctor Carruthers about a pacemaker. Okay, I will." She ended the call, her smile gone. "Elevator on the left, third floor."

A nurse was waiting for them when the elevator dropped them on the cardiology floor. "You're the, um, police officers?" She wore her long hair in a large, twisted bun at the back of her head. The weight of it pulled her head up, giving her posture dignity and class.

"Yes, Detectives Sharp and Hanlin."

"Follow me, please." Hands in the lab coat pockets, she walked soundlessly on wedge shoes with rubber soles, moving quickly on the endless corridor until she reached a group of offices clustered together near a small reception area. "I'll show you in."

She knocked twice, waited a second, then opened the door enough to stick her head inside. "Doctor Carruthers? I'm sorry, but this is urgent. I have SFPD here," she added, then opened the door widely to let them in.

The doctor, a middle-aged man with a tall forehead and buzz-cut hair, stood and beckoned them inside. He wore a white lab coat, pristine and starched, and a stethoscope folded inside his chest pocket. He was lean and tall, not an ounce of fat on his body, probably a consequence of the life lessons he'd learned as a cardiologist.

Kay shook his hand, surprised at how dry and warm it felt. "Detectives Sharp and Hanlin. Thanks for seeing us on such short notice, doctor."

"What's this about?"

"An eight-year-old girl with a pacemaker has been kidnapped. I hope you can help us locate her by using the device."

He crossed his arms at his chest. "I sympathize with your search, Detective. Health information laws prevent me from sharing such information without a subpoena."

"I'm her father," Brian said. The doctor raised an eyebrow. "I'm an SFPD cop *and* her father. It's possible, you know. It can happen." His unwarranted sarcasm brought a frown to the doctor's forehead.

"Y—yes, absolutely," Dr. Carruthers replied, sitting at his desk and typing into his computer. "Name?"

"Holly Epling," Brian said.

"Holly Flynn Epling," Kay added.

The doctor typed. "Date of birth?"

"December thirtieth," Brian replied.

"Address, for verification?"

Brian gave Rachel's address, and the doctor seemed satisfied with his answer.

"And your name, sir?"

"Brian Hanlin."

The doctor hesitated a moment, frowning at the screen. "We have her, yes. The device she's wearing is network capable and can be located if it's connected to the internet." Kay drew closer, silently urging him to give her something she could use. "The device is not online right now. It was last seen thirty-four minutes ago."

Kay felt a pang of fear ripping through her gut. "What

happened? Is she still alive?" Her throat constricted as she spoke the words.

"I can't be sure," Dr. Carruthers said with the voice he probably used to reassure his patients. "All I know is that she was alive thirty-four minutes ago, and her device was working properly at that time."

"Do you have a location?"

He shook his head with sadness. "No, I don't. Our system doesn't automatically locate our patients. We can get locations, but we have to manually request it when the device is online." He cleared his throat quietly. "I don't have to explain to you what the stress of being a kidnap victim can do to her heart."

"How can we find out where she is?" Kay asked again, realizing her voice pitch was higher. "Can you help us?"

"Yes, we'll call you the moment the device is active again." He looked briefly out the window facing the parking lot as if that view held answers to their questions. "You might be able to get more details from the hospital that actually did the procedure."

Kay glared at Brian in disbelief. He seemed frozen in place, staring straight ahead at the doctor. "Which location is that?" she asked, her voice barely above a whisper.

"Mount Zion. We're all part of the same network and have the same system, but they might know more. In any case, we'll notify you the moment the pacemaker registers on the network again. We'll trace that for you, Detectives, and hope you can get your little girl back safely."

He shook their hands and showed them out after Kay left their phone numbers with him.

Walking briskly to the car, she kept her mouth shut until they reached the parking lot.

She unlocked the door and climbed behind the wheel, feeling sweat breaking at the roots of her hair. "What did you do, Brian? Gave me a random hospital to shut me up?" Her acute voice ripped through the air in the Ford.

"I forgot! I already told you I didn't know for sure. What more do you want from me? At least I got the right hospital system, didn't I?"

As always, he twisted things around, making her look like she was the bad guy in the conversation. She was growing tired of it. Beyond tired.

She drove off, heading to Mount Zion. Racing thoughts swirled in her mind, going over what she knew and didn't know, all the assumptions she'd made, all the facts she'd verified. She doubted everything, every single thing that her ex had said. How could a parent not know where his daughter had a pacemaker implanted?

But he'd already explained that, and satisfactorily, if she could only accept that he was a cold, egotistical bastard who'd never wanted a child in the first place. What more was there to ask or doubt? In his immense selfishness, he'd been brutally honest. His parenting had been limited to paying the bills and signing alimony checks, and it was a miracle he even did that much for Holly. Philandering wasn't what Brian sometimes did; it was who he was, all the time, nothing but a narcissistic sex addict on the prowl.

A thought pulled at her heartstrings, bringing the threat of tears in her eyes. With Rachel gone and Ciara in the hospital with little chance of recovery, who would take care of Holly once she'd be found? Brian? Some parent he'd make.

The Mount Zion Medical Center couldn't offer any additional information, only the renewed commitment to locate the device the moment it appeared online, and a promise to ask the pacemaker manufacturer for help. Bracing herself to start looking for Holly using Brian's method of busting doors and faces, Kay started driving toward Oakland.

"All right, we'll do it your way. Where do you want to

begin? Any particular gang member in mind? Do you have an address?"

Before Brian could answer any of her questions, Kay's phone rang. The media screen displayed the caller's name.

Elliot.

FORTY-SIX

BASEMENT

"It's been three hours," Edmundo shouted at the two cowering men. "Three hours and you couldn't find a little girl? Running barefoot out there?" He racked his gun and waved it in their faces. "*Mierda!* The boss will have you shot." He paced angrily. Isabela's sobs drove him insane. "No, *I* will have you shot right now."

He didn't pull the trigger, just stared at their sweaty faces, enjoying the sight of fear rattling their bodies. They knew better than to say anything, but Isabela wouldn't stop crying since he'd shoved her against the wall.

"Now get out there, and don't come back without her."

"*Si, jefe,*" they mumbled and rushed out the door.

Still angry, Edmundo called one of them back. Pale as a sheet, the man stumbled inside, holding his hands clasped in front of his crotch. "*Si?*" he said softly, obviously expecting to be shot.

"Did she run out in the street?"

The man shook his head so vigorously that his potbelly bounced and his jowls trembled. "*No, es impossible.* We were out there all the time, Rico and me. The fence is eight-foot tall, solid concrete, except for the gate, and that's where I was. All the time."

"Did you get coffee, take a piss, anything?"

The head shaking repeated. "I was there, boss, I swear."

Edmundo waved him away, and he vanished, leaving the door open in his wake. A kick from Edmundo slammed it shut, the thud fueling Isabela's lame-ass whimpers. She'd fallen into a heap by the wall and had stayed there, begging for mercy she didn't deserve.

The boss was going to kill him for that kid. Slowly, taking his time, making an example out of him so that everyone else could see what happened to those who defied his orders.

Ciguatera.

It was slow, agonizing, and deadly when the angels had mercy on the poor bastard's soul, and the boss ended the unspeakable torture with a bullet through the head. It was all he could think about since the girl had vanished. How would he die?

"And it's all because of you!" he bellowed. Isabela flinched and withdrew to the corner, sobbing louder and raising her hands to protect her head from the blows that she expected to follow. "You couldn't lock that damn door, could you?"

She looked at him with swollen, tear-filled eyes. Her makeup had smudged and circled her eyes with blackness, like a ghoul's empty eye sockets. She clasped her hands together at her chest. "I swear I locked that door, Edmundo! Why don't you believe me?"

Edmundo's hand rose, about to fall heavy on her lying mouth when his phone chimed. "*Maldito bastardo,*" he muttered, then read the text he'd received. "What the hell?" He scratched his greasy goatee, staring at the screen in disbelief. Isabela looked at him with worried eyes. "I'm turning the Wi-Fi off. Keep it off, all right?"

"Sure, Edmundo," Isabela whispered. "Who cares about Wi-Fi now?"

Groaning, he walked into the next room and found the modem on a large desk filled with all sorts of junk and Isabela's computer. He yanked the power cable out of the wall socket. "There. No more Wi-Fi." He stopped in front of Isabela, whose whimpers had ceased for a moment. "The man has gone *loco* in the head."

He considered slapping his woman again but felt too tired to do it. Instead, he drew a wooden chair closer and sat on it heavily, looking at Isabela. She kept her gaze lowered. Tears quietly streaked her face with smeared eyeliner.

"He's going to kill us both," Edmundo said, grinding his teeth and clasping his hands so tightly his knuckles turned white. "I can't do anything about it unless I find that girl and pop her." He muttered a long string of oaths. "Just tell me what time you went there last? She could've gone away four hours ago, and she could be with the cops right now, spilling her guts. Tell me the truth, Isabela."

She stood with difficulty, touching the wall for support. Then she looked straight at him, intently, for a long, silent moment. "Edmundo," she said, "for the last time, I had just been down there to feed the little bitch, and I swear on my life I locked the damn door. If you could only believe me." A sob swelled her chest, but she kept herself from whimpering. "You kill me, or the boss kills me, whatever. I know this is not on me."

"And you didn't let her go because you're a stupid bleeding heart and didn't want *la chica* killed?" His voice reflected his opinion of Isabela's earlier concern with killing a kid.

"No, Edmundo, I swear."

Edmundo stood abruptly, then angrily kicked over the chair. "I went down there after you, and the room was empty!"

The faintest shred of doubt started creeping inside his head. He'd been downstairs, looking everywhere, and the kid was gone. He'd checked under the bed, in the toilet, behind the door. There was no place she could've been. He couldn't remember how he'd found the door, locked or not. After a few shots, he couldn't think straight. But with the girl gone, it must've been unlocked. Otherwise, where the fuck was she?

He climbed down the stairs quickly and barged into the basement, with Isabela lagging a couple of steps behind him. A ray of sunshine came through the window and cut across the room through dust particles, shining its light over the stained concrete floor. The bed was empty, and the girl was nowhere in sight, just like the last time he'd checked.

But something caught his eye.

He stared at the concrete closely, where ash and cinder had fallen out of the fireplace as if someone had stirred up tinder. Right next to the fireplace, on the concrete, there was a small, partial footprint in ash, a few toes and the ball of the girl's foot as if she'd tiptoed through. The print led away from the fireplace.

He crouched, reaching under the bed, and touched the girl's leg. She shrieked and wriggled away, but Isabela quickly circled the bed and grabbed her by the hair, pulling her out screaming.

"Gotcha, you little piece of shit."

FORTY-SEVEN
EXCHANGE

"Ah, I get it now." Brian's suggestive chuckle made Kay cringe. "Who is this Elliot, anyway?"

The phone continued to ring, amplified by the media system in Kay's SUV. She tapped on the screen, switching the call to her mobile device instead, and the trilling dropped to a barely audible sound coming from her left pocket.

She took out the phone and answered Elliot's call, keeping the phone flush against her left ear. "Hey," she said in a low voice. Brian chuckled again. He leaned back, hands intertwined behind his head as if he were about to watch a very good TV show.

"Kay," Elliot said. The sound of his voice made her forget all about Brian and his infuriating demeanor. "How's everything? Did you find the missing girl?"

"Not yet, and it's not looking too good." She weaved through traffic at a slower speed than before, her mind focused on the call.

"Oh." There was silence between them for a moment, a loaded silence filled with unvoiced questions and things that needed to be said. "Well, I'm on my way down—"

Her mind switched into high gear. She didn't want him in San Francisco, tagging along with them and putting himself in danger for nothing. "Elliot, we talked about this—"

"Before you tell me off, just know it's about the case."

"Which case?"

"My case." She could hear the smile in his voice. "The Taylor Lorentz murder?"

She breathed, feeling embarrassed for a moment. Not everything revolved around her. She'd spent too much time with Brian; she was starting to think like him. "What's going on with the investigation?"

She could hear traffic sounds for a while. "Well, it's a hell of a case, partner. I had a few leads, but they didn't pan out, not for the murder, anyway. Video surveillance from Katse's patio showed me a number of vehicles that drove on the highway that morning. I spoke with most of the people, including our old acquaintance, Frank Livingston. His Hyundai was one of those cars."

"I remember him, yes."

"He saw a black SUV stopped on the side of the road, then it peeled off and drove northbound at high speed."

A sense of doom unfurled in her gut when she heard Elliot's description of the vehicle.

"Did you run the background for that?" she asked, her voice choked.

"Yeah, it's registered to a San Francisco LLC, a company named I Dream of Shannon. Weird name, isn't it?"

Her blood instantly turned to icicles. "Are you sure about that information?" She kept her voice calm and measured, almost indifferent.

"I'm positive," Elliot replied, speaking slowly, probably picking up on the angst in her voice. "Why? What's up? The weird name ring a bell?"

She didn't reply; instead, she slowed her speed, looking for a place where she could stop. "What address do you have for that suspect?"

A moment of heavy silence. "You're with him, aren't you?" He sounded disappointed and worried at the same time.

"For now, but I'm working on fixing that." She didn't ask about the address again; she knew she didn't have to.

"It's eleven seventy-five Cedarwood Drive in Millbrae."

Cedarwood.

Her old home address. Hers and Brian's.

Memories rushed to her mind, good and bad, overwhelming. Heart-wrenching.

As if reading her thoughts, Brian leaned forward, studying her face with an inquisitive smile.

She pulled into a small parking lot in front of a dry cleaner's shop and a small bakery with a few wrought iron tables set on the sidewalk. Cutting the engine, she turned to Brian and said, "Stay here." Then she got out of the vehicle and put a few yards between the Ford and her.

"I can talk now, Elliot," she said when she was sure Brian couldn't hear what she was saying. "It's just you and me." She kept her back turned to the SUV, knowing Brian was adept at reading lips and facial expressions like most cops are. "Where are you?"

"I'm about one hour north of the Golden Gate."

"Remember when you said if I changed my mind—"

"Tell me what you need." She could hear Elliot's engine revving faster, and his siren turned on. "I'll make it in forty minutes or so."

"Don't go to that LLC address, Elliot. Just trust me and meet me north of the Golden Gate Bridge. There's a busy vista point on your left as you're coming down, very close to the bridge."

"What are you not telling me?" She didn't reply. "Kay? Please be honest with me."

She paced, staring at the horizon like a trapped fugitive searching for a way out. "I think our cases might be connected. That address you gave me was our house when I was still married to him. He kept it." She fought tears she didn't see coming. "Please, don't ask me for more, not now. I'll explain when we meet."

Silence.

"You got it, partner," he eventually said in a low but warm voice. "You could find a whisper in a whirlwind, Kay. No one's better at this job than you are but watch your back. I need to know you're safe."

"Copy that," she replied. Funny how Elliot's words brought tears to her eyes, tears she couldn't explain. "See you soon," she managed to add without sounding emotional before she ended the call.

Dizzy and feeling drained, she sat on a wrought iron chair, her back still turned toward the Ford where Brian was. She closed her eyes and tried to make sense of her feelings. Betrayal, unspeakable betrayal, worse than she'd ever felt yet at the hands of Brian Hanlin. Guilt and shame and a sense of foreboding so strong her hands trembled. It was just like Elliot had uncannily said before she left Mount Chester. Her hairs were now standing on end, the tickling at the back of her head in resonance with the sense of dread coiled in her gut.

"What can I get you, hon?" The waitress smiled, waiting with a notepad and pen in hand. She was young, barely eighteen or so, and wore a pristine white apron with ruffles over jeans and a knitted top.

Startled out of her introspection, Kay jolted. "Coffee," she said, feeling her throat parched dry. "Just black." She quickly glanced at the Ford and saw Brian staring out the rear window with a look of angry consternation on his face. "Make that two to go, and make one a long decaf, please," she added.

The waitress scribbled something on her pad. "You got it. Anything else?"

"No, thank you."

Moments later, the waitress brought the coffees. "This is the decaf," she said, smiling and setting it aside, then put the other in front of Kay.

"Thanks," Kay said, her mind still wandering as she pulled out some cash from her wallet. "Keep the change."

The girl took the bills with a smile and vanished.

But Kay's mind was elsewhere, on one of her most enjoyable days as Brian's wife-to-be. Before she'd had an inkling of his cheating. A day when she'd been happy, blissfully so, unaware of what was really going on.

In more ways than one.

They had visited the San Francisco car show, walking hand in hand for hours and looking at every single vehicle. Brian talked excitedly, pouring endless engine statistics and performance numbers out of his prodigious memory, while she just enjoyed seeing him happy, hearing him talk, being with him. They weren't married then, just planning to be in about a month.

They ate waffles for lunch that day and burgers for dinner long before the show closed its doors at nine in the evening. The two of them were among the last ones to leave after the exhibit had started turning off the lights. On the way home, he'd held her hand almost the entire time, driving expertly with one hand, and she'd been the happiest woman alive.

They'd made love that night, passionately, her craving for him insatiable, his desire for her arduous, consuming them like a shared fire. Then they lay in each other's arms, spent yet unwilling to fall asleep.

"When I'll be able to afford it," Brian whispered, wrapping her in his arms and nesting her head on his chest, "I'll get me the biggest, blackest, shiniest Suburban ever made. There's no

SUV like it." He caressed her hair with gentle, rhythmic moves that made her eyelids heavy. "Why do you think law enforcement uses them? And I don't mean us two-bit cops, I mean the FBI. They don't go anywhere without their Suburbans."

"Uh-huh," she mumbled, trying to stay awake so the day wouldn't end.

"No, I'll get five of them, not one, and all black. I'll register them to a business, so I can expense the lease, and I'll make them work for me."

"What business?" She lifted her head and looked at him, surprised. As far as she knew, he wanted to be a cop, a detective, someday soon. Not an entrepreneur.

"Well, I don't know yet," he laughed. "But it will be called I Dream of Shannon." He placed a kiss on her forehead. "Very memorable and unique, don't you think?"

Fully awake from the jolt of uneasiness caused by the business name referencing another woman, she leaned into her elbow to look at him. "Who's Shannon?"

He touched the ridges on her brow, caressing them until they leveled off. "Nothing to worry about, babe, but I'm shocked you don't know who Shannon is."

She mock-punched him in the ribs, then settled back in his embrace. "Just tell me already."

"Shannon was the 1971 Plymouth Hemi Cuda in my favorite movie of all times, Gone in 60 Seconds. It's blasphemy you didn't know that; I'm appalled." He sounded only half-joking.

She laughed at his youthful enthusiasm, relieved that Shannon wasn't a real woman who could steal him away. "How can I keep track?" She ran her fingers over his chest and felt his body responding to her touch. "Stacey is in the driveway, you obviously dream of Shannon, is there room for a Kay in your life?"

He kissed her forehead, then lifted her chin until he could

reach her lips. "You're my dream turned reality, my sweet Kay." He kissed her lips thirstily until she was out of breath. "So, what do you say, LLC or corporation?"

She wanted to be mad at him for ruining the moment, but she loved his playfulness. "Well, it depends. What will your business do?"

He'd laughed so hard his entire body shook. "Isn't it obvious? Figure out, hustle and bustle, and whatever, until it makes me rich enough to have Shannon for myself."

His voice still resonated in her mind as she stood and walked toward the SUV with the coffee cups in her hands. With bloodcurdling accuracy, all the puzzle pieces had fallen into place, leaving her breathless, her heart thumping in her chest like a caged bird, staring at Brian as if she'd never met him before.

Then she snapped out of it, regaining some control over her emotions. She wasn't out of the woods yet. She smiled casually and opened the back door, and offered him the tall paper cup.

The gift of coffee calmed Brian somewhat, although he immediately commented on the quality of it.

"Another decaf swill from my dear wife?" His voice sounded tense, loaded with an unspoken threat.

"Ex-wife, Brian. Once and for all." She started the engine and turned into traffic. "Take mine if you don't like it."

"Nah, that's fine. I'll live." He propped his head between the front seats again. "Where are we going? I thought we were finally going to Oakland to find my daughter. You don't seem to care about her that much. Not saying I blame you, considering—"

"Yes, well, listen, if you want me to help you with this case, I can't work like this, in the car, on the road all the time. I need my computer, database access, and all my systems. How can I run suspects like this? How can we find Holly like this?"

"What are you saying, Kay?" He looked at her with undisguised suspicion. Seemingly absent-minded, he took out his gun and checked the load, then racked it and slid it back into its holster.

The sound of metal scraping metal sent a shiver down her spine. Her breath caught, but she didn't flinch. "I'm saying you need to trust me or I'm out. Completely."

"Oh, boy, this again," he groaned. "I trust you with my life, Kay. I thought I'd proven that already."

"Then we're going to Mount Chester, where I can work." She turned onto Park Presidio Boulevard, heading for the Golden Gate Bridge.

"Son of a bitch... really, Kay? You're throwing my ass back in hillbilly jail?"

"No, you'll stay at my place this time, as long as you don't drive me insane and you sleep on the couch."

"It's a promise, and you're an angel." He leaned back against the backrest, visibly relieved. "My guardian angel." He didn't seem to care they were leaving town when his daughter was still missing.

Her phone chimed, announcing a new message. She skimmed it while waiting for a light to turn green. It was from an unknown number, a screenshot of a map with a red dot. The map was a section of West Oakland near the foot of the Bay Bridge. Then a text message saying:

Manufacturer had the last known location for the device. Good luck. Dr. C.

They'd found Holly.

The excitement washed over her, but she breathed it away slowly and quietly, steadying herself.

She waited for a while, hiding her emotions and expecting Brian's phone to chime, but it didn't. For some reason, Dr. Carruthers had only texted her. "That Brockett is a stupid, stubborn son of a bitch," she said, seeing Brian's suspicion rekindled by the text message she'd received. She slipped the phone back into her pocket. "No matter how much evidence we serve him, he won't drop the charges."

"Finally, you see it too," Brian replied. She shot him a glance as she drove past the Golden Gate Bridge toll readers. He looked out the windshield, his elbows propped against the back of both front seats. Not a wrinkle on his forehead, not a shred of worry in his eyes. The man never ceased to amaze her.

But then again, he was an experienced undercover cop who'd spent years pretending he was someone he wasn't. A born liar who'd found his calling to weave thick webs of deception and pull off whatever act he was playing.

There was no saying what Brian Hanlin was really thinking.

As soon as she crossed the bridge, she turned into the Vista Point rest area and drove slowly, looking for Elliot's vehicle.

"What are we doing here?" Brian asked coldly. "Not that I don't trust you, but I'd like to know."

"We're meeting someone who can help me help you." As she drove along the curved parking lane, Elliot came into sight, leaning against the back of his Ford. His wide-brimmed, black hat cast a shadow on his face, doing little to mask the tension in his jaw.

"I don't know about that," Brian muttered, visibly uncomfortable. The Vista Point was busy, filled with tourists snapping their cameras incessantly, and under video surveillance. He seemed to check the pedestrian traffic carefully, then resigned himself to not doing anything but pout and wait with his arms crossed at his chest.

She pulled a few yards from Elliot's car and cut the engine, then walked over to him quickly. His eyes lit up when he noticed her, and a hint of a smile fluttered on his lips.

"Hello, partner." He touched the brim of his hat with two fingers. "Glad to see you took my advice."

She frowned a little, unsure what he meant, but decided to let it go. "I need your help, Elliot."

"Anything." The smile had disappeared, leaving a look of determination and strength in its wake.

"Please take Brian to Mount Chester and wait for me there. I won't be far behind, not more than an hour."

"Kay, that's not what we discussed."

"Elliot, please," she whispered, smiling nervously for the small group of Japanese tourists who'd gotten too close for her comfort, snapping cameras in their faces and grinning at Elliot's attire.

Ignoring them, Elliot bit his lip, visibly torn. "All right, partner. Hand over the merchandise, and let's get the hell out of here."

She rushed to her SUV and opened the back door, inviting Brian out. Noticeably uneasy with the situation, her ex frowned and glared at Elliot with suspicion.

"Elliot will take you home, Brian," Kay said calmly.

"Ah, the famous Elliot," he mumbled, giving the man a head-to-toe look filled with undisguised contempt.

Elliot grabbed Brian's arm in typical cop fashion. "Let's go." Brian resented that and didn't refrain from showing it with a loaded glare and a forceful arm jerk, but Elliot didn't release his grip.

"One more thing," Kay said, raising her hand to stop them. "My colleague has a rule about passengers in his Interceptor. Only he can carry a gun." Swiftly, she reached for Brian's belt and took his weapon, leaving both men slack-jawed. "Don't worry, you'll get it back tonight when we get home." She tucked the gun in her belt, under the sweatshirt, hoping not too many people had noticed the weapon.

A glint of rage lit Brian's eyes briefly, then he lowered his eyelids, hiding it well. Elliot took him to his SUV and opened the back door. Brian held on to the Ford's roof and shouted, "Where are you going, Kay?"

Several tourists stopped their stroll to watch the scene, their backs turned to the breathtaking Golden Gate Bridge.

She walked over briskly to Elliot's SUV. She hated every second she wasted, knowing Holly was out there, but she didn't have a choice. Her ex needed to stay calm for a while longer. "There's something I need to do before I leave the area," she told Brian. Suspicion still lingered on his face. "Ciara had a stroke and is in the hospital. She's probably not going to make it. I just want to say goodbye."

FORTY-EIGHT
FOUND

Holly sobbed, her face burning where Isabela's hand had struck. Her heart beat hard and fast, choking her, crushing the breath in her lungs. She pressed her hand on her chest and tried to steady her breathing, but this time it didn't work.

No one was coming to get her. She was going to die here, in this basement.

Petrified, she watched the man pull out a gun. She felt faint, yet she believed she could bolt out running if she could somehow make it past him. A rush of energy, of desperate courage, flushed through her body.

"My father's a cop," she said, looking the man in the eye. He scowled at her and pointed the gun at her head. "They always catch cop killers, and they put them in jail forever." Her voice was weak and filled with tears. "They do worse to people who kill cops' kids."

"Shut the fuck up, *pedazo de mierda*," Isabela shouted, then struck her across the face, hard, sending her tumbling across the floor until she hit the wall. "I got beat up because of you, so shut your piehole."

Holly panted, looking around in panic, still seeing stars

from the blow. She wanted to throw up, the thumping in her head making her feel sick. She dry-retched once, but Isabela grabbed her arm and pulled her up.

"Oh, no, you better not barf here, where I have to clean. Take your vomit with you to the grave." She shoved her toward Edmundo, who was looking at the girl with a strange look on his face. "Do it already, Edmundo. I'm tired of this shit."

"She's right," Edmundo said. "She's a cop's kid. They won't stop until they find who killed her."

Isabela shrugged. "So?"

Edmundo grinned, showing two rows of crooked, yellow teeth. "So, who do we pin this on?"

Holly watched the exchange between them, only half-understanding what was going on. All she knew was she wanted to run and go someplace safe where she could throw up and make the unbearable thumping in her head stop. She was afraid, more than she'd thought possible, fear rattling her body so hard it felt as if it was going to break apart.

Isabela smiled and licked her swollen lip, wincing. "Pin it on Big J, *mi amor*. He always looks to get ahead, and he'll stab you in the back when you least expect it."

"You're still going to jail," Holly said, shaking but standing up slowly, expecting another blow.

Edmundo grabbed her arm, and she shrieked. He propped the gun barrel against her temple, pressing hard. She tried to wriggle free but couldn't; his grip was like an iron claw, crushing her flesh.

The sound of commotion came from upstairs. Rushed footfalls, a distant gunshot or two, some distant shouting. Edmundo listened intently, aiming the gun at the door, then back at Holly's head. "Who the hell is up there?" he whispered, looking at Isabela. Her eyes, wide open in fear, were the only answer he got. Then footsteps on the stairs approached.

The gunshot reverberated in the cramped space. A loud

thud marked Edmundo's body falling to the floor, blood gushing from his forehead. Holly screamed and rushed toward the door, landing squarely in a woman's arms, sobbing.

The woman put away the smoldering gun and wrapped her arms around Holly's shaking body. "You're okay," she whispered, holding the little girl tightly in her arms. Behind her, a tall man with a gray mustache and a loud, raspy voice directed his people to get Isabela and clear the rest of the house.

"Don't shoot," Isabela said, holding her hands up and sobbing hard with her mouth wide open. "It wasn't me; it was him; it was Edmundo." She struggled with the cops handcuffing her but was easily overpowered. "You killed him," she sobbed. "Motherfucking pigs, you killed my husband."

They hauled her screaming and kicking out of there, not before Holly glared at her with tear-filled eyes from the safety of the woman's arms and stuck her tongue out.

Just like Mommy would've done.

FORTY-NINE
CLEANUP

"Nice shot," Brockett said, holstering his weapon.

But Kay didn't respond. She caressed the girl's silky red curls and wiped her tears with her fingers. "Your mother was my best friend. You have all her freckles, all of them, including this one." She touched the tip of the girl's nose. Through her tears, Holly smiled.

Kay scooped her in her arms and climbed up the stairs. Brockett followed in his heavy gait.

"What's gonna happen to her?" she asked Brockett, lowering her voice to a whisper.

"You know the drill. We'll call social services, but we'll try to locate the family first. Anyone who could take her. Too bad about Mrs. Epling. Maybe if she gets better, she could try to get custody of her later."

There was no family. Rachel's father had died many years ago, and so had Brian's parents.

Letting Holly go broke Kay's heart, but the little girl needed immediate medical attention. She entrusted her to the EMS crew and slipped her business card in the child's hand. "Call me, okay? For any reason or just to talk." The little girl nodded as one of the EMTs fitted her with a nose cannula.

Then Kay returned to assist with the crime scene.

Two bodies were being loaded into the coroner's van. She'd taken one of Edmundo's goons down herself, while Brockett had taken the other's life just as he was pulling a gun on them. There would be hell to pay for the jurisdiction issue and all that, but it was worth it.

"Now what, Detective?" she asked Brockett.

He grinned widely, looking at the ambulance as it drove off. "Now you go home, Detective Sharp, and do whatever it is you do in your own ZIP Code." Those were words he'd said before but this time it was with none of the earlier animosity, just light-hearted humor. "You're one hell of a cop."

"You're not so bad yourself." She shook his hand, enduring through the steel grip of the old Marine.

"The hell I'm not..." he mumbled, pushing his glasses up his nose. "I'd barely drafted the subpoenas for Holly's pacemaker by the time you found the girl."

Kay felt her cheeks on fire. "We got lucky, that's all."

Brockett waved at her, intending to leave, but then stopped. "How about your ex? What are you going to do with him?"

She shrugged, smiling bitterly. "Nothing. I made sure he was processed correctly and legally represented at the arraignment. He got out on bail, and my role ended."

He scratched his head and stared at her in disbelief. "So, you're not going to investigate Rachel's murder on the DL?"

"Nope. I'm driving home right now. I'll leave the investigating to Brian. He's got time on his hands."

He patted her on the shoulder and laughed. "Smart lady."

"But let me ask you something," Kay said. "Why did you charge him? The case against him is weak and circumstantial at best. What do you have?"

His salt-and-pepper mustache moved as if his nose was itching. "A fingerprint. A single one."

"What?" She propped her hands on her hips, failing to understand. "Whose?"

"Brian Hanlin's." The cop smiled enigmatically.

"But the house was covered in his prints. He lived there half the time."

He massaged the back of his neck as if looking to squash the pain nestled in there. "This particular fingerprint was on the back doorknob, and there was residue of the roast we found on the table."

"You're saying—"

"I'm saying he pulled a piece of roast with his fingers, probably ate it, then opened the back door, while his fiancée was lying dead at his feet. And you, the unbelievable country cop, somehow knew to ask me about the missing items on that table." He looked in the distance and smiled, a tired, overworked smile. "Go home, Detective, and drive safely. It will be dark soon."

FIFTY

IN THE BOX

Kay felt as if she'd been away for months when she entered the white, single-story sheriff's office building in Mount Chester. It was late, almost seven, but almost all her coworkers were still there. Novack waved at her, and Denise Farrell shouted, "Hey, look who's back."

Kay smiled and shook their hands, then chatted with them for a few seconds, until the sheriff appeared.

"You're back," Sheriff Logan said, a statement, not a question. She smiled and nodded. He studied her with squinting eyes and a deep frown, the kind a parent wears on their face when the curfew-breaking kid is finally home safe. "Any fallout for me to worry about?"

Her smile waned. "There might be a small issue, but that's only if the SFPD chooses to investigate a particular hostage rescue involving an eight-year-old girl. A couple of gangbangers might or might not have been shot during said rescue efforts."

"Ah," Logan said, pursing his lips in disapproval. "We'll deal with that if and when it happens. Welcome back."

"Thank you." She walked past him and stopped at her desk. A file folder awaited, with a yellow Post-it note affixed to the cover. In Elliot's handwriting, the note said, *This is what we have on the Taylor Lorentz case, plus what we got from a Detective Brockett on your request. We're in the box.*

She took the case file with her into the observation room adjacent to the interrogation room and set it on the small table by the two-way mirror. For a while, she looked at the two men inside "the box," as the cops liked to call the interrogation room. One stood casually, cowboy hat on, arms folded at his chest, leaning against the wall, his legs crossed at the ankles. The other man fumed, seated on a metallic chair, his elbows rested on the bent and scratched table, his expensive suit wrinkled and stained.

Starting her review of the Lorentz case file, she paused at the enlarged detail of the bullet stopped by the victim's cell phone, and the photo of the enlarged fingerprint. Another wave of memories flooded her mind, of a day that had started well, a few weeks before the wedding, but ended in a hospital emergency room.

Brian had wanted to open a bottle of Burgundy for dinner but couldn't find the corkscrew. Suspecting it had been thrown out by accident, and unwilling to interrupt dinner to go shop for one, he'd grabbed a pillow off the bed and the bottle, and headed with a determined gait for the living room wall.

"Oh, no," she'd shouted. "You can't possibly want to do that. If the glass breaks you could cut yourself badly."

He chuckled, full of self-confidence, and positioned the pillow against the wall with his left hand. "Don't worry, I've seen it done."

Before she could say anything else, the bottle hit the pillow and broke instead of spitting out the cork. He screamed, holding his bleeding right hand with his left and turning to her for help.

He'd needed stitches for his thumb that night, and painkillers, and something to help him sleep. For days, he was grumpy and avoided her as if it was her fault any of that had happened. Now, as she stared at the fingerprint detail, she wondered if there was a chance the fingerprint matched.

It had to... with everything that meant about Brian, about who he was. Yet her mind clung to the reasonable doubt she still had until she compared the prints, unwilling to accept reality.

Hope is the most addictive drug of all.

"How much longer is she going to be?" Brian said on the other side of the two-way mirror.

"She's already here," Elliot replied calmly.

"How do you know?" He leaned forward in his chair, an expression of contempt on his face.

Elliot didn't reply.

"So, tell me, how long have you been screwing my wife?" Brian asked, obviously not willing to give up.

"Damn you, Brian," Kay muttered, cringing, watching the scene as if it were a train wreck in slow motion.

Elliot's fist landed squarely on Brian's jaw, knocking him off his chair and hurling him toward the wall, where he fell into a heap. Brian groaned, feeling at his jaw and swearing under his breath. Elliot approached him and bent over with a hand behind his ear. "Would you please repeat that? I'm not sure I heard you the first time."

Brian picked himself up from the floor, glaring at Elliot but keeping his mouth shut. Kay closed the case file and rushed inside before any real blood could be spilled.

"What's going on here?" she asked the moment she stepped inside the box, looking at Elliot first, then at Brian.

Elliot shrugged. "He fell. I was lending a hand."

"I fell," Brian confirmed. "Nothing happened."

She drew up a chair across from Brian's, the scraping of metal on concrete grating to her ears. "Sit down, Brian."

He didn't obey. He leaned against the table, towering over her, his eyes filled with rage. "Why am I here, Kay?" Elliot's hand pressing on his shoulder forced him into his seat. "Why did they take my phones? I need my phones," he shouted, his pitch increasingly higher. "What if the hospital calls? It's my daughter out there!" He tried to stand, but Elliot's hand found his shoulder and changed his mind.

"Sit down, Brian," Kay repeated.

"I'm not a fucking perp in your sweatbox, Kay," he hissed. "I trusted you. My kid's out there, and you don't give a fuck."

She didn't flinch and didn't think it was worth it to update him on Holly's whereabouts. "I only have one question for you." She paused for effect. "On Wednesday morning, when you turned yourself in, how did you get here?"

The question left Brian speechless for a moment, eyes wide open, staring at Kay as if in shock. "How did I... Jeez, what kind of question is that?" He ran his fingers through his disheveled hair nervously, pressing hard on his scalp in a signature gesture she knew well, when powerlessness and frustration got the best of him.

"Yeah, it's a simple question. How did you get here? Did you take an Uber?" He continued to stare at her in disbelief, his mouth agape. "It wasn't Stacey, was it?" She smiled crookedly, looking him straight in the eye, noticing the slight dilation in his pupils.

Fear.

"She was home, in your driveway, wasn't she?" Kay smiled derisively. "Because you couldn't bear the thought of someone else driving her. So, Brian, how did you get here?"

His consternation instantly turned to rage, catching fire faster than dry hay on a windy day. "You have no right to question me, Kay. You have no jurisdiction, and I'm out on bail anyway. What the hell are you trying to accomplish?" He stood and walked over to the door, but Elliot blocked his path, pointing silently at the chair he'd just vacated. He turned away from the door but remained standing, pacing back and forth restlessly. "I keep telling you I didn't kill Rachel. You keep finding evidence I didn't, and still, you're just like that piece-of-shit Brockett, you suspect me. You're jealous of Carly, aren't you? Is that it?"

Kay's lopsided smile widened. She wasn't going to gratify that ridiculous question with an answer. "This isn't about Rachel's death, Brian. It's about the morning you showed up here. A young girl was killed that morning, and we were hoping you might've seen anything, something that could help us out." His relief was visible in the line of his shoulders and the waning tension in his swollen jaw. "My partner," she gestured toward Elliot, "whom you've met, said we should ask you."

"Oh," Brian said, stopping his agitated pacing and taking his seat causally as if he were in a lounge, about to order drinks. "I didn't see anything. It was dark when I got here. Someone drove me."

"In what? In one of your black Suburbans?" His pupils dilated and the blood dropped from his face, turning his skin ashen.

"What are you talking about? What Suburban?"

She watched him lie with astonishment. Unlike before, when she was a young, naïve woman deeply in love, now she knew when he was lying. Still, except the reaction in his pupils and the pallor that had shrouded his face, he'd shown no sign of deception whatsoever. No fidgeting or touching his face. No movement or reaction that didn't fit his legend, the story he was sticking with, of innocence wrongly accused.

Many cops who worked undercover for extended periods of time developed the skillset, but some were born with it, pure naturals, able to lead multiple lives concurrently without a glitch. He was one of those few.

A pang of unspeakable sadness tugged at her heart.

The girl she'd been eight years ago hadn't stood a chance once the charismatic predator had set his sights on her. And neither had Rachel.

It had taken her years of training with the FBI and countless cases worked to develop the skills she needed to see through his lies, and still, she got duped by him. At first, and with some reserve, she'd trusted him.

Again.

As if the lesson eight years ago hadn't been enough.

A heavy sigh left her chest, cleansing all the remnants of sadness from her heart. It was time to make him pay. "You know what's around the hill from here?"

He shook his head and crossed his arms at his chest, looking at her as if she'd lost her mind. "What?"

"It's the bottom of a valley, a place locals call Frozen Falls, because of some stone formations and a small creek." He frowned and shrugged, visibly impatient. "Well, south of Frozen Falls, about a mile, there's Katse Coffee Shop. It's really nice, with a patio and all." She placed her hands on the cover of the case file. "And video surveillance."

Brian sprang to his feet and pounded against the table with both fists. His chair fell backward with a scrapy thud. "In the middle of fucking nowhere? You have got to be kidding me!" The agitated pacing resumed, punctuated by mumbled oaths.

"Yes," she replied calmly, opening the case file and flipping through the photos. "And Golden Gate Bridge has high-resolution cameras. We have you driving the Suburban on the way north, and Edmundo Buendia driving it back to San Francisco."

"Who?" He looked at the photos with real interest. "You could get facial recognition off this?" He tapped his fingernail against the photo. The enlarged detail of Edmundo's face was grainy and partly obscured by a reflection in the Suburban's side window.

"I didn't need to," she replied, smiling. "Don't you love it when perps make it so damn easy for us with their face tattoos?"

He propped his hands on his hips. "Huh?"

"See this?" She pointed at the man's cheek. "These four

teardrops inked on his face, you know what that means, right, Detective?"

He looked at the floor briefly. "Um, it's a prison tat, and it's one teardrop for every life taken. He killed four people. Great. But what does that have to do with anything?" He stared at her, a look of deep disappointment on his face.

A quick knock on the two-way mirror interrupted her roll. Elliot walked out and closed the door. She didn't break eye contact with Brian.

"He's second in command in your organization, isn't he?"

"Wow... You're insane! You've completely lost your mind!" He leaned over the table, closing the distance between their faces, scrutinizing her. She didn't flinch, only smiled calmly. "Was seeing me again a little too much for you to handle, Kay? I didn't think you still cared—"

The narcissistic son of a bitch. Swallowing her rage, she flipped to the next photo in the case file. "The same Suburban was seen near the shooting that Rachel witnessed, with you behind the wheel. Here." She pointed at another grainy photo, so grainy one could barely see the driver. "An ATM camera puts you and the Suburban on the same street and at the same time as the shooting of Oliver Galaz."

He collected the chair and sat on it as if his knees had given on him, a look of pure stupefaction etched on his face. "That's not me, in that photo. How can you tell it's me? No lawyer would struggle with this for one minute."

She took out her phone and recalled a number from memory, then initiated the call on speaker. Brockett answered immediately.

"Do you have the test results yet, Detective?"

"Yeah. The Suburban has Hanlin's fingerprints all over it, and gunshot residue on the inside of the driver's door."

Kay stared at Brian the entire time Brockett spoke, nodding

slightly. "Remind me, Detective, what's the nickname of the head of La Vida Sangrienta?"

"It's Barracuda, why?"

"Just checking, thanks!" She tapped the red circle to end the call, still smiling and looking at Brian. He was slouched on his chair, arms hanging limp from his shoulders. He looked so desolate she almost took pity on him.

Almost.

"You know, I didn't see the connection until I remembered who Shannon was... A barracuda, the love of your life. That's what Hemi Cuda means, right?"

He ran his hands through his hair, his eyes staring into emptiness. "I don't know what you're talking about, Kay. You're not making any sense. Coming here to surrender to you was a huge mistake. You're biased, still hurting obviously, a woman scorned. You're out to see me bleed."

She scoffed at his lame attempt to deflect. "You know, I believed you, when you showed up here on Wednesday morning. I wanted to believe you. I had some doubts, but I put them aside. It was a touch of pure brilliance when you staged the shooting at the SFPD precinct. It had me swearing to people you didn't kill Rachel." She shook her head, disappointed with herself. "That took some serious guts, I'll give it to you. Who was the shooter?"

Brian didn't answer. He just stared in her direction, his pupils unfocused.

"Well, I have it here that before his dishonorable discharge, Edmundo Buendia used to be one hell of a sniper. He won competitions and was selected for several black ops missions in Afghanistan. Did you know that?" Silence. "But of course you did. Who better to entrust with your life, than a champion sharpshooter?"

"None of this makes any sense, Kay," he said, but his voice

sounded off, unconvinced, defeated. "You think I asked someone to shoot us? Really? How delusional can you get?"

"I think you felt I wasn't buying into your story and you panicked."

"I can't believe it—" He stopped in the middle of his sentence when the door opened.

Elliot came in, holding a phone. He placed it on the table in front of Kay. "We found a text message on Brian's phone instructing Edmundo to kill the Wi-Fi. He didn't want his kid found."

"Yeah, because his kid wasn't missing," Kay replied. "She was entrusted to a subordinate's care. But why, Brian? Why take Holly to Edmundo?"

"Wait a minute," Brian said, leaning forward with a glint of hope in his eyes. "How do you know whom I texted? You're making shit up."

"No, Brian, that's your specialty. We have Holly, and Edmundo, and during the process of rescuing Holly we seized a number of phones."

That last statement lit a flicker of panic in his eyes that immediately subsided. "Again, I don't know what you're talking about. I'm already going to stand trial for Rachel's murder, a crime I didn't commit. So, charge me with something or let me go. This has gone on way too long."

He didn't even ask if his daughter was okay. Son of a bitch.

But he was right. The charade had lasted long enough.

"Then, what happened?" Kay asked. "Why kill Taylor?"

He gave her the are-you-crazy look again. "Who?"

"The nineteen-year-old jogger who saw you get out of the Suburban and start on foot across the hill to get here. You couldn't leave a witness behind, could you?"

"I don't know what you're talking about." He sighed and stood, a little wobbly as if drunk, probably feeling exhausted and defeated.

"It doesn't matter if you cop to it or not. It's all about timing," Elliot chimed in. "When our medical examiner found your fingerprint on the bullet taken from Taylor's body and the brass you left at the scene, you weren't in the system yet. AFIS didn't return any matches. They booked you the following morning, *after* our ME had run his search."

"Ah, but a thumbprint like yours is one to remember, isn't it?" Kay asked, standing and walking over to Brian. "Much like a certain bottle of Burgundy, isn't it?" Brian instinctively plunged his hands into his pockets. "I told you that was dangerous, didn't I? But don't worry," she laughed, "it's not going to kill you, Brian. It's going to get you life."

FIFTY-ONE

FAMILY

Novack had taken Brian away and locked him up in one of the detention cells, awaiting processing. Kay's ex had gone from disbelief to shock to spewing insults, making threats, and offering large amounts of money, all compressed within ten endless minutes of her time.

"What's going on with him?" Elliot asked after Novack took him away.

"You mean, this meltdown?" Kay tilted her head with a smile. "It's what happens when a narcissist is exposed and humiliated. He just can't handle it."

"I was wondering why he came to you to feign his innocence. He came looking for trouble, didn't he?"

"He came looking for someone he'd duped once before. A sure bet," she replied, her smile gone, washed away by a wave of sadness. She paused for a moment, feeling the threat of tears burning her eyes. "I started my life all wrong. I believed his lies back then, I still believed him this morning, up until you mentioned the company name and it all fell into place. But why me? And why did I believe him?"

Elliot didn't say anything, just listened, supportive and strong and nonjudgmental as he had always been.

"I'll tell you why," she continued, lowering her eyes, a little embarrassed. "He's showing no signs of deception, only anger, frustration, hurt—all normal emotions for someone who's been wrongfully accused of murder. He's got no remorse. He would've killed his own daughter to cover this up."

"But why kill Rachel the way he did, instead of setting his goons on her or something?" Elliot removed his hat and let it fall on the table. "I don't get it."

"Arrogance, maybe? Perhaps we'll never know. The unsubs we end up collaring are the ones who think they're too smart to make mistakes. The rest we never catch."

Elliot scratched the back of his head. "Another question I have is why did Rachel come back to her house, when she knew who shot that street dealer? She spoke with the ADA the next morning, right? She had to have known it was Brian, right?"

"Another good question, one that won't let me sleep well until I get the answer." She sighed, knowing there was more truth in her statement than she cared to admit. "Rachel had backtracked at the DA's office as if she'd gotten cold feet. Maybe she realized the man she'd noticed was Brian sometime later, not at the time of the shooting. But I'm speculating now. Truth is, I don't know."

A knock on the door, and Novack popped his head in. "Detective?"

They both turned and said, "Yes?" then laughed heartily.

"Him," Novack said, pointing his finger at Elliot and grinning. "Your perv awaits, my liege."

Kay stood and followed Elliot, glad to wrap up the whole Brian business. "Perv? What perv?"

Elliot grinned and tilted his head toward the holding cell next to Brian's. "Meet Darrell Bates, forty-four and loaded. Taylor was pregnant with his baby—"

"Pregnant?" Kay asked, surprised. "Poor girl."

"Like you said, not very smart. He volunteered a DNA sample to be excluded for her murder. Turns out this other model citizen, Mr. Melby," he pointed at the third lockup cell, "the owner of the local strip club, was filming the pervs who had to bid for the privilege of raping his girls. So, now we have Mr. Bates for rape and soliciting."

She patted Elliot on the shoulder. "You've been busy."

"But I collaborated, didn't I?" Melby said, holding on to the bars of his cell and shouting after them. "Hey, cowboy, you promised to drop the trafficking charge!"

Elliot stopped and leaned over to Kay's ear. "Watch this," he whispered, then walked over to Melby's holding cell. "I'm a man of my word, Melby. I'm not charging you with sex trafficking, only the other charges, the more minor ones, like facilitation of prostitution and conspiracy to commit rape."

"Thank you," Melby said, his voice a bit hesitant.

Novack overheard and rushed over. "But why drop the sex trafficking charges, Detective? You've seen what he was doing."

Elliot grinned. "They weren't going to stick in the first place. Trafficking involves some form of transportation, and the girls weren't taken anywhere."

Novack laughed. "Ha! The charge was bogus?"

"I like to think of it as leverage."

The bullpen roared with laughter, barely covering Melby's cussing. Kay's phone rang, and she withdrew to the interrogation room to take Brockett's call, beckoning Elliot to follow.

"I've got more news for you, Detective," Brockett announced. Kay put the phone on speaker and set it on the table. "Our techie managed to retrieve a text message stuck in Rachel's phone."

"What do you mean, stuck?"

"It was meant to be sent to you, but apparently, it didn't go through."

Kay sat down, her heart thumping in her chest. "What does it say?"

"It says, *I'm so sorry I didn't call sooner to apologize for what I've done. I don't blame you for not taking my call. But I need you now. We need your help. Brian isn't who I thought he was. I didn't know at first. I just realized that it was his ruby cuff links I saw that night. He's dangerous and I'm*— That's all there is. Something must've interrupted her."

Kay swallowed with difficulty. "Yes, the killer did. Rachel threw the phone into the dishwasher with Holly's plate and place mat, and the phone lost connection with the network." She frowned, weighing the chances of that happening, and of the message still remaining intact in the phone's memory after it had lost nearly all its power during the week. But it was there, confirming what she'd only guessed, that Rachel had realized who Brian was, sometime *after* going to the ADA, perhaps when she'd returned home. "I guess it can happen," she said, sounding doubtful. "I've got news for you too, Detective. We're charging Brian Hanlin with murder."

"Huh? Whose murder?"

"He shot a local girl the morning he showed up, a poor soul who had the misfortune of seeing him get out of the black Suburban."

The old cop stayed silent for a moment. "Well, then, I guess you won't be trying to disculpate him in the Rachel Epling case, will you?"

"Nope."

"One more thing, and you're not going to believe this. Little Holly will be okay. Family showed up to take her."

She frowned, staring at the phone in disbelief. There was no family left. "Who?"

"Brian's parents. Yeah... alive and well, if you can believe it. I checked their ID, their backgrounds, 'cause I couldn't believe my eyes."

"He told everyone they'd died, and left him money and that house," she whispered, shaken. "Including me."

"Well, guess what? He lied. Good night, Detective." Brockett was laughing when he ended the call.

She sat there silently with her head spinning, the last remaining fact she'd thought she knew about Brian uprooted and shred to bits. At least Holly didn't have to enter the foster care system. And perhaps the Hanlins could do a better job raising her than they'd done with Brian.

"Can I buy you a cup of coffee?" Elliot asked.

She stood and they walked out of the box together. "I'm so done for today. Let me sign off on Brian's paperwork and I'm ready to go." She walked over to the front desk, where Deputy Hobbs was pulling paperwork duty. "Show me Hanlin's paperwork," she asked, holding a pen in her hand.

Hobbs pushed a clipboard with some forms over to her. She signed and pushed it back. "Thanks."

"Any special treatment for your ex, Detective?" Hobbs asked as she was walking away.

"Oh, hell, no," she replied over her shoulder. "Have at him."

"You go, girl," Denise Farrell shouted from across the bullpen. "Woot, woot," she called, pumping her fist in the air.

And like that, all embarrassment disappeared. She was home, with family, and Elliot waited for her by the door. She dashed over to him with a beaming smile while butterflies flurried in her stomach. "I'm starving. How about a steak dinner and some beer instead of that coffee?"

He shook his head with a sad expression on his face, but his eyes glinted with laughter under the brim of his hat. "I don't know about that; I can't risk it. My professional reputation will be damaged if I'm seen in public with someone whose ex-husband is a crime lord."

"What ex-husband?"

A LETTER FROM LESLIE

A big, heartfelt ***thank you*** for choosing to read *Missing Girl at Frozen Falls*. If you did enjoy it and want to keep up to date with all my latest releases, just sign up at the following link. Your email address will never be shared, and you can unsubscribe at any time.

www.bookouture.com/leslie-wolfe

When I write a new book I think of you, the reader, what you'd like to read next, how you'd like to spend your leisure time, and what you most appreciate from the time spent in the company of the characters I create, vicariously experiencing the challenges I lay in front of them. That's why I'd love to hear from you! Did you enjoy *Missing Girl at Frozen Falls?* Would you like to see Detective Kay Sharp and her partner, Elliot Young, return in another story? Your feedback is incredibly valuable to me, and I appreciate hearing your thoughts. Please contact me directly through one of the channels listed below. Email works best: LW@WolfeNovels.com. I will never share your email with anyone, and I promise you'll receive an answer from me!

If you enjoyed my book and if it's not too much to ask, please take a moment and leave me a review, and maybe recommend *Missing Girl at Frozen Falls* to other readers. Reviews and personal recommendations help readers discover new titles or new authors for the first time; it makes a huge difference, and it means the world to me. Thank you for your support, and I hope to keep you entertained with my next story. See you soon!

Thank you,

Leslie

www.LeslieWolfe.com

 facebook.com/wolfenovels
bookbub.com/authors/leslie-wolfe

ACKNOWLEDGMENTS

A special, heartfelt thank you goes to the fantastic publishing team at Bookouture. They are a pleasure to work with, their enthusiasm contagious and their dedication inspiring.

Very special thanks to Christina Demosthenous, who makes the editing process a pleasant experience and who is the best brainstorming partner an author could hope for. She is my guiding light in all things publishing and doubles as a muse when I need a nudge. I can't thank you enough.

A special thanks goes to Kim Nash and Noelle Holten for tirelessly promoting my books across all channels. Alba Proko is the wonderful audio manager who turns my written stories into audible recordings, nurturing the productions throughout the process and making me proud of each and every one of them. Your work with my stories is nothing short of inspiring.

A huge shoutout for the digital marketing team, who work seamlessly and tirelessly in ensuring that every book launch is better than the one before. You are simply amazing.

My warmest thanks go to Richard King and his enthusiastic efforts to bring my work to other markets in translated versions and perhaps, one day, to the screen. A heartfelt thank you for everything you do and for your keen interest in my work. It's much appreciated.

Made in United States
North Haven, CT
07 April 2024

51008009R00198